CHAPTER 1

CHRISTMAS BREAK

Myrna awoke in her mother's bed with a blanket wrapped around her. The bright African sun filtered through the trees and the birds had stopped singing. She was sweating and her school jumper was bunched around her waist. Myrna smelled an unknown odor and couldn't wait to wash herself. As her feet touched the polished floor, she realized her school stockings were still on. Myrna walked towards the bathing house. She was sore and stiff in her upper legs. She rubbed her thighs with her hands and smelled an unfamiliar cologne waft up as the cold water poured over her body. What had happened the night before? Her head throbbed and her vision blurred. Her mouth tasted metallic, and was so dry, her tongue stuck against the inside of her cheeks. There was no one to ask about what had occurred — her brother and his fiancée had left, her mother and father were at the coast, and her sister Violet was visiting relatives. Only her Uncle Dodge and his guest Festal were in the house, and Myrna was too embarrassed to ask them what had happened and why she was sleeping in her parents' bed. When she was clean, she gathered her clothes and went to the small room she shared with her sister. She sat on the mat to put on her tee shirt and *chitenge*. She began crying and could not stop.

Back at the Royal Academy, the long Christmas break was over and the classroom was abuzz with chatter as the boys talked over their adventures during the break. Some bragged about their sexual exploits with gestures and rude guffaws trying to outdo each other with their tales. Others were groaning about being back in school after their vacations. For Myrna, it was a relief to be back in the classroom, even though she was the only girl in this prestigious all boys secondary school. She listened to their teasing and bragging and knew that something had changed in her life. The joking and jostling of the boys now seemed childish. Myrna's body felt different – the vacation had lasted over a month, and her period was almost three weeks overdue. Every morning when she ate her sorghum gruel or smelled cologne, she was nauseous. She leaned over her notebook and began reflecting on her Christmas break.

Christmas vacation over the last six weeks at the Chitundu house had been a confusing time. Myrna's mother, Beatrice, was due to give birth to her eighth child. Her father, Bishop, was caught up in the poor economy with no one buying the bricks he made at their brickyard on the edge of Blancville. Uncle Dodge seemed determined to make Myrna's month long school vacation a continuous party – Dodge was known as a notorious matchmaker. Myrna had no idea she was his current transaction.

Dodge began by picking Myrna up from the Royal Academy boarding school in a taxi. He helped her into the backseat and gave her an apple from South Africa, her first taste of this exotic fruit. He also handed her a tan cashmere scarf which Myrna immediately wrapped around her head of soft curls to keep the red, laterite dust off of them. 'Paper Roses' played on the radio. Myrna tried to make out the words but the lyrics were a little fast for her to translate. She recalled one refrain played over and over, *Oh, how real those roses seemed to me. But they're only paper roses, like your imitation love for me.* At thirteen Myrna had never dated a boy, but she could feel the possibility of love and pain, and an end to dreams in the emotion of the singer.

Her brother Stephen and his fiancée Esther were at her parents' house when Myrna and Uncle Dodge arrived, along with Festal, a man in his early forties. Uncle Dodge was entertaining the group with stories and drinks, treating Myrna like a privileged adult rather than a young

The Bride Price

Suzanne Popp

This book is dedicated to women who persevere in obedience to their calling, and sustain the dreams of those around them.

A portion of proceeds from this book go to support VillageSteps in the education of children in Africa.

Suzanne Popp

ACKNOWLEDGMENTS

My friends and the supporters of VillageSteps, who encouraged me to put my stories into a book, the publishers and editors of PNWA conference and PAWA members, who affirmed my vision for this novel, my church, Calvary Presbyterian Church in Enumclaw, whose members helped to build schools in Zambia, and saw the dedication of Africans to care for children in difficult circumstances, and all the beautiful and courageous women I have come to know in my years of living and traveling. Most importantly I would like to thank my loving family; especially my husband, Ken, who inspires me daily.

teenager. Dodge brought her gifts to share with her friends and family —
a bar of lavender soap, a special diary with violets on the cover, and a
tiny key to give to Violet. Her parents prepared a special dinner of
chicken and yams. They praised Myrna for how dependable she was and
how the family had always relied on her as the strong one, while her
mother Beatrice kept slipping the best pieces of meat and fried yams to
Festal.

Festal said nothing throughout the meal, silently looking down at his
plate for most of it, pulling the meat apart with his fingers, while
occasionally glancing at Myrna. Uncle Dodge slipped Myrna a bar of
chocolate as she left the dining table to clean the dishes. He hinted she
had an admirer. Without questioning her uncle, Myrna accepted the
chocolate, happy for her family to have the food and drinks Dodge
provided.

Myrna studied Dodge's face. Surely he didn't think she would be
interested in Festal, the older man. Festal must be a relative or a
business associate, she decided. If only she could talk to Violet about
what was going on. She signaled her sister to meet her in the kitchen. As
Violet pulled back the curtain to enter the room, Dodge intercepted:

"Your cousins have invited you to come and visit them. They want
you to stay for a week. I have your bus ticket for you to leave tomorrow.
Your mother and father will be going on a little vacation to the coast to
enjoy the beach before the baby comes. You had better get packing
before it gets dark. Don't worry about the dishes. I will help Myrna."

By the time Myrna finished in the kitchen, and returned to the
sleeping room, Violet was already asleep, her diary open beside her,
and her basket packed for the holiday. As she lay on her mat the
following night, Myrna began reflecting on the treats and copious
amounts of sorghum beer she had received from Uncle Dodge after her
parents left for the coast. Since she had never tasted alcohol before
and had never known the effects of it, she wasn't sure how she got into
bed.

It had been a year of drought, with business slow and food scarce. Business must have been good for Uncle Dodge though, because his generosity was impressive. His friend Festal had been markedly quiet, lacking the easy banter that continuously poured from Uncle Dodge. Myrna paid no attention to Festal's hovering around her father's compound and his looking at her, plying her with small gifts and treats. She did not connect it with herself. It was unusual to be noticed by her brother Stephen as well. He introduced her to Esther and mentioned what a help Myrna was to him. Stephen usually just wanted Myrna to iron a shirt for him, or make him something to eat or drink. Now he held her up as the valued sister. Esther had even asked Myrna for her opinion about bridesmaid dresses and which flowers suited her. *Stephen must want something.*

Myrna was flattered by the gifts and little outings. She found it a little heady to be the focus of so much attention. Violet and Myrna didn't like or trust Uncle Dodge, but there was a side of him that could be fun. He knew a lot of people and had a way of skirting around parents.

Myrna avoided thinking about the gaps in her memory when she couldn't recall what had gone on in the house during her parents' absence. She missed having her sister to bounce ideas off of until the two of them could figure them out. It was the first time she had slept alone in her own home.

There was one night when Uncle Dodge came into the kitchen when she was washing up the dishes, dressed in her school uniform – a royal blue jumper and white blouse with a Peter Pan collar. She had wrapped a cloth around herself to protect the wool fabric. Myrna felt secure in her uniform as it reminded her of her place, a girl who was attending secondary school and going places. She had worn the jumper each day of the vacation, to make a statement of where she belonged.

Dodge made a special cup of tea for her with lots of sugar. As she stood washing the dishes and rinsing the mugs and plates, Dodge spoke in a soft voice to Myrna. She felt her head reeling as she finished the doctored tea, and a creepy feeling come over her, as though she was losing control of her body and didn't know where the conversation was leading

"Myrna, the whole family is so proud of you, how you put your family first, and what a hard worker you are. You are so fortunate to be able to help your family during these tough times. Stephen and Esther are counting on your support. I know you are not going to disappoint your family. Don't worry about drying the dishes, I will finish the job."

As Myrna put down the mug her uncle brought had given her, she noticed some sediment in the bottom. She just wanted to be in her bed and away from Uncle Dodge. "Finish the job." Those were the last words she remembered of that evening.

Now, back in the classroom at the Royal Academy, there was order and predictability. Myrna had time to catch up on her reading and prepare for the new classes being offered this semester. She decided on biology and critical thinking, and English and African literature. She wanted to find out why her body was changing and why she was nauseous. Everything about her body felt different; her breasts were tender and her period was late. But at least she was comfortable being back in her own bed and private dorm room, instead of sleeping on the reed mat she and Violet shared at home.

Myrna looked up and saw Wellington Taylor looking at her. He was her tutor in English language arts and had promised her a gift when she returned from vacation. He smiled as he handed her a large book. She felt her face heat up as she accepted it— a new biology book.

"You didn't think I would forget my promise to my star pupil, did you?" As Wellington went to his desk and began preparing his class notes, Myrna turned to the chapter on reproduction. She looked around to make sure no one was watching, then began leafing through the pages. There it was— illustrations of male and female reproductive organs, so pink and small, and then the description of pregnancy. She felt nauseous as she read the words. *Cessation of the monthly flow. Enlargement of the breasts.* Her eyes glazed over with tears. She had missed her period. She was never late. A thousand questions welled up in her head like the flow of the Zambezi when it was in flood stage. Nothing could hold it back. What had happened? When did it happen? Then she slowed her thoughts down and went over everything.

It was a blur, the actual act. There was the cup of tea; she now recalled some pushing and prodding. The image of dried blood on her new tan scarf suddenly came to mind. She had wondered how it got there. Did she cut herself? All she remembered was soaking the scarf in water in the morning so it would not stain. Surely, this man/woman marriage act could not be what had happened. But her mind reeled. She shut the book quickly. Her life was over. The school would never allow a pregnant student to continue.

Myrna was the first girl admitted to the Royal academy, and now, because of what she had done, she would be the last. She didn't know how soon they would find out. She could never explain this because she didn't really know how it happened. Nor could she tell anyone her secret. Wellington Taylor was the first European she had ever met and he had been so proud of her rapid progress. He always called her his jewel, telling her she was not like the other students who could not control their animal instincts. He disliked their coarse jokes and their innuendoes about their sexual prowess. What would he say if he found out his star pupil had betrayed his faith in her? Just then, Wellington Taylor turned around and looked at her.

"Miss Chitundu, are you feeling well? You look like you are about to pass out. Go outside and get a drink. I think you are overheated."

Myrna rushed from the room, banging her hip on a desk in her hurry. She barely made it to the ablution block before she threw up the gruel she had eaten for breakfast. She cleaned her teeth, rinsed out her eyes, checked her blouse and straightened her pleated jumper before heading back to the classroom. She couldn't think straight. Maybe she would have some weeks before she needed to tell anyone. But who could she tell? Maybe she was mistaken. After all, she had never been with a boy before, so how could this happen? In the pit of her stomach, she knew it had.

When Myrna left the classroom, Wellington Taylor went back to her desk and pulled open the book where the pages were bent. He saw the pictures of the naked figures and thought this might have disturbed the girl. Myrna was thirteen, but she was protected by her family and very innocent. Maybe the anatomic drawings had been too graphic for her. Wellington straightened out the pages and returned to his class notes, resolving that he would be available to the girl if she had questions. He would talk to the biology teacher to ensure the girl was not ridiculed by the boys or made to feel unsure of herself. This girl was the brightest student in his class and it would be a shame to have her discouraged or intimidated. What a difference it could make in the country to have girls educated, especially one who wanted to go into medicine.

Wellington thought about his two years at the exclusive boys' school. They had been difficult, but the possibility of having an African girl pass her exams and move on to the university would make it all worth the effort. He had been diligent in encouraging Myrna, and they had such a good rapport. Wellington's eyes scanned the sea of blue uniforms, white collars, and closely cropped black hair. His eyes lighted on Myrna; the girl with glossy curls that cascaded down her back, a wide smile that lit up the room, and a nature as gentle as the antelope. He would talk to her biology teacher. It wouldn't do to have such a gifted student discouraged.

CHAPTER 2

ANNOUNCEMENT OF PROPOSAL

In early February, Uncle Dodge went to visit Myrna at the Royal Academy. He spoke with the headmaster and said that there was an emergency at the Chitundu household, and Myrna's parents needed her at home. When the headmaster went to Wellington Taylor's classroom to call her out, Myrna jumped up from her desk and gathered her papers, hurriedly following Uncle Dodge to the waiting taxi. *Something must be wrong with my mother's pregnancy*, she thought. Neither of them said a word to each other on the three hour drive back to Blancville. Myrna was convinced her mother was ill, and Dodge didn't really want to answer any questions about taking her from the classroom.

When they got home Myrna's mother was very direct. She sent the men into another room. Myrna could see the baby had dropped and her mother was ready to give birth at any time.

"Myrna, we are very proud of you, as you have always put your family first. You know that our brick business is difficult as people cannot afford to buy fired bricks or build right now. Your father and I have received a very good offer for you in marriage. The expense we have gone to provide your education, is about to pay off. We have the chance to see your brother married and you married to a man of means who is willing to care for you and aid your family. Festal is well established and is of our belief. We hear no bad reports of him and he is healthy. Think over whether you are willing to be his wife and can be faithful to this man." Beatrice looked at her daughter's figure and noted the increase in her waistline and her breasts. She felt her own child kick and thought that Dodge could be right; this daughter could be pregnant.

Uncle Dodge waited with Bishop in the next room. Dodge had introduced his sister Beatrice to Bishop when she was fourteen, and the two young people had made an excellent marriage. Bishop, however, was not excited to see his own daughter marry at fourteen, especially to a man a year older than he was. He and Beatrice knew they could not afford to continue to send their daughter to the secondary school. Stephen, their oldest son, was desperate to marry his girlfriend Esther and needed to come up with the bride price before Esther was forced to marry a better financed suitor. Thomas needed money to continue his schooling. Uncle Dodge insisted that Myrna was the answer to their difficulties, she just needed their encouragement. He also indicated that the girl had shown Festal special favors over the Christmas holidays. Bishop wanted to punch Dodge for that remark, but he remained quiet and waited for the women to make a decision. Then he would announce whether he was in support of the price the suitor had offered. It was ten cows and a small parcel of land as well. A fortune. Bishop could not help but think what it would mean to their family during this lean time.

Myrna looked at her mother in disbelief. Her words of praise had been the same as Dodge had used earlier.

"Are you asking me to give up my scholarship and my dream of becoming a doctor to marry a stranger who is older than my father?"

Beatrice said nothing. She dropped her hands below her bulging abdomen and bent her back slightly as if in pain. Her face was a mask of determination.

"What about Violet? She doesn't want to go to school or to travel. She has always wanted to be married and not have to work in the market. Why don't you marry her off?" Her mother's face went taut, the lips pulled into a straight line. Myrna saw the pain this question caused her mother. Violet had always been her favorite after Eunice died. Maybe she blamed Myrna for her twin's death. They both had the dysentery, but Myrna recovered from it and her twin sister died. Myrna set her face. She was silent while thoughts raced through her brain.

Festal was old. How could her mother bring up the subject of the bride price for her brother while at the same time talking about Festal? Her brother was twenty, marrying a girl his age, yet Myrna was expected to marry a man three times her age. In addition, the man lived far away from Blancville, so there would be few, if any, visits from friends or family.

Festal had never been to school. She couldn't imagine him being a good match for her. Then Myrna remembered that she was pregnant, and what alternative did she have? She could be the hero for the family, or the shame of the school. Both women stood facing each other in complete silence, then Myrna felt herself nodding her head up and down in submission. She would marry Festal. Her mother left the room immediately to give the news to her husband and Dodge that their daughter had accepted the offer and was ready to be married.

A month later the transaction was nearly complete. The only thing left was the wedding. Cattle had been exchanged, along with the title to land in Copperfine, food and cloth, a sewing machine, and the enormous three-legged cooking pot that had been Beatrice's wedding gift from her mother. When Myrna saw the pot being given to her, she cried, feeling that she was now bound to her mother by a history of submission and sacrifice. Like the pot, she would be useful, durable, and a legacy.

CHAPTER 3

THE WEDDING OF MYRNA AND FESTAL

Beatrice's hands worked to help Myrna slide into the muslin wedding dress she had sewn for her with her new treadle machine. It was snug, especially across her breasts, but there was no mention of these changes. The young girl's eyes were dazed. Her full head of hair was pulled back from her face with a braided coronet and curls hanging down on either side.

Beatrice recalled her own wedding day; she was also married at fourteen. Her brother Dodge had been desperate to raise the bride price for his own engagement, and had pressured her to marry Bishop. She had not attended school and her own dreams were gone— erased like Myrna's dreams of being a doctor. Beatrice had wanted to become a seamstress and design dresses that would appear in catalogues. Instead, she became a wife and mother at fourteen. Life had turned out all right for her. Bishop had been a kind husband. Now, after fourteen years of marriage, she could not imagine a life without him.

Beatrice saw how upset Violet was about the wedding. She stood beside her sister Myrna biting her lower lip to stop from breaking into tears, and frowning the entire time. Beatrice could not separate the girls, in spite of calling Violet several times to assist with different chores. Violet made it clear to everyone how she opposed the marriage and the dreams Myrna would be giving up. She was outspoken and was going to ruin everything.

"Violet, I need you to go to the market now and run the stall. I have to keep working on this dress. Take the money box with you and pay attention to the bills. There are counterfeits being passed." Beatrice handed Violet the moneybox and ignored the attitude of the girl. She knew this was no time to correct her manners; it was all the girl could do to avoid sobbing. She leaned over her treadle machine and studiously pedaled away, feeling the baby shoving against the fabric as she pulled it away from herself and pushed it under the needle. After twenty years of marriage, Beatrice was thirty four years old, and in spite of her age, she was a beautiful woman. She had produced seven live children, and was carrying her eighth. She knew her husband would rest easier when they had the money for the bride price, although neither of them discussed what a godsend it would be. She maintained herself in the community, and Festal would be some distance away, but she had heard no ill of him, and information traveled rapidly in this country of few newspapers and fewer radios. If Myrna had gone any further with her education, she would not be as eligible for a wife. She was pretty full of herself as it was. Beatrice stifled this thought and concentrated on her sewing. She could imagine how beautiful her daughter would be going down the aisle in her white dress and veil. *She takes after me when it comes to her features and her carriage. I never had her confidence though. She must have gained this from her schooling. She has always been a girl who speaks her mind. We need to get this wedding completed as soon as possible. Babies don't wait.*

Violet knew her mother did not want her to talk to Myrna. She was angry about that as well as being angry with her sister for not telling her about this engagement. She was also angry at her mother for the part she played in all this drama, and angry at losing her best friend to adulthood. As for Festal, she reviled him for taking Myrna away, and Dodge for executing the plan. She called her uncle a predator, knowing that Myrna had not realized she was his next transaction. Violet refused to stay in the room if Dodge was present.

At the market, Violet dawdled, making her way slowly to the stall where her mother usually set up their mat ready to sell the vegetables. She wandered from row to row, making her way to the clothing section. A lacy bra hung on a rack, catching her eye. It looked expensive and when she looked, it was. But she had never owned one, nor did her mother. She pulled out the money she had been saving for the choir tour and bought it for her sister. It was a token of womanhood and romance such as she had seen in magazines at the beauty salon. She wanted her sister to know how much she loved her. She wrapped it in paper and put it in the hamper of clothing they were preparing for Myrna's trousseau.

When Bishop hugged his daughter on her wedding day, Myrna noticed tears in his eyes. Neither of them spoke a word about the arrangement. Myna knew her father had his regrets about not earning enough to keep his daughter from being given to the highest bidder; that Dodge had manipulated them into this union for his own profit, and that Bishop lost another child.

Myrna wanted her father to know the pain she felt, the pain of leaving her dream of an education behind. She wanted him to see her sacrifice and say it wasn't necessary, that she could stay with them. Instead, she heard her father tell Festal that he knew he would value this woman, that he was welcome to come and stay with the family at any time.

Bishop wanted to hear that Festal loved his girl. He didn't say how relieved he was that his daughter relented to marry Festal, saving her family from losing their business and position in the community. Now Beatrice could give birth to this next child in a hospital. There would be a second wedding with Stephen and Esther, and their younger son, Thomas, could continue his schooling.

Bishop walked his daughter slowly across the grass, leading to the small arch covered in bougainvillea. The head pastor was away and an unfamiliar associate pastor filled in. Festal waited for Myrna and as she approached him, she saw him wipe his eyes with his handkerchief. Then the pastor looked down at his notes and began the ceremony.

"Myra, do you take this man to be your husband?"

That is not even my name. I am not even here.

"I do."

Myrna repeated the vows after him as she looked at Festal and how uncomfortable he was standing in front of the crowd of well-wishers. Sweat appeared on his forehead, and he flinched in his tight-fitting suit. The wool gabardine was too warm for a late February day. Myrna allowed Festal to place the ring on her finger. She did not have one for him. The pastor asked them to turn and face the crowd.

"Mr. and Mrs. Festal Phiri, I now pronounce you man and wife." Myrna could hear the Brahmin cow wailing in the distance and saw the tears well up in Violet's eyes as the bouquet of red lilies was handed to Esther. Esther would now be able to marry Stephen. It was finished.

There were hugs all around. Many small gifts had been set on a table. Myrna didn't recognize many of the people who came to congratulate her, but she kept hold of Festal's hand. The photographer wanted them to stand under the bougainvillea arch, but Festal pulled Myrna over to the large baobab tree which was flowering. Festal leaned over her and whispered "The baobab is our family totem." The photographer took a single black and white photo. He wanted to take more, but the couple was reluctant. They were led by the pastor to the head table and took a few bites of the food heaped on their plates. Everything was rushed and yet time stood still. Myrna listened as Uncle Dodge proposed a toast to the newlyweds, and did not even look at him as she heard him describe the happy couple, and how generous Festal had been, and what a dutiful daughter Myrna was to her family. Dodge wished them a fruitful marriage, and many children to bless their home. It was a commercial for his matchmaking skills. *Painless pandering.* The guests raised their hands and ululated with the message.

Myrna did not want to be here any longer than necessary. It was over. She gave her mother and father a cursory hug, then hugged her sister and her brother Thomas. She gathered her belongings and loaded them onto the cart where the presents had already been packed. Festal was right behind her, helping her keep her balance and steadying her as she mounted the seat of the oxcart.

The couple headed to Copperfine, the iron pot trussed to the back of the wagon with its three legs in the air, even as the newlyweds wondered who they had joined themselves to, and were afraid for the unveiling.

CHAPTER 4

IN THE MARKET

I am stressing over this wedding of my sister and cannot get it out of my thoughts. It could have been me. I know Myrna never saw it coming. Here I am sitting on a mat of reeds in the market tying onions by their stems into a swag while I wait for my mother to return. The market is smaller today than it is on the weekend, or when the holidays are about to begin. And so is my world. The row where I sit to sell our vegetables is facing the hand pump where most people come to fill their clay water jugs. Our space is back from the puddles of mud that surround the tap, so I can stay dry. Flies hover above the moist ground, and especially near the meat market, which is at the far end of the row.

That must be how it is everywhere in Copperfine where my sister will be living. Each week I see an animal being hauled live in a wheelbarrow or driven with whips to the butchery. Sometimes a goat is held by its hind legs like a wheelbarrow itself and walked to his fate. It reminds me of Uncle Dodge with his forced marriages. When I see the animal go by standing on its front legs, its head nearly touching the ground and the owner holding on to its back hooves making it go where it doesn't want to, and joking at its helplessness to escape his grip, I want to scream. There are always a couple of sparse-haired dogs with curling tails and dribbling tongues sidling alongside, waiting for a scrap to fall their way when the animal is butchered. By noon, the meat is finished. If you buy it later than that, it is covered with flies, spongy and sizzling with germs.

Our spot is sunny and clean. I used to smell the fish, the open sewers, and the rotting produce when I first came here to help my mother. Myrna would tell me to look at the colors of the people's clothing, the beautiful fabrics hanging on the rail near the tailors, their machines humming away as they pedaled out a new skirt or shirt, and the textures of all the produce; yam leaves, pinto beans, red peppers, green lentils, and golden rice. Just near the clothing section, the hair dressers sit, plaiting the hair of women. They have a mouth full of hair ties, and various hairpieces hanging behind them. Sometimes on the branches of a tree an old towel hangs frayed, and a woman sitting with her head cocked to one side for hours, is being braided up in an acceptable style. There is always laughter and an audience that encourages her. That is when I first came up with the idea of sketching what I saw.

At first I just did pencil drawings of the fruits and donkeys with their carts of firewood. I would color them in when I had materials to make paints. It allowed me to take my mind to another place without leaving the market. In the past year I have started making portraits. They are not complicated, just lines and shadows to recall the features of the people I see. There are many faces in the market, people of all ages and classes, or their servants, looking to secure good prices, or to sell for a profit what they have produced. The face that keeps coming up in my mind is that of Myrna with her large eyes and her trembling mouth. I don't even want to think of Festal.

The women in our row make little piles of produce on their mats and arrange them to attract attention from the shoppers. My sister used to tell me how magical it was to see brown burlap sacks of beans and lentils change into neat designs of color and texture, encouraging people to notice and buy. It is not so magical when you are the one shucking rotten layers off the onions so someone will choose them. I try to recall people's names and smile at them so they will remember our stall and come to shop.

After eight hours of sitting in the sun, I am ready to do something else. I have to concentrate to make a sale and count the change correctly. It is easier than taking care of baby brothers, I have to say that. I always hope I will meet someone interesting in the market, but women are the only ones who seem to shop for fruit and vegetables. I stay away from the area where the local beer and fetishes are sold. There are plenty of men and flies hanging out there, but they are not the kind I want to attract. My mother handles the weekend market, where more sellers and buyers come from further away.

Eight months ago I watched my sister Myrna go off to boarding school, wondering at the time how she could find it so interesting to sit in class all day reading books. I know she has wanted to be a doctor ever since our sister Eunice died, so she worked hard at her studies. She learned to read when Stephen was in school because she made him teach her. She saved food from her breakfast, or biscuits from the market to give him in trade for teaching her everything he learned in class. As soon as he got home from school she would borrow his books, making use of the late afternoon light to read the assignments. Soon she was doing his essays, and the teachers were remarking how good they were, and questioning who had written them.

A tutor finally visited the house to encourage my father to let Myrna attend class. Then the government stepped in with a scholarship after she received the highest marks in the region on her exams. But this time Myrna has left for good. It's final. Finished. She married that man Festal that Uncle Dodge dreamed up for her, and she is on her way to the cow town of Copperfine. I am not lonely. There are sellers to gossip with. I have worked in the market with Mother since Myrna started boarding school. I have friends in the market and I have my brothers to keep me company. Not Stephen, though. He is tied up with Esther day and night. My friends in the choir always want me to come visit them and sing for their events. My mother and father are at home in the evening, Dad counting up the receipts for the day, Mother mending the boys' clothes. We could talk about what is going on in our family or our country. I could get a newspaper and read it to them. But we don't. We usually just get ready for the next day, as there is always more work to be done. We don't talk about Myrna. My father would cut that off pronto. What I want to understand is how Myrna married that man Festal. He is way out in the bush, he's old, and he can't even read.

When he was here, he didn't even talk. I watched how he used his hands to eat his food, picking up pieces of meat and sauce with his long slim fingers, and wiping the drips off with his pointer finger. I saw how he looked at Myrna as she used her napkin and her cutlery, ignoring him. She was so proud of her school uniform and wore it every day, even when she was home. It meant she was somebody going somewhere. I think she felt safe in it. Invincible.

I am in charge of the market stall today while Mother attends a funeral. She makes the most money on onions, although she doesn't grow them. Our brick yard is slow right now because people can't afford bricks that are fired. We have stopped adding any cement to them and even the tailings that we burn to fire them are hard to come by. Tobacco is not selling well and people are raising less of it. When people have no money they just cut mud bricks out of earth and use them. If we had more money, Myrna would still be here and she would be in the school studying biology and critical thinking. She said she wanted to learn how to think and make important decisions. I asked her, "Don't you think we know how to think already?"

"'No," she said. "We just hear something enough times and we think it is true, or even our own idea. We don't question it and we repeat what we are told. We learn by rote method. We are a nation of clichés. I want to learn the truth about life and how to decide for myself. Right now, we don't even know what we have or what we are missing. We are like the termites that turn up precious stones and heave them out of their towers of mud."

Myrna is two years older than me. She is very strong and not afraid to say what she thinks and what she wants to do. When we played together she could come up with a hundred games, while I was still thinking what I wanted to do. So how could she marry that man? I just didn't see it coming. She was happy when she came home for Christmas break. We were having a good time, just sleeping in our special room, or sitting on our carved stools in the courtyard near the kilns, shucking the hard corn from its cob and spreading it on mats to dry. We roasted groundnuts on a sheet of roofing and sketched out fashions we could make out of scraps from our mother's sewing. Even taking care of the little brothers was fun when there were two of us. Little did we know, Ma and Uncle Dodge were hatching plans to marry Myrna off.

I think our brother Stephen knew about the plan because he was so flattering to Myrna, asking her advice and getting her to like his girlfriend Esther, and totally ignoring me, even though I am just about as old as Myrna, and I certainly have a better fashion sense. So why were they just asking Myrna what she thought about their bridesmaid dresses? She won't even be one.

I don't think my Dad knew of the plan to marry Myrna off, because Myrna has always been his favorite. Ever since my sister Eunice died of the runs, Dad has wanted there to be a doctor in our village and Myrna was on her way to becoming one. He backed her when she won the government scholarship and stood up to my mother, even though he worried about Myrna going to a school that was all boys.

Here comes a customer, poking at the tomatoes. She's not a regular. No one comes this late to the market, when all the good produce is picked over and what is left is going limp. There, she has bought some and some of the onions as well. I saved our paper and just dropped the vegetables into her basket. I'm going to use it to make drawings. I will wrap the money in the corner of my cloth, as I have already counted out the cash for today. Mother should be back by now.

Myrna should have figured out what Dodge was up to. Maybe if we could have talked about it in the dark, like we did with our dreams and so many other things, maybe we could have figured it out. I was supposed to stay with my cousins a week, but it must have been a month or more, because when I returned, the winter break was over and Myrna was back at school.

I am glad I have my diary to write down what is going on. I write in it before I go to market. This morning I wrote about the baby brother or sister that is coming any day. I am hoping for another girl, as now there is just me in the family. Stephen is away with his girlfriend and Thomas is back in school. The others boys are small and know nothing of grown-up matters.

Uncle Dodge found my father for our mother, and that was years ago when he was only my brother Stephen's age. Dodge gets paid when he works out a marriage contract, but Dodge also likes poking around and getting people excited. Well, it isn't going to happen that way for me. I am not going to marry anyone he suggests. I have to like the way the man looks first. Then he has to agree that we will stay in Blancville and not go off to some god-forsaken cattle station filled with flies and snakes and people we don't know. My husband has to agree that we will have friends over and visit my parents whenever we feel like it, and that we will have lots of children and never be alone. My husband can't be that old to start with; just old enough to earn money. I do not want to travel and see the world. If my husband wants, he can bring it to me, because I do like nice things, I won't deny it. I want all my children to be born in the hospital. I will need a nanny for them.

I miss Myrna to death. We slept together since we were little. So where is she sleeping now? They probably have a hut made of dung with a sick calf in the front room tied to the big kettle Ma gave them. She should have given the Dutch oven to me, because at least I won't have to sell it to buy medicine for a cow. It is the first thing I will have my husband buy for our house. After the bed. I am not going to sleep on a mat forever. It makes lines on my skin. I also could use a satin pillow so my hair stays smooth and doesn't frizz up or break off.

Uncle Dodge bragged in town that he got the highest *lobola* for my sister that has ever been given in our district. I bet that is true. How he convinced that old man to pay such a high bride price is beyond me, even though Myrna is beautiful. But she never dressed up for him, or paid him any attention. She is really smart and kind as well, much kinder than I could ever be. She seems to always have a purpose in her life. Sometimes she is so busy seeing the big picture, she might forget the smaller details. Like me. Her only sister. So how did Dodge get her to marry the man? She wanted to be a doctor so much and she could remember anything. Dodge must have put a hex on her, that's all I can think. I wouldn't let him near me, even if he was giving me gifts and lining up a suitor. No, I am going to find a man who loves me and wants my parents close by, and who can make sure we never go hungry.

It was tough when Stephen was afraid of losing his girlfriend Esther, and Father could not come up with the money to help him. Stephen and Esther will be getting married this month and it will be a nice celebration with a whole roast goat. I am going to have a new dress and dance with everyone in my store-bought shoes. Everyone except Uncle Dodge. He is slippery as cow guts. If I see anyone talking with him, they will have my good riddance. It worked out for Ma and Father, but that is the exception to the rule.

Myself, I will be courted and make up my own mind. I remember how Joseph looked at me at Myrna's wedding. I didn't know his name then, but I saw that he was looking for something. I was afraid that Uncle Dodge had gotten involved in my business. I miss Myrna so much, but I don't think she could give me any advice because look where she ended up. I have not been to see her. I haven't asked to go. I am afraid of what her life must be and that the same thing could happen to me. She was so much smarter, but she couldn't avoid the bride price. I am more practical. Festal makes me nervous. It seems he can see inside a person, even though he says nothing. If Festal is the lion waiting to feed, Dodge is the hyena. Myrna must be even more lonely than I was when she left for boarding school. Maybe she even had a boyfriend there at the school, and now it is over. I can't imagine Myrna sleeping with Festal. Those long greasy fingers. Now I am going to get out my drawing pencils and make a little sketch for my diary. It is the nicest thing I have owned. I wonder how Myrna found it. Probably when she was away at school.

My drawing is finished. It is a dress I want Ma to sew for me. It has leg of lamb sleeves that bell out above the elbow, and a dipped waist that comes to a point. The color is fuchsia like the African violets I love, not the pale blue everyone calls violet. I am more towards the colors of the sunset. I will wear it for Stephen's wedding. Esther has asked me to be a bridesmaid and sprinkle the bougainvillea flowers for her processional. I hope that Joseph will come. I can't think how to let him know that I will be there. I don't think Myrna will come, I don't think anyone has invited her or knows her address except Dodge. 'She is a past customer now,' I bet he says. The market is closing and they are lighting the kerosene lamps at the food stands. The mosquitoes are coming out and the bar is overflowing with men. Here comes Father. Something must have happened to the baby.

CHAPTER 5

ALL IS WELL

It was late afternoon when Festal and Myrna arrived at Copperfine. They had taken five days to make the trip, traveling by oxcart over the cracked red earth, and stopping along the way for pieces of fruit, roasted ears of corn, and kebabs sizzling at roadside stands near the small towns. For Myrna, it was a time to observe who this man was that she had married. She had left Blancville with a sense of resignation that her life was over. As they continued on their journey, there was an awakening to new possibilities. She grew used to Festal's habits; of checking on his oxen, loosening their harness, and putting a handful of cotton under the part that was rubbing them. He made sure they had food and water each time the wagon stopped for the night, checking their hooves for a stone and cleaning the yoke to remove the dirt of the day's pull.

Festal walked a long ways out in the bush to relieve himself. He asked her several times if she needed to stop, if she had enough to drink or was hungry. He had packed two large wool blankets in the wagon bed and when she wanted, he would stop and she could stretch out. She was still nervous doing this, and preferred to spend the daylight hours perched on the wagon seat beside him. The first day she watched as the pair of oxen labored, one starting to pull, then the second joining in, each matching the other in their steps, even when they decided to urinate. They were a well matched team, in strength and in temperament. One was a brindle bull and the second a solid red-colored bullock with a white tuft of hair between his set of long horns. They worked methodically along, neither paying much attention to what lay on either side, but very aware of the track they were following, and when it was time drink or to rest.

By the third day, Myrna had lost all interest in the oxen, the cart, or what direction the wagon was heading. Her neck and back were stiff from tension and the jolting of the cart. She accepted Festal's hand as he helped her down and into the wagon bed. Festal had never tried to touch her body or to embrace her during the entire trip, and it surprised her. She didn't know what she had expected, but it wasn't this shyness, almost deference that he showed towards her. She saw he was well muscled and his strong back from the wagon bed where she reclined, and how he slouched with the jolting of the wagon, his spine giving to the jerks and bumps of the unpaved track. Myrna liked the way he handled the animals. They had never had animals at their home in Blancville as the bricks and the firing ovens left no room for grazing or stalling an animal. The family had chickens but these were kept in a small coop and not let out. Her father had hired a driver when he needed to go somewhere, or used the local donkey wagon and driver to haul in water if they were building an addition to the house.

When they got to a larger town, Festal suggested that Myrna buy a book for herself. He watched her pour over the bookshelves before selecting a slim volume. "No, go ahead and get a bigger book," he insisted.

She smiled and said "This is the one I choose." He paid for it eagerly and squeezed her hand as he helped her back into the wagon with her small package. Both of them heard the laughter of the store clerks, and thought it was directed at them. It was their first transaction as a married couple.

The red and dusty road to Copperfine was rugged laterite with few travelers along the way; each of whom greeted them and asked how the road lay. The rains, which normally fell this time of year, were delayed and the wind built each afternoon with clouds bunched across the horizon. At first Myrna said nothing, but by the end of the second day she was looking forward to meeting with fellow travelers, no matter how slight the conversation, as Festal had said few words the entire trip.

At night Myrna and Festal stopped at guest houses where the two of them could refill their water bottles and take a shower and they could get feed for their oxen. Each night Myrna brushed the red dust from her hair, which the scarf could not keep out, and wiped her face clean. Then she coated her face with shea butter to stop its drying out. Festal was fastidious with his bathing and smelled fresh, even in the heat. He used a scented dusting powder on his feet which were covered with leather sandals. Then a little pomade for his hair.

Each morning he scraped his face clean of whiskers with a straight razor that he sharpened with a leather strap, but by nightfall it was once again covered with stubble. They slept in the wagon, as it the nights were dry, and they had blankets to keep out the cold. Festal slept on the seat and Myrna nestled down in the wagon bed, covered in her sleeping cloth and wool blankets.

By the third day, Festal's face took on a worried, tired look. At the same time, he had a vitality about him that showed Myrna his powerful side that was not to be trifled with. Her lips were starting to crack from the dry heat and she found herself wanting to make sure they did not. She gathered some shea butter from her toiletries and applied it to them, and to her nose. She frequently had to urinate, and tapped Festal's arm so he would stop for her.

Festal taught Myrna how to recognize different animals by their silhouette, and how to tell which way they were heading. He could spot an animal on the horizon before Myrna even noticed a herd. Sometimes he answered bird calls with a perfect pitch and listened for their response.

"None of my relatives live south of Copperfine or we could bed at their place," Festal explained.

"I like sleeping in the wagon under the stars," Myrna said.

"Yes. I like to do things in the way I am used to. We can make better time as well."

Myrna couldn't imagine traveling any more slowly. But she was in no rush to get to the cattle station. It had been described so negatively to her by her sister. But after a few more days of traveling behind the dust and heat of the oxen, she was ready to arrive somewhere and get down to walk around for a while.

With no increase in words or speed, they slowly made their way towards Copperfine.

How had Festal ever come across Dodge and ended up married to her? Myrna doubted Festal would share that information any time soon. For now, it was enough that they were making their way together towards their future home, and where their baby would be born. She stopped for a minute to wonder if Festal knew she was pregnant. How would he, if she didn't tell him? She let that thought drift away with the cloud of red dust the wheels had churned up. She began to pray, for the first time in her life, that she would know the right things to say and do so that she would have a father for her child. She hoped he would love the baby the way she was beginning to, even as it jostled along inside her. Why did Festal make no allusion to their coming together or their wedding day? Was he as much in the dark about what had gone on as she was? Then a new possibility dawned. What if he was not the one who had taken her virginity? She could not bring herself to use the word rape. Rape was something that happened in the open savannah when you strayed too far from your tribe or family, or in the dark alleys of an unknown city when men had been drinking—not in your own home in your parents' bed. If Festal had not taken her...

The cart stopped with a jerk. Festal stepped down from the cart and led the oxen. "We are very close to the cattle station," he said. "I don't want to risk the oxen charging to get home and upsetting the cart, or you. Over there is the post office. If you receive letters, you can pick them up there. I have never received a letter, as I don't know how to write."

Myrna realized now how difficult it must have been for Festal to make all the arrangements for the cattle, the marriage license, and the land without being able to decipher a word. He had to trust Uncle Dodge for everything, and that was hard for her, his own niece, to imagine.

"If you want to write anyone, just let me know what you want to say and I will write the letters for you. You will have to drive me to the post office though, as I have never driven even donkeys." Festal reached over and placed his hand over hers.

Ahead on the top of a ridge was the house he had built. It was a rondavel with curving, smooth dark red walls. Black poles supported the thatch roof. At the base of the walls it was surrounded by a two-foot wide gutter that carried away the rainwater, if it ever came. At the back was a smaller building with a wall around it that Myrna guessed was the wash room. At the side was a grove of mango trees and a large round cistern taller than a man. It was made from clay and blackened by fire, and had a small spigot with a drain flowing into a catch basin and the vegetable garden below. Near the cistern was a small kitchen with a thatched roof and a low wall circling the fire pit. An iron arm across the fire pit allowed you to hang a pot from it above the coals. A platform with purple and red bougainvillea climbing its sides flanked the front courtyard. Round black clay pots, sheaves of roofing thatch, and calabash pots sat on top of it. A ladder made of poles lashed with rawhide leaned against the arbor. Under the platform, yellow calabash gourds and green watermelons twined around each other, their shadows making a filigree beneath the arbor. The courtyard in front of the rondavel was about 20 by 40 feet, and surrounded on three sides with a low curved wall of adobe and an opening at the front. There was a small storage shed for their goods and firewood. Her mind took in the scene like a still life painting that would remain in her imagination through the years for its beauty and clarity as she had never seen a landscape quite like this.

Myrna started down from the wagon, and felt Festal unexpectedly swing her up into his arms and carry her into the house, pushing the hand-hewn door open with his knee.

She was slightly dizzy from the motion and surprised at how powerful Festal was. She was also amazed at his knowledge of a custom she had only read about. He placed her on her feet in the room and she looked around. It was tidy and cool with a single bed made of leather strapping against one wall, and a small oval mirror above the table that flanked the opposite wall. The thatched roof was held up by a spoked arrangement of timbers stained with black pitch. The adobe walls were plastered with a coating of white wash.

After her eyes adjusted to the darkness, she saw the neat rows of shelves built into the mud walls forming a cupboard, and the two carved stools near the doorway. The floor was polished cow dung as hard and smooth as linoleum with a curved ledge around the edge which strengthened the foundation and could be used for seating. She walked over to the single window, closed with a dark wood shutter. She could see the door was made of mahogany planks, carved with birds and flowers. It was left open during the day and needed a curtain across the opening to keep out the flies. This would be her home for her married life. She loved the simplicity and order of it.

Myrna felt Festal's eyes follow her as he watched her face. "I've got to put the oxen away," he grunted, wiping his eyes. Myrna reached her hand out and touched his cheek. She would need to ask him in a few minutes where the latrine was, but for now, she swept her eyes over the room. She would be happy here, she decided. This would be a house of love.

By the time Festal returned from unhitching and hobbling his oxen and shoving the cart closer to the storage shed, Myrna had removed her smaller books from the bag and lined them up on the shelves, along with their tea mugs, the enamel plates, and a small package wrapped in red paper. Her clothing was in woven hampers and she pushed them alongside the bed. She pulled her wooden pick from her hand bag and went to the mirror above the table to see how her hair looked. Dusted in red, it reminded her of one of their roosters. She cleaned and smoothed the edges with her pick pulling each curl into its ringlet.

The rest of the day was spent putting away the items from the ox cart and opening the wedding gifts. Each one recalled the friend or family member who gave it to them. There were more gifts than Myrna or Festal had ever received. She noted them on a list so she could thank the giver when she saw them again.

In the evening after the fire was built, the water heated in the large pot, and the door closed, Myrna reached up on the shelf and took down the red box. She handed it to Festal. He wasn't sure what to make of it.

"Open it," she commanded. He did. Inside was a leather punch and red cow bell. Festal was pleased and set them on the shelf beside the books. He couldn't think of what to say, but they showed him that she had thought of him and what he might like. That was enough.

"The bed is for you, Myrna. I will sleep on the mat. It is what I am used to," he said. Myrna climbed onto the bed with its mattress filled with soft grasses, then she pulled the red wool blanket over her, smoothing out the quilt. After she blew out the candle, she found she was wide awake. After a few minutes, she asked, "Festal, are you asleep?"
"No."

"I want you to be happy."

"I am."

"Goodnight, then."

"Goodnight."

The following morning, Festal was gone. Myrna woke to the hee-hawing sound of love-sick donkeys braying in the far pasture below. She pulled her legs from the warm covers. The room was so cold she saw her breath. She removed her nightgown, arranged a *chitenge* around her hips, and wrapped up in her sweater. Then she pulled her wool socks on and up her legs before swinging her feet onto the cold polished floor. The room smelled of fresh thatch, smoky pitch, and Brazilian floor wax. In the outdoor kitchen, Festal had built a fire and water was heating. She heard the popping of the firewood as pitch flared up, and smelled the fragrant smoke.

Immediately she headed for the latrine and noticed a bowl of water, soap, and a towel set out in the small building. The walls were freshly whitewashed and on the back wall there was a crescent-shaped opening so she could see the valley below. She had not noticed this the evening before in her rush to relieve herself. She washed and returned to the house, her legs damp and stinging from grasses that had brushed them.

Myrna put leaves in the china pot then went out to the kitchen where she dipped boiling water from the large iron pot for the tea. By the time Festal returned, she had made small sandwiches with hard biscuits and barbecued eggs her mother had packed. She opened a can of sardines. Until they bought some provisions, it was the best she could do. Festal came back from checking on his calves and Myrna said she wanted to see them.

"Let's eat something first, then I will show them to you."

They ate without talking and drank the hot tea from enamel mugs with fresh cow's milk. When they were done he led her out to see his cattle. Morning sun sent a glow around the corral. Gigantic Brahmin, Watusi, and Holstein-cross cows, as well as some white face mixes stared at her as she entered the area. Festal named off the breeds to her. She was startled by the length and thickness of their horns and the sudden tossing of their heads. Their warm breath made puffs of blue against the morning cold and she could see how damp their noses were. The calves lay in a small paddock piled in the corner for warmth. Their heavy coats of black and white hair were tufted up as though they had just been licked. Their eyes were heavy with sleep as they had just finished their morning milk and were ready to nap. Festal had rigged a leather milking bucket with a nipple for those without a mother.

"Most of the ranchers just abandon these," he explained. "But this is how I got ahead. I saved them and started my herd." He didn't tell her how many cattle he owned, but she could see there were six healthy calves of all colors that he had just fed. She reached over to pet them and rub their soft sides.

"After we finish putting the supplies away, the neighbors want to meet you. If you're not too tired," he added.

As Myrna walked back to the house with Festal she felt the heat on her face. The flies were beginning to come inside the house. She decided that while Festal was away at work, she would make some curtains for the window opening and the door. This should keep the majority of them out. She would also have to make covers for the bread and fruit dishes, she thought, as she looked at the onions and yams that were now covered with flies. She stepped outside to the kitchen and put the cover on the large cauldron of water over the fire, pushed the fire logs beneath its legs, and placed the dirty dishes in a metal basin to rinse. She asked Festal where she could bathe.

"I made you a place where no one can see you," he said. "I will show you."

Myrna, was raised in a large family, and had never worried about anyone watching her bathe, it just didn't happen. At home, she took her bath behind the reed screen when the boys were at school and the men were working, as did her mother and sister. Well, she would have new ways to learn, that was for sure. She followed Festal behind the rondavel to a building with a spiral opening like the shell of a snail, so that no one could see the bather. The leather bucket above her head was on a pulley and when she pulled a rope, the bucket would empty onto her to rinse away the soap. There was a metal pan to stand in to catch the water that would then be used to water the orchard. She touched the new towel that hung on a wooden peg and felt the roughness of the loofah sponge hanging beside it. A bar of green soap was on the washroom floor. Festal filled the leather bucket above her with heated water, then left her to finish her bath.

CHAPTER 6

VIOLET MEETS HER MAN

It is the weekend and I am at home reading my diary. So much has gone on in my life in the last few months. I have just jotted down brief notes. I want to read it and catch up. Mother has gone to the market with the baby Jethro and Father is talking bricks with someone. The boys are playing and this is my chance.

February 19 – Dear Diary. I met someone at Myrna's wedding. He came alone and by the time he reached the reception, his shiny black shoes were all dusty. He said he wanted to see me and had caught a glimpse of me in church when I was singing. His name is Joseph.

Actually, I had noticed Joseph earlier. He is not from these parts. I liked his face and the way he lost his thoughts when I smiled at him in church. I saw him stop singing and lose his place. He is about 20 and works for the Indian shopkeeper at the mercantile store.

When Mother and I first went to Joseph's shop for cloth, he put some extra cloth in her bag, and made sure she counted her change. I was with her and know he wanted to look at me, but he never took his eyes off my mother. Even pregnant, she is an impala woman, as my dad calls her. Her skin glows golden and her large eyes take on a startled look when she first hears something. Her cheeks pull in with two tiny puckers when she smiles. *Dimples.* That is the word. Sometimes I start to say *pimples.* I have to think about it each time I go to describe them. Dimples. Mother did not comment on her condition, but I know it pleased her when I told her she was the most beautiful pregnant woman in our house. After she had baby Jethro, she turned slim almost immediately. I am writing this diary in English as I want to keep up my languages. Joseph says this is important in any business. I am making short entries in my journal, just enough to remind myself of what is going on, so I don't run out of pages. Love, Violet.

The second Sunday in February, Joseph returned to the Full Gospel Presbyterian church. Violet's choir was performing at another congregation at that time, but he didn't know that, so his eyes roamed the sanctuary, looking for the girl who he secretly called his impala girl. His disappointment at not seeing her among the singers was noted by Dodge, who approached Joseph in the narthex shortly after the rains had started. The two men, along with the majority of the congregation, were trapped inside, until the deluge ended. Dodge put his arm around Joseph and said, "I have been watching you for some time. I have a niece that sings like an angel-perhaps you have heard her in the youth choir."

"Yes. There is one girl I have noticed that is tall and has large eyes." Joseph went into a reverie as he thought of the girl that sang so beautifully and who he couldn't take his eyes off of.

Eyes so widely spaced so that the white of them made you look only at her face. She was a slim and tall girl, tall like himself. I didn't pay much attention to anything else, although I tried to follow the logic in the sermon, and dutifully opened to the passages in my-new Bible It is leather bound with gold edged pages, and the cover of it is embossed in gold with my name, Leibitsang. It gives me pleasure as it is the first book I have ever owned. While I cannot read it, I can find the page number and chapter, and follow along with the reading, and depend on the pastor to tell me what it says. It feels powerful to be a man who knows book, and this is where I will record my wedding and the birth of my children.

Dodge was going with what resembled a sales pitch on the family, lineage and pedigree of the girl. Joseph tuned the man out, but nodded occasionally as Dodge went on, in case there was something in his words that could help him with his pursuit of the girl.

"You are looking very downcast, as though you have lost your best friend. I came over to welcome you to a family gathering, as my lovely niece is getting married."

"The Chitundu girl?" Joseph couldn't control his voice.

"Now don't look so crestfallen. It is Myrna, the older sister who is having her nuptials. Your girl is still in the running. Myrna is marrying an older fellow from the north. She was in secondary school, but now she is a bride. I helped seal the deal, and it wasn't the easiest transaction." Dodge laughed with the memory of how this uppity girl had been trussed and brought to the altar with scarcely a whimper.

Joseph was relieved to hear it was not the girl he admired, so let his defenses down.

"Where is the wedding being held and how should I get there? I am not sure what I should wear. Will they welcome me? I need your advice."

"Don't worry about being welcomed. I am inviting you. Wear a sports coat, or a suit, and I will come and pick you up next Friday at the mercantile store and take you to the event. It's going to be in the large park next to this church. You can count on me."

"Do not mention me to the girl," Dodge added. "I don't want to take any credit. Let her think that the caterer told you to come, and that this is not your usual habit. She will be busy at the wedding, as she is the maid of honor, so you will see her and note if she is what you are interested in. I can tell you, you won't find a better family, myself notwithstanding." Dodge smiled at his skillful disclaimer, and thought what an attorney he could be, if he only had the desire to study those long hours.

Friday, Joseph was ready and waiting for Dodge. When Dodge didn't show up, he hired a taxi and made his way to the wedding of Myrna and Festal. The grounds beneath the majestic baobab and flame of the forest trees were filled with wedding guests and spectators.

A truck with a cow standing in the back was parked under canopy of the trees, and her bellowing punctuated the service that followed. Joseph stood at the back of the seated throng of guests. The tent was filled with visitors, all dressed in their wedding finery. He recognized the fabrics and traditional cloths of regions he had traveled. The bride was beautiful and tall; young, and a little tearful. She was dressed in a simple muslin gown with a lace veil and a bouquet of red lilies. The groom, who seemed to be in his forties, was slightly shorter in stature, even though the bride was wearing sandals. He wore dark clothing and his nervous gestures may have made him seem older. He didn't smile, and the deep lines at the corner of his eyes indicated long hours in the sun. His hair was thick and cropped short, but no silver showed in it and his eyes were amber in color, with long curled lashes. Intense, and not to be trifled with, this is how Joseph would have summed him up, had he been called to do so.

Festal held on to the girl's hand even after placing a gold band on her finger. The cow in the truck continued to bellow, now with continuous giant sobs of sound. The couple turned and faced the crowd and the bride handed her bouquet of flaming red lilies to a short, voluptuous woman, who was standing beside Violet, then the family headed to the reception in the adjacent field. Joseph followed the crowd of relatives and well-wishers.

In the park, colored papers something like small flags lined the pathways. The food sat under small tents, and it was abundant. The bride and groom stood against a baobab tree while their picture was taken. Drinks were brought to them and plates of meat, breads, rice and groundnuts were served to the 300 or so people gathered in the park.

Joseph tried to get close to the sister. He caught her name as the relatives congratulated the bride. *Violet.* It was the most beautiful sound he had ever heard. He stood at the side, watching the event take place, and comparing it with the celebration he would have when Violet made him her husband. *Violet.* Even the sound of it made his heart sing. He would provide dresses for all the bridesmaids, there would be at least five of them, and have plates for all the guests; even small napkins with their initials intertwined. There would be music and they would dance into the small hours of the morning.

Just then Dodge came up to him, with no mention of the missed ride. "So, you are becoming part of the family," he proclaimed. "Have you met the mother and father? They will need some persuading. I can help you with that. I don't require much of a retainer. This is the ideal time to make your case, while they are still enjoying the fruits of the first pairing." Dodge laughed at his poetic rendering of the event. "Then the newlywed couple is off to cattle country. But you could keep their last daughter, and her children to come, closer to home. This is a real benefit. You will have to tally up what it is you offer, if I am to negotiate this in all of our best interests."

Dodge gave Joseph a sideways glance to see if he was following the course of the conversation and was in agreement. His niece, Violet, was too tall for his liking, and she had always seemed a little lackluster when it came to chemistry, for his tastes in a mate—not that he intended to tie himself down with a woman anytime soon. Violet had stopped attending following graduation from basic school, but she had a beautiful singing voice. Her mother doted on her and she was given to superficiality. Dodge knew the girl looked down on him, and he thought she needed to be knocked down a few pegs, but Violet seemed to have registered on Joseph's radar. He led the young man over to Violet's parents and introduced him.

40

"This is a friend of mine who owns the store where many of these fabrics are sold," he said by way of introduction. Joseph bowed his head in greeting and lowered his right arm, supporting it with his left hand, to shake the hands of the parents. They said nothing but they saw the respect he offered. Dodge prattled on as usual. The parents' focus was on Myrna and Festal, making sure the presents and goods were loaded onto their wagon and that everyone had been able to congratulate the couple.

When Violet saw Dodge corner Joseph, and smiling, she had immediately ruled him out. But the young man had arrived at the reception alone, so maybe he had come of his own volition. She noticed his height and the care he took in his dress. His shoes were polished and his fingers were long and slim with buffed nails. She also noticed that he watched her, then would turn away with some shyness when she caught him looking.

Violet was not doing much that hot season, and she found herself running errands for her mother, going to the mercantile store and buying fabric for the children's uniforms, picking out a print to make a new skirt, and a top for the choir tour. The choir would be touring two other countries, and she wanted to distract herself from the loss of her sister and the revulsion she felt for the man her sister had married. Festal was a predator, just like Uncle Dodge. Violet could tell that from his eyes. He looked straight at her when he spoke, which was not often. Violet noticed how striking his eyes were in color and shape, with their curled lashes, and she had sketched them several times. She tried to capture the intensity of how the man looked at a person, and why his gaze was so piercing, but her drawings did not reflect his animal magnetism.

Violet obsessed on Festal and how her sister connected with him because her Uncle Dodge had just told her that Myrna was pregnant, and she couldn't imagine how this had happened. She was considering a piece of lace when she saw the young clerk looking at her intently and she said, "Didn't I see you at my sister's wedding?"

"Yes. I didn't know your sister at all, but I had to come."

"Was it the catering that interested you? That is what my Uncle Dodge told me."

"That is what he told me to say. He knows I am interested in...I didn't even know your name when I came. Now I do. Violet, it is you that attracted me."

"I am glad you said that. I will mention to my father that you have a solid business."

"I do not own this business. I am waiting for the right partner to make my ventures worth the effort. I want someone who can make something together with me, so that we are equals in life. That someone I have not had time to think about or find, but now I have hope."

Violet reached for money to pay for her dress goods, but Joseph shook his head. "These are a gift to you."

"I could never accept a gift from a man directly. What are you thinking?" Violet pulled three bills from her purse and pushed them across the counter, refusing to meet Joseph's eyes. She looked out the open door as he put her cloth in a brown paper and carefully folded it into a neat packet, tying it with twine.

"Violet, I have much to learn, but I am willing to be taught."

She blushed as she left the store, just as the owner of the mercantile walked in the door.

"Good afternoon, Valoo."

"Joseph, who is that palm of a woman? Call me the next time she comes to the shop."

"She is my future wife," Joseph heard himself say.

"Well. Congratulations." Valoo was puzzled at how he and his wife could have missed such a happening. This girl was quality, and now Joseph might be thinking of leaving. Valoo decided he had better give the boy a raise to keep him in the harness a little longer.

"Joseph, I have been noticing how thorough you are with the inventory and the cleanup. I appreciate your attention to your work. I am going to give you a bonus at the end of the month for the extra hours you have put in. My customers always ask for you when I make the buying circuit. Keep up the good work. By the way, when is the big day?"

"Thank you, Valoo. You and your wife and daughter will all be invited. We haven't firmed up a date as of yet. We have to consider the mother, you know."

"Oh, yes. I saw she was expecting. Has the child come?"

"Yes. Another boy."

"You have made an excellent choice of family. Family is really all that matters in the long view. Family and reputation. And tradition." Valoo looked for a moment as though he wanted to add something to this list of instructions for life, but what it was eluded him. "Well, keep up the good work."

"Yes sir. Thank you again, Valoo. You are a generous man."

Later that evening, as Valoo handed his daughter the tickets and told her she would be going home to care for a dear relative who had fallen ill, he remembered what he had wanted to add to his advice. Values. Like Valoo. Values. That is what was needed for a successful life. He would have to try to remember to tell that to Joseph. Maybe at the wedding.

CHAPTER 7

JOSEPH'S HISTORY

Joseph began his courting of Violet by going over his history. He knew Violet would want to know all about him, and have information to share with her parents when they asked. As he could not write it down, he rehearsed what he wanted to tell them about himself, and if need be, he would have the church secretary write it out for him. As he thought about the decisions he had made so far in his life, he was positive that the choice of Violet would be one of the most significant he would ever make.

Joseph came from the region where the Kalahari begins. His people were hunters and gatherers and had been for eons before the other groups began to take over the land. He was tall and had a mind for figures. At an early age, he could take inventory of what was in the granary, the *boma,* the garden. While his brothers and sisters were busy herding goats and cattle, or wrestling in the sand, Joseph lined up sticks to keep track of his calculations. It wasn't long before one of the Indian merchants discovered his gifts and asked him to come and work in his mercantile warehouse. Joseph often took yard goods or a tool for his pay, and then would trade or give them to local people in need. By the time he was a teenager, the merchant offered him the position of store manager, encouraging him to travel with him when he made his purchasing trips.

Joseph loved to travel and while he did not attend formal school, he knew how to trace his voyages on a map and to record what he had seen by making a symbol in the margins. He also learned the price of goods. He probably would have continued to work in the large warehouse store if he had not overheard a conversation between Valoo and his wife discussing the marriage of their daughter.

"We are going to have to get the money together and send Pearl back to India to provide a suitable husband. I have asked my uncle to line up a matchmaker to work on behalf of our family. I know it is expensive to put together a dowry, and she is young, but we don't want her to fall for some *kaffir* that she comes across in the marketplace" Valoo told his wife. The Valoos thought they were alone for the evening as he and his wife counted out the cash from the cashbox at the back of the store. Joseph was tidying the dry goods shelves and could hear every word.

"Husband, I have had the same worry. I see her go to help do inventory and I am afraid the girl is not thinking about how many yards of cloth we have. There is no one here of our social status or class. We may have difficulty in finding someone willing to take her if we wait too long. She is already fifteen. I was thirteen when we were betrothed."

"I will arrange to get her a ticket for next week. We will wire my uncle and have him look after her until a match is made. You tell her she is going to visit a sick relative to give comfort. I can forward him the dowry to seal the arrangement. He knows what we want for our family in a mate."

The gist of the conversation was that they needed to get her back to their homeland so that she would marry a proper husband, and not find herself tying up with a *kaffir.* Joseph had heard this derogative before, but he had never applied it to himself. Valoo and his wife had shared meals with Joseph and he had spent much time with Valoo on road trips and in guest houses along their travels, He never thought himself less than this man, except in age, wealth and experience. Now, he realized he needed to go out on his own and set up his own business. He did not share this information with Valoo, but was even more polite and deferential to the older man than he had been before.

Joseph volunteered for more tasks and sought advice as to how things were done. When Valoo asked Joseph about his plans for future, Joseph would tell him his goal was to learn everything about the business, for Valoo was so knowledgeable. In this way, Joseph learned the skills from a man who had started out with nothing and made a fortune among the middle class Africans in the community of Blancville. Valoo was respected by members of the community and the governing leaders, giving money conspicuously to well-known causes, such as the resettlement benevolence and the hospital guild. Privately, Joseph knew what Valoo really thought of the people and their potential. Joseph resolved that he would be a person with integrity in his business dealings, and his home life. Joseph joined the Presbyterian Church and began to give some thought to his social connections, as well as the idea of meeting a woman of virtue to help him succeed in his goals of being an independent business owner.

CHAPTER 8

JOSEPH VISITS CHITUNDUS

It was the following Monday when Joseph decided to make a call on the Chitundus, parents of Violet, his impala woman. He left them a note at the church on Sunday, penned by the church secretary who had also helped him write out his history, and they agreed to meet with him on Wednesday following market.

Joseph ironed his shirt twice to make sure he would make a good impression. He spritzed his jacket with aftershave, checked his shoes to make sure they were polished, and checked his pants for lint. Then he made his way to their home on the outskirts of Blancville. He took the bus so he would be fresh on arrival, not realizing their driveway was three hundred feet in length, and a dusty track at that. On the way, he checked himself a couple of times to make sure he was not sweating and that his hair was not dusty like the powdered beignets at the bakery. He carried with him a small set of photos of his family. There were also a few photos of the Brahmin cow at Myrna's wedding. Another was a sunrise over the Zambezi with the double rainbow and the cascading water between two nations. He didn't know what he was going to say, but put it all in the hands of fate, and Violet. If she had any interest in him, she would have said something to the parents.

When he arrived, Bishop Chitundu had gone out for an emergency in the village. He had been called to mediate between the parties. Mrs. Chitundu apologized and invited Joseph in. He was glad to talk to her alone.

"Mrs. Chitundu, I am Joseph Leibitsang. I am wanting to be the husband of Violet and the father to her children. I have seen your family, and I want to be a part of it. I work in provisions, that is, I provide. Here are some pictures of my family. Last week, I attended the wedding of your oldest daughter. I had to come because I am in love with your daughter Violet and I wanted to see you all."

Beatrice looked Joseph in the face. "Please, call me Beatrice. As you can see, we are a large family, and growing larger. I am missing my married daughter very much. I cannot have another leave me so soon."

Joseph glanced shyly at Beatrice. "I am a man who values family. I have several brothers and sisters. I will not take your daughter away. She will be here to assist you whenever you need. Here is the design for the house I will build for my wife. She will have a room for her parents and family to come and stay. I will build it close to you so you can walk between houses. Family should stay close. I also expect to provide for my extended family as we will always have supplies and provisions for them. I keep a close eye on the markets and buy before there is famine. My plan is to open my own warehouses once I have a partner to share with me. I want that partner to be your Violet." Joseph let out his breath after this long and practiced appeal. Beatrice handed him a cup of tea with a smile. He drank it and thanked her for her hospitality.

"I will put in a word for you with Mr. Chitundu, but only after I have a chance to talk with Violet. Thank you for coming, Joseph Leibitsang"

Joseph had made his case, and Beatrice had agreed that she would put in a word with Mr. Chitundu. As he left, he recalled the fragrance of mangos and the immaculate polish on the traditional floors, the vase of lilies on the table, and the colorful yellow antimacassars on the arms of the chair. The clock on the wall said 11:00 when he arrived, and 11:00 when he left. Somehow, he liked the lack of punctuality in the household, where natural rhythms took precedence. Most of all, he appreciated that Dodge was nowhere in sight.

As he walked back down the long, dusty driveway, Joseph thought over the conversation. The ground had been laid for staging an understanding. There could be no formal engagement until the father determined that the girl would be adequately supported, that a bride price was negotiated, and that nothing was rushed.

Beatrice had been resigned to her daughter Myrna leaving the area because she had already been away at boarding school, and her absence had become a reality. The possibility that Myrna was pregnant and that the father of the child had paid a hefty bride price made acceptance of Festal more palatable, also he was of their tribe and knew the customs. They would always be welcome in his home, even if he lacked some of the social polish of an educated man. For Violet, a child who had always been close to her mother, the biggest argument in favor of this young man Joseph was that he was direct. He intended to keep close ties with the family and not live far from them. Violet would be cared for, he had shown the mother his plans for a house with room for her mother and father to come and stay with them whenever they wished. He wanted a family, He had made a success of his business and was just waiting for a partner in order to become an independent merchant.

He had served his apprenticeship and could aid the family with the products he had access to. He did not mind having a wife that had little formal schooling. He said he recognized in their home that she had been trained in what mattered. Joseph was in good health, he was not a womanizer, and he wanted children. He said he was not the owner of the store where he worked, but he was the owner of his future, and he wanted to marry for affection and stability in the family.

Beatrice Chitundu had five sons and two daughters. She wanted husbands who would support their children and keep the family ties.

The case put forward by Joseph met with her approval. Now, she would hear what her daughter Violet thought, before presenting the situation to her husband. She knew not to ask her husband a question unless she had the answer. And for her, the answer, at this point, was a qualified "Yes."

CHAPTER 9

WELLINGTON TAYLOR VISITS CHITUNDUS

Beatrice and Violet, sat on the verandah watching the afternoon sun dry up the rain. They discussed the suitor Joseph and his strong points, the conversations he had had with Violet, and the love Violet felt towards him. They were waiting for her father to return home, when a young man stepped into view. He was slim and athletic, with a tweed hat on his blond, wind-tossed hair. He introduced himself.

"Hello and good afternoon. I am Wellington Taylor, Myrna's tutor."

"Myrna is no longer living here." Violet immediately translated for her mother who did not speak English.

"That is what I heard. We miss her at the school. She is an excellent student," he said, blocking his eyes from the sun.

"Myrna is no longer in the area," Violet said.

"Can you tell me where she is? I have some things that belong to her."

"It is better if you just forget about Myrna."

"Can you give me her address so I can at least congratulate her?"

"She will not want to hear from you. Uncle Dodge said he had taken care of her things."

"Well, he hasn't. She has some personal effects that I am going to keep until you give me her address."

"We are not giving you her address. She is gone. She doesn't need to be reminded of what she has lost."

Violet knew she was being loose with her translations, as her mother kept asking what the man wanted, becoming upset, and wondering what the teacher was doing here. Violet felt a little guilty. After all, she would be able to marry Joseph because of the bride price Festal had paid, and she didn't want to risk any upset of this arrangement.

Beatrice did not want Myrna to be upset either. It was better this way. Just let him leave and Myrna go on with her life in the cattle station. If he was interested in Myrna, he should have said so before Festal got her. The family was better off now. Stephen and Esther were together, Thomas was back in school, and Violet would soon have the husband she wanted. They had made the right choice for their family.

Wellington saw he was getting nowhere with the sister and that the mother could not understand what he was after. In frustration, he took the books and the diary he had brought and returned them to his office.

When he left the school the following year, the diary and the essays Myrna had written were packed up with his things. It would be a few years before he came across them and read the young girl's confusion of events that Christmas break. She had no idea that her uncle might be scheming to force her to drop out of school and marry an older man she did not know or want. Wellington Taylor never forgot Myrna's face or her sense of responsibility. He was frustrated at not being able to communicate with her. The smugness of her sister and mother refusing to answer his questions, or allow him to have Myrna's address was upsetting. The fact that Myrna would never know how much he admired and respected her, was Wellington's deepest regret.

CHAPTER 10

BEATRICE TELLS BISHOP ABOUT JOSEPH

Bishop listened as his wife described the young man from church who was interested in Violet. Bishop had made it past the crisis in his business, and really was not eager to have this last daughter leave the household.

"Bishop, I talked with the young man we met in church and at the wedding of Myrna. He is Joseph Leibitsang and he runs the mercantile and provisions store here in town."

"I was sorry after Myrna married. I was boxed in by the need to get a bride price for Stephen. I don't want another daughter leaving the house so soon. We have Stephen married, and Myrna. Why can't this wait?" The torment was seen in the lines around his mouth and eyes.

"Bishop, you are ahead of me already. I just wanted to let you know that if we decide to let Violet marry this young man, they will be living within walking distance of us. He assures me that she can be here whenever we need or want her to come. He showed me the house plans he has had drawn up, and they include a guest room for us to stay anytime we want. He is only waiting for us to give our blessings to an engagement."

"What about the family? Did he say anything about his people?"

"He said he wants to be a part of our family. He has several brothers and sisters and values family. He had pictures and ideas that were respectful of our wishes and of Violet. He knows others will have more to offer in the way of money or position, but he offers us a future of providing for us and his family, as they arrive. He wants children, and most of all, he wants his wife to be a partner with him as he builds his business."

Bishop looked at the pictures that Joseph had left. He liked that the man traveled and saw the beauty in what was around him, not just the money to be made. It was very thoughtful to have taken pictures at Myrna's wedding. Bishop also liked the idea of planning ahead with the house and living close by. He wasn't ruling this young man out.

Beatrice and Violet prepared dinner and no more was said of Joseph as they listened to news about the father's day, and how he had worked out a settlement for the townspeople whose problem he had been called upon to mediate. It was a domestic problem. One of the relatives was accused of taking the house away from the widowed sister. After some discussion, it was decided that she could live in the storage hut of another brother, as she had only one child, and the older brother was within his rights to take the property when his sibling passed. No signature of the wife was on the title, and she had no means of paying rent. She had lived in the house for ten years, but her husband was killed in an accident, and no provisions had been made for the event of his death.

"This sounds like a hard case. Did you have difficulty deciding what should be done?"

"The woman was not prepared to leave her house. She thought she owned it with her husband because they had worked together to pay for it. But she was not on the title and the brothers were very sharp. They had lawyers and were even willing to make it difficult on her reputation if she decided to go to court. She was lucky to have one of the brothers give her space to live. He could take her as his wife, but I don't think he wanted her. She is not so young."

"It is always the money that decides these issues. It is good you were there to sort it out. Am I on the title of our house?"

"No. We have no paperwork as we built the house on tribal land given to us by the chief. If we wanted, we should have someone write down what to have happen if I die. I don't think my brothers would make you leave, but you are right to think on these things before it happens." No more was said about ownership of houses, or people passing.

After his wife had gone to lie down and rest, Violet sat alone with her father on the verandah in the dark. "Father, I have made it clear to Joseph that he must stay close to you both if he is to consider me for his wife. He said his own father was very important to him, and he misses him every day. He was killed working as a U.N. Peacekeeper in Zaire. Joseph wants to earn your respect."

"He seems like a thoughtful young man. I will give it my consideration. Your mother was very impressed by his presentation of his prospects."

"Joseph really liked her as well. He was so pleased she let him hold the baby."

"Was he? I was always a little afraid of them when they were that small. I don't think I really carried any of you until you were about a year old. You all seemed too fragile. Well, as I said, I will think on his proposal and he is welcome to come and visit again when I am home. There is no rush." Bishop listened to his daughter and thought what a loving girl she was. It was natural she would want a man who knew how to express himself and give her the words of love that meant so much in a marriage. He would hear Joseph say them to her, and know that she would be cared for and valued.

Uncle Dodge stopped by that evening and saw his niece and his brother-in-law sitting on the porch. He joined them, and Violet left immediately. Dodge began his litany of what Violet needed, and that he was the only one that could insure the family would not once again slip into scarcity. Bishop heard him out. It would be the first of many harangues about the suitability of a mate for his niece. The more Uncle Dodge suggested dropping this Joseph prospect and letting Dodge find a suitable husband for the girl, the more Bishop leaned towards letting the girl have the husband she wanted. Violet's choice was Joseph. Bishop had not known this compliant and loving daughter could be so persistent. Bishop had to admit the boy had presented himself well. He was cordial to all the family, including Festal. Joseph had won Beatrice over in their first meeting and she was a strong advocate for letting Violet make her choice. Joseph had made his plans known to them and had not inflated his attainments, but emphasized that he would give Violet a future. What had impressed Beatrice was how he genuinely listened to the girl and consulted her on what her preferences were, and that he was not going to take her from the bosom of her family. What convinced Beatrice was that Joseph was a provisioner and knew his market. The family would be protected from sudden famine or need. She also saw he was ready to be a father.

After a month of nonstop campaigning by his daughter, Bishop gave his consent. They could marry with the stipulations that the Joseph and Violet would make their home within walking distance of the parents, the family would benefit from the provisioning, and Violet would be secure and provided for. Joseph's words of love for the girl were openly spoken, and her affection for Joseph was already abundantly clear.

Joseph had shared a brief history of his family, which concerned Bishop and Beatrice less than the proximity of their daughter and her future family. Neither of the parents had realized how much they would miss Myrna when she moved out of the area, and this was not to be repeated. With those stipulations, and a great deal hugs and tears, the couple was betrothed. Wedding plans began. Joseph invited Beatrice to come into the store and confer with himself and Valoo what the best choices were for the bridesmaids' dresses and the wedding linens. Valoo appreciated sharing his expertise. He admitted that his own daughter was recently engaged, and that he and his wife were missing the initial preparations.

When it came time to pay for the fabrics and the notions, Valoo stepped up to the counter. "Joseph has been like a son to me. I want to make this my gift to you and your family. I hope your marriage will be blessed, and that I will be a guest at your wedding."

"We will be honored by your presence. We appreciate all you have taught Joseph, and that you will be a friend to our family."

CHAPTER 11

LETTERS AND INVITATIONS

The neighbors came early and late to visit Festal's new wife. She was on display. No one went away dissatisfied with this woman, about whom the stories had already spread. Lottie, who lived closest to the Phiris, was the first to come. She wasted no time giving Myrna a big hug and pressing a little jar of honey into her hands.

"You come over and visit as soon as you get settled in. Our house is the one next to you on this same side of the ridge. My husband is away most of the day with the cattle and I welcome a visit."

The first day more than twenty people came by. She received many gifts; an egg from one, a handful of greens, a bunch of onions, a young goat, a basket of roasted corn ears, tomatoes, two towels, a whisk, and a fly switch, to name the ones she could recall. To welcome the visitors, Myrna had put on her best muslin dress with small patterns on the sleeves. She tied her hair in a patterned head cloth and on her wrist she wore a simple copper bracelet her sister had given her. Festal watched her.

"What is that scent of flowers you are wearing?"

"Do you like it?"

"Wear it always."

As her visitors poured in she wished she had something to give them. Festal told her there would be time ahead to pay a visit in return. There was no hurry. When they were alone, the two of them decided where their belongings would be stored, and how to sort out the food and dry goods.

"Make a list of the things you need and we will go to the market tomorrow to get them," Festal said,

"I know some of the things to get, but tell me what you like to eat then when I fix them you can tell me if they are made to suit you. Otherwise, I may be cooking what you don't like so much. Help me make a list." Together they made a list of what they would eat for the following days. Some of the choices were unexpected, such as a cattleman such as Festal having to buy meat at the market.

"One cow can feed so many people, but it needs to be killed in the market for the meat to be distributed. Also, we have the *halal* butchers in the market that do it so it is clean. The whole animal needs to be distributed early in the day, so each Tuesday one is butchered for the village."

"I have never selected the meat before."

"I can help you do that and let you know what prices to expect."

The following day, Festal took her to the market to buy produce and show her where the butchery was, and how to select a good piece of meat. The market was even larger than the one in Blancville, which surprised her. Festal said it was because this was the sole place to buy goods, as there were few stores in Copperfine. The selection of goods varied with what was in season. There were always animals for sale, along with produce, fetishes, clothing, some carvings, and native medicines. He showed her where the cloth and sewing notions were, as well as the man who tailored clothing, the tinsmith, and the tire repair shop. There was also a crafts market where the buyers would come to buy wholesale to distribute in the tourist and safari areas. Festal told her what a fair price was for various goods, and left an allowance for the groceries in a pouch under his mat. And so the first week went by.

Festal did not approach her physically, other than to rub her ankles when he saw they were swollen from nettles she had walked through on the way to the privy, or to help her untangle her mane of hair when it became caught in a strand of fly paper he had hung near the kitchen. He slept by her bed at night. He also listened to her tearing fabric for curtains, and sometimes singing a short song as she tended the calves. She had taken over feeding them and brushing them and they followed her about like a flock of ducklings. Festal delayed leaving for the hills with his cattle. He hovered around the house long after he had finished his chores, watching this woman make the place her own. Finally, he got up the courage to leave for his work. It was a Monday.

CHAPTER 12

LETTER FROM VIOLET

Festal recalled the day the letter came. They had been in the house for just over a week when it arrived. Since the postal people had never had to deliver a letter to his cattle ranch, the postmaster had one of the clerks take it out to Myrna. There it was. *Myrna Phiri.* The cattlemen joshed Festal about her receiving a love letter. That thought festered in his mind until he got home to see the letter for himself. When Myrna showed it to him, she pointed out his name, Phiri, on the envelope. It was from Violet. Festal was relieved and somewhat embarrassed by his jealousy. Myrna ignored his eagerness to see the letter, and instead traced his finger over the name Phiri.

"That is our name," she said. "Try writing it in the dust." He followed her fingers, soon writing for the first time. He practiced it over and over until he could write both names in the sand.

Myrna waited until Festal had gone to the fields before reading the letter. She had a surge of loneliness when she saw the careful penmanship of her sister.

Dear Myrna, How is your state of health? I trust it is fine. I have been working in the market every day. While I was there, Mother gave birth to a boy named Jethro at the hospital and it is fortunate she was there as the baby was not an easy birth. He is well now and at home. I was so frightened when Father came to collect me that evening instead of Mother. The family is busy preparing for Stephen's wedding. I am going to be a bridesmaid and mother is making me a dress of fuchsia pink taffeta. The big news is that I have met a man named Joseph, and he is everything I want. He is young, tall, and handsome. He has a great future as he is a provisioner. He is interested in me. If you come to Stephen's wedding you will meet him. I am sending you a little sketch I made of him, but it doesn't even do him justice. We are all thinking of you. Love, Violet

A second letter arrived the following week, addressed to Festal Phiri. When the postman delivered it, Festal was not home, but Myrna said she would make sure he received it. She gave the man letters she had written to her sister, and money for postage. She also placed a small coin in his hand to thank him for bringing it all the way out. He thanked her. Now he could give a full report to his fellow workers of the ten cow wife, and when he did, he said she was worth every one of them and more. Her reputation began to grow.

Myrna watched Festal's long fingers open the letter when he came home. Myrna had propped it on the shelf beside the red cowbell, as though this was a daily happening. She asked Festal if she should read it to him, as he was washing up. He nodded.

This is your invitation to the wedding of Stephen Chitundu and Esther Phiri on the 17ᵗʰ of April The Chitundu Family.

Uncle Dodge will pick you up at the bus station that morning.

Festal shook his head in disbelief. His first mail and he was invited to a wedding.

"I do not want to go, as we have just made the journey," she said. "But you can go and report everything back to me. I will care for the calves. If you want to go." The wedding was a month away and Myrna was sure she would be showing, which is why she was unwilling to go.

Festal liked the idea of being invited. Everyone had made him so welcome. But how could he leave his new wife alone? He already woke in the night thinking she had gone missing. They were so newly married. It would be a chance, however, to get supplies for the cattle station, he thought. He might also be able to secure a harness for the pair of donkeys he had trained. Then again, who would watch over his young bride? She was so agreeable to what he wanted. Maybe someone else would persuade her … He didn't allow himself to finish the thought. Tomorrow he would decide. He went out to wash up for dinner, still unsure what to do.

In the morning Festal announced he was going to attend the wedding. He would take letters from Myrna for the family. The trip would take him a week. He was relieved that he had made a decision and the moment he did, he regretted it. She would be alone. He would be away. He had to do it. Was he a fool to leave his greatest treasure unguarded?

Festal returned home by mid-afternoon, before Myrna finished preparing the evening meal. She was cooking Festal's favorite dish. The ingredients were lined up on the table, while the chicken stewed in the pot. When he walked in, he reached for her and picked her up,

"You have been eating well," he said. Myrna was surprised at the remark. She had been gaining weight, but he had to know she was pregnant. It was now mid-March.

"Yes, you are feeding me well. I hope you also have a good appetite. I am making you a special dish tonight." Myrna picked up the hot towel from the lid of the Dutch oven and smoothed it over Festal's dark face then put it against her own. Within minutes the two of them were on the bed, and he was on top of her. She hoped no one would come to their door, as there was no screen and no hallway to protect them from view. Festal was afire in his passion.

She felt his member penetrate her and it seemed it would not stop. She moaned with the pain and the suddenness of it, and as soon as he was spent he wrapped her in the sheet and headed to the washroom.

Myrna lay on the bed dazed at the heat and the passion of his mating. She would remember this afternoon. She took some time before getting up from the bed, pulling the sheet from around her and dropping it into the hamper beside the bed. Then she cleaned herself with the towel before Festal returned. When he did, he took her in his arms and smoothed her hair, then ran his hands over her body and slowly began to caress her. She felt something she had never felt before—and it was totally different from the first fierce thrust of penetration. Now, she was the one waiting for the pleasure of the ebb and flow of his movement above her. He was taut, and tender. He fashioned his lovemaking as though she was a fine instrument that needed to be tuned. She moaned and wanted to rise to meet him, but she let him take the lead entirely. This was a stranger she had not expected—one filled with passion and tenderness.

When Festal rose from the bed, he brought a hot wet towel to Myrna and carefully washed her, tenderly putting the shea butter on her female parts after warming the oil in his hands so that it became a slippery warm film that made her skin, from her breasts to her thighs feel as though they were satin. She didn't move as he looked at her with the eyes of a worshipper. She noticed how golden they were, and how languorous they became as his lashes half closed over them. He brushed his lips across all of her parts, skimming them without any pressure—making her want this flicking of the tongue and touching to never stop.

She repressed another moan of pure pleasure, wondering what other skills this husband of hers had concealed behind his intimidating face.

It was after dinner when they made love for the third time that day. This time, Myrna was eager for her lesson. Festal laid her carefully on his sheepskin mat. She found her body beginning to respond and arch toward her mate as he balanced above her, withholding his weapon of pleasure until she reached for it with her body moistening in anticipation. The oils from the earlier tryst had stimulated and intensified her nerves so she could feel every thrust of his body. She felt his penetration when he lowered himself into her crevice, with a thousand needles of desire. The hardness of the floor made her buttocks rock forward with each thrust, enjoying the muscular tension of response. They fell asleep tangled in each other's' bodies. When they awoke later that night, they were ravenous and went to the table to finish the meal she had laid out for him.

CHAPTER 13

ENVY

Winnie Kafuma, wife of the fetish priest, came to the edge of the Phiris' courtyard and paused. She could hear laughter inside and while the door was open, both hunting dogs were standing on the threshold wagging their tails. She had not expected Festal to be at home in the middle of the afternoon. She had missed the welcoming party for the new bride and decided to stop by and make her own judgment of this wife everyone was talking about. Winnie had known Festal for several years, even thinking at some point that he might be the husband she needed. When her father married her to the local fetish healer, she moved Festal to the inventory section of her library of likely candidates for her daughters. As the girls grew, she had sized him up for each of them, but Festal had shown no interest. Then she placed him in the category of men who were more spiritual and less likely to find women a pressing need. She never thought of Festal as a man who sought out other men. But why had he never been attracted to her? What did this girl have that caused him to break all his reserves and empty his *boma* of so many hard-won cattle? She had to find out.

Inside, there was love-making going on. No visitor was there or the dogs would have been tied. It was only mid-afternoon and the rest of the men were in the fields, their wives busy with the weeding or washing. This girl was making herself more laundry. Winnie waited longer than she needed before turning back to walk to her home. She would have nothing to report, but that would not prevent her from raising her eyebrows and letting others think she knew more than she let on. She unwrapped the small cake she had made for the couple and ate it herself as she climbed the hillside to her rondavel. This girl would waste Festal's resources if she kept him from his work and couldn't budget her own time well enough to do her chores. She lingered a little at the edge of their own clearing, imagining what they had been up to in the house and how Festal was in bed. She saw her own husband carving a fetish and thought maybe he needed a little attention. He didn't. He said he needed to finish his work and the girls were probably in the house anyway. She did not mention where she had been or how her errand had ended.

Winnie gathered the laundry and checked the hens for eggs. She had used two in the cake and there were three more waiting under the hens. The women in the village had reported to her that this new wife had hair like a wild colt, thick and long when she did not braid it or cover it with a head scarf. She was expecting a child already and she appeared to be very young, about the age of Winnie's youngest daughters.

Winnie called to her girls to ask if they had visited the woman. It wouldn't hurt to let them get to know her. Neither of them had attended school, and this woman was educated, or so she had heard. The village could use someone to help them know what was going on. In the interest of her husband's trade, information was important. She leaned on her kitchen ledge and called to Salina and Pillar to come inside.

"Have you met the new wife who lives in the rondavel at the end of our lane?"

"No."

"Well, I would like you both to visit her and report back to me on what she looks like, and what she knows. Can you manage that? Just listen and look around. Don't be obvious."

"When should we go?"

"Just wait until you see her coming to the river to do laundry, or out with those orphan calves. Don't let Festal see you sneaking around, make sure you just talk with her."

"Sure."

The day broke with the heat of the sun on their courtyard. Lilies were bathed in sun and birds of paradise were almost painful in their beauty. Myrna had never felt more beautiful, and Festal reveled in the passion he had roused in her. He had breakfast, and then left for the fields.

As he was out in the pastures with his fellows, the beast of jealousy began to gnaw at his innards. He coveted the very sight of Myrna's body, recalling the first time he saw it. He had been questioning whether he should marry the girl. She seemed so aloof and disinterested in him, wearing her shapeless school uniform and using her prissy manners at the table with her fork and knife. He was ready to leave the Chitundu's home and head back to Copperfine that morning in December, when Dodge pulled him over to a hiding place outside the bathing room at her parents' home. There the two men crouched and watched her strip off her uniform, seeing her ripeness and her innocence as she soaped and lathered her supple young body, the ringlets of her hair and the bubbles of white shampoo cascading over her breasts and down her thighs. She knelt in her little bathing tub with perfect balance, her arms reaching up to squeeze the water from her hair, her buttocks shimmering with the water and filtered sun.

He had been captive to the intensity of the lust that her slim form and upturned breasts had roused in him, and in Dodge. This image of her beauty was now layered over with the pleasure he had known in their lovemaking the previous night. He could not bear to have anyone mention her name, for fear that what he had discovered and won would be taken from him. Everyone wanted to talk about her and congratulate him on his woman. He wanted no one to see or touch her, even in their imagination. The passion he felt at the thought of someone taking her from him made his eyes fevered with arousal and fury.

When he returned to the rondavel, Festal was fretful and could not be easily soothed. The more Myrna stroked him and tried to please him, the more disturbed he became. At last, she realized that he was unbalanced by the passion they had enjoyed, and she concentrated on doing small errands around the house. There was a tear to be mended in the pants he wore. She pulled out a pretty little sewing basket and began mending the rip. As Festal watched her, he calmed and could again control the searing passion rising in him. He came close to her and breathed in her scent, then he pulled the pants from her lap and laid her body against his hardness like a shield. She did not resist his embraces, nor did she return them. Instinct made her submit and let him bring her to desire by moving against her, stroking her until she could not resist him. She allowed him to unfasten the buttons on her blouse and pull it from her breasts. She was wearing the white lace bra, but made no effort to remove it, letting him root at the valley between her full breasts until he begged her to help him get it off. Then she slowly pulled the straps down and let him unwrap her beauty, slowly unhooking the back until it slid down her now naked body.

Festal was fully aroused when he pulled her pliant form against him. He plunged into her heat and she felt the searing sharpness of his manhood. He rocked her again and again until he was spent and she was warmed and soothed, falling into a satisfied sleep.

In the morning when she woke, Festal made her a cup of tea and watched as she sipped it, her lids heavy with love and slumber. She let her hot tongue touch his forehead as he leaned over her before leaving for the fields. He was sated with her smell and her languorous goodbye. Evening could not come soon enough

That night, after he finished cleaning up and came to his mat beside her bed, Festal was looking a little sheepish as he pulled a tiny impala he had carved from his pocket. He watched Myrna's eyes as she felt it and accepted it. She pulled a black waxed thong from her sewing basket and tied it neatly to the slim mahogany charm. Then she put it over her mane of loose curls and let it drop between her breasts. She did not say thank you, or compliment him in any way. She simply opened her arms and her legs to him and took him in. He was hard in an instant and she moaned in pure pleasure at his response to her invitation.

Festal left the next morning for her brother's wedding, carrying her image in his mind so that all he had to do was sniff the scarf she had given him and he could recall the pleasure of her love and picture the love amulet he had carved suspended between her breasts.

CHAPTER 14

HOSPITALITY

Dodge met Festal at the station and took him to the small stone church where the wedding of Stephen and Esther would take place. Violet was the maid of honor and dressed in a florid pink dress that matched the flowers the bride carried. Esther was much shorter than her husband Stephen, and her curvaceous figure was overwhelmed by the tulle and ruffles of the dress she wore. Her full breasts bobbled at the neckline and the train of the gown dragged behind. Festal took in the details, thinking how little he recalled of his own wedding, other than the beauty of his bride coming down the aisle in her simple white gown, ready to take his hand. He made himself pay attention to details so he could share them when he returned home. When the ceremony was over, Violet stayed close to him, asking how Myrna liked the ranch.

"She is doing well. The calves and my dogs love her and the neighbors say I have done well. I am happy."

Violet pressed a small envelope into his hand to take to her sister, along with a photo of herself and of Joseph. Festal met Joseph, the young man interested in Violet. He was friendly, even cordial to him, as they discussed the market for beef, and what the best foodstuffs were, and how best to preserve them. Joseph was interested in the possibility of making cheeses, and wondered if there were mushrooms growing in the Copperfine region. Finally, Violet reclaimed Joseph, who was enjoying his conversation. Festal greeted the parents, and saw the new baby Jethro. He had carved a small bull for the baby and gave it to Beatrice. When he was ready to leave, Joseph gave him a bolt of fine chambray to take to his wife. It was bulky and cost Festal extra on the bus ride, but he carried his trophy home to his wife with pride.

Pilar and Selina, Winnie's daughters, stopped by Myrna's house one afternoon when Festal was away and spent a couple of hours with her, talking about Blancville, and how it was at the school she had attended. She told them about her tutor, her sister, and the classes she had taken. They were fascinated by her biology book and wanted to look at all the pictures in it. Myrna saw that they were shy about what they saw. They couldn't think of any questions to ask her. They would have some talking to do with each other when they were alone, she was sure. Then the three of them took turns playing *mancala* and munching on popcorn she made for them. When they returned home, they made such a fuss about going over to visit again soon, but had so little information about Myrna, other than what a kind and beautiful woman she was, how she was just their age and could make patterns from anything she saw. Winnie discouraged them from visiting again. This was not the report she wanted to hear. She would have to visit the woman herself and form her own opinion.

Myrna and Festal had been getting to know each other and arranging their household to meet their needs. They had not visited the neighbors who had welcomed her to the cattle station. During Festal's absence, Myrna prepared small gifts of dried teas and fragrant spices, such as the cinnamon that grew at the edge of her father's brickyard. She tied up sachets of them with ribbons and took one to each of the neighbors, spending a little time with each one, getting acquainted while their men were away with the livestock. She wanted to know what life was like on the cattle station. Her closest neighbor, Lottie, welcomed her warmly. She had two children already and it looked like another was on the way. Myrna offered to watch her children if Lottie needed to get away for a bit. Lottie laughed at the offer.

"You will know soon enough how good it is to have another hand willing to do that. I have to take the two of them with me to the privy just to make sure we don't have one fall into the cooking fire. You are so blessed to have a man who planned ahead and put a wall around your kitchen."

"Is that right? Don't most of the houses have a protected place to cook?"

"No. It's a shame but that is a big cause of accidents with the young children. They trip on the firewood and fall into the cook fire, or play with the fire, then get burned. There is little we can do to save them as the burns get infected."

"I am going to really watch that," Myrna said, wondering why the woman had realized the danger of a child's getting burned, but did not build a wall around her own fire pit. She would ask Festal about it when he came home and whether something could be done.

"Thank you so much for the bit of spice. I will put it in my soap I am making this month. I do like a soap that has a smell to it."

"I would like you to teach me how to make soap. I have never done that."

Lottie agreed, and with that promise, the two women parted. They would exchange many duties and recipes over the next years. People stayed put in cattle country and once you had a friend, it was almost as good as having a diary, since they would remind you what you had said, what the situation had been, and what they had advised you. For sure, they would have a proverb to highlight the meaning.

The visit to the next neighbor was troubling. Alicia had invited Myrna to go to the local church with her while Festal was away. She dressed and waited for Alicia to come by for her, but the woman did not show up. When Myrna saw it was getting late, she walked over to the woman's house. There she saw Alicia inside the doorway, and heard the children crying. The husband was sitting on the stoop just outside the doorway.

"What are you coming over here to snoop where you are not invited? Can't your husband take care of you without you sneaking around?" He did not invite her in, nor did Alicia dare to respond. Myrna could see her peering out and the cartons of sorghum beer lying scattered on the ground. She immediately turned back to her house and did not attend church that day.

Monday was wash day. Alicia was at the river gathering water, her eyes were swollen and she carried her arm in a makeshift sling. Her youngest child hung on her back   No one said anything about it, but they helped her lift her bucket to her head and balance it with a rolled towel. Alicia was a quiet woman who seldom spoke up, and Myrna realized that she would never have known what her life was like if she had not happened upon the scene that Sunday morning. She knew better than to tell Festal about it because he would worry that she could have been assaulted as well, and he might restrict her from going out to pay visits, especially when he was away. She had learned not to add to his worries.

One by one, the guests who had brought her welcoming gifts were greeted and each given a small token of appreciation. One house that Myrna visited was at the end of the path, the property overlooking the valley from three sides. It turned out to be the house of the local fetish priest, Emmanuel Kafuma. His wife was not at home when Myrna came to call, but he would let her know she had stopped by.

As soon as her husband told her the news, Winnie was pumping him for a description of the woman.

"She is tall, healthy, and young. You don't need to be getting into her business. You will meet her soon enough. She is going to be a big part of this community, I tell you."

"I thought I would have the girls get to know her. She is educated and may be able to teach them a skill."

"You can teach them any skills they will need. Don't get them thinking above what they are. Not every girl can be like her."

Winnie needed to know what it was this woman possessed that she lacked. Festal had eluded her and she would find out why. She began to plan how she could ingratiate herself to the woman to get her daughters aligned with her because she believed what her husband said, this woman would be a force in their community. This time, she would give them some coaching as to what to ask and say, and a gift to present.

When Festal returned from his trip with the bolt of cloth, Myrna knew which of the women could use a pretty head tie or a little top for a child. She liked having something to share and knew she could make good things from the chambray he had brought. She mentioned her visit to Winnie, and that the woman had not been at home.

"Stay away from that woman, and don't have her girls coming to this house."

"Did she have an interest in you?"

"Don't be getting into my business. I have said enough."

Full stop. Myrna knew not to press Festal. He was not going to talk about the matter and asking him again would irritate him. She dropped the topic. She was curious to meet this woman and learn more about the community. She turned back to her husband. "That is an enormous bolt of cloth. How did you ever carry it?" Myrna was stunned by the weight of the bolt of chambray. Festal swelled with pride at the praise. He hoisted her again off her feet,

"You weigh more than the bolt!"

Myrna laughed, thinking he was making a joke. Together, they sat down on their bed to share the happenings of their time apart. He gave her the photo from Violet and the letter, which she put up on her shelf to enjoy later. That night, it was cold in the room and Myrna coaxed Festal into the bed. She felt his body heat, then the hardness of his maleness against her, then the pain of such a deep penetration as he plunged into her. There was less room for him as the baby was growing, she thought. He shuddered as he pulled away from her, patting her shoulder and going to wash himself before returning to his mat. It was not as enjoyable as what she had experienced before, but why had he been so surprised that she had gained weight? Why didn't he realize that she could be pregnant if he had had sex with her during the Christmas holidays? She had protected this baby the only way she knew, they would be a family soon enough. She walked slowly to the washbasin, taking a pitcher of hot water with her, and enjoyed the smell of the lavender soap cleaning her. She took her time before returning to her bed and putting out the candle.

The following morning, Festal was tender around her. He brought her a cup of warm milk and asked if she had liked the material he carried to her. She brought his hand to her lips and brushed it against them. When he came in for the evening meal, there was fresh steamed nshima and chicken stew over it, with a small scoop of fruit jam and a biscuit on the side. Festal came to her bed again that night and she welcomed him with a touch, opening her body to him. It was not as painful this time. Festal fondled her breasts which had become enlarged and tender. They were new at their love-making. Myrna realized they had somehow missed the first chapters. It would be better between them. This would be a house of love.

CHAPTER 15

THE CATTLE STATION

At the cattle station, Myrna made good use of her time. She gathered berries from the hillside behind the house and made jam, using the honey Festal's neighbors brought them. After preserving the fruit with sugar and honey, she sealed the tins with wax, then lined them up on the little mud shelves with a piece of bright fabric ribbon around each lid. She now had the fabric to complete the covers she wanted to make for the table and the bed, and she pieced together a curtain for the doorway to let in the breeze and keep out the flies. She weighted the bottom hem with small pebbles so the breeze would not displace it from the doorway, then mounted it above the door with a dowel running through a casing in the fabric. Two pegs held the dowel away from the wall. In the calves' pen, Myrna spread fresh grasses for them to lie on, and it reduced the amount of mud and the flies.

In the last week, she increased in size around her waist. It was now difficult to wear the school clothes she had brought with her; the jumper was tight across her breasts. She relied on the wrapped traditional skirt, the *chitenge,* which was also cooler in the heat, and a loose blouse on top. She had her hair wrapped in a twist up the back and a wrap of satin across her forehead and over the sides ending in a tie at the back of her neck. When Festal was away, the hunting dogs stayed at her side wherever she went, leaning their long muzzles back and exposing their necks for her to stroke. When she walked to her neighbor's house, the dogs dropped to the ground outside the courtyard and waited for her to return. At night, they guarded her by lying on either side of the doorway and occasionally she would hear their low growl if an animal approached. She fed them treats from her meal and taught them to sit when she patted her side. They would be a good protection for the baby.

When Myrna decided to read Violet's letter, it was full of information about Joseph. His picture showed him to be as handsome and as strikingly tall and young as Violet had described. Festal had also been impressed by his outgoing and friendly nature. Myrna tried to imagine her little sister married and settling into a routine of domesticity. She could not. She read the paragraph about Wellington Taylor stopping by the parents' house. She could feel his frustration and her own in the interruption of their correspondence. It was a wound that festered as she thought about her sister getting the man she wanted, surrounded by her family, friends and activities, while Myrna had no access to her former life, her tutors, her books, her friends. Myrna asked for forgiveness for this envy, but it would spring up again, and she would have to rid herself of the thoughts many times over the months ahead. There was no one she could share it with, least of all Festal.

Myrna had talked to her neighbor Lottie about buying a couple of chicks so they would have eggs. She located nesting baskets and thought they might go atop the platform where the gourds were stored. She asked for Festal's approval before making this purchase.

Lottie had two children who were toddling about her house, pulling at the cloth on the window, and knocking over the pot of water sitting on the floor. Lottie laughed as she gathered the smallest one into her arms, the small waist beads showing off the chubby buttocks of her little girl. "You just wait," she said. "You will know how sweet it is to have a guest pay a call and give your mind something to think about other than keeping babies clean and safe."

The calves were a special project for Myrna. She liked their cool wet noses and rough hot tongues that eagerly searched for the nipple when she brought them milk. She did not have to milk the cows; one of the young boys did that chore. Then he would bring the warm milk back on his cart. After each of the calves nursed, Myrna wiped the nipple clean, then refilled the bucket from the can, and went on to the next calf. At first, the calves crowded her, spilling the milk and almost trampling her in their eagerness. In time, they learned to wait their turn, and after all of them had their fill; she brushed them and checked them for ticks, then bed their stalls with fresh grasses. The pen was made of thorn bushes, so Myrna had to watch not to get her skirts hung up on the plants. She had mended a few tears already. The calves were given names and they learned them. If she called to one, it would answer with a bawl which set the herd to calling out.

The hunting dogs dropped at her feet when they returned home from the fields. Myna liked their silken ears, some bearing the notches of the relentless wait-a-minute thorns that would tear them when they were coursing through the underbrush. She asked Festal if they might have a pup from one of the litters to raise in the house, but Festal was of the belief that every animal on the station should earn its keep, and what did they need in their house with another mouth to feed? Myrna had no answer.

It was shortly after this pronouncement that two hunters carrying spears and wearing loincloths stopped by the house and brought a baby duiker for Myrna. They did not speak the same language as Myrna, but they pantomimed having killed the fawn's mother, and their remorse. She understood their intent, nodded yes, and reached for the fawn, uncertain of what Festal would say to this foolishness. The men left as silently as they came. When Festal returned and saw the tiny fawn, no bigger than a kitten on his sheepskin sleeping mat, he stroked it and pulled it into his arms.

"What did you name it?"

"!" (Click).

Festal called the hunting dogs into the rondavel and Myrna had a moment of dread, until she saw him training them to accept this tiny antelope, making clear to them that this was part of the family when they started to lunge for it. Soon they realized they were to protect it, so it would be safe from them and any predator that might come near the yard. "Click" was the sound of its tiny hooves on the pounded floor, and the Xhosa language of the hunters that had brought it to their home. Myrna wrapped its feet in dampened cloth to keep the fawn from slipping on the slick floors. It would come to her each morning to be let out, then bounce around the yard with all four hooves off the ground. It always nestled behind Festal on his mat at night. Myrna took his gentleness and affection with the antelope as a good sign that he would be tender towards their baby. She couldn't wait until the baby was born.

When Winnie Kafuma realized she had missed meeting Myrna, and her husband warned her against delving into the Phiris' business, she resolved to go and visit Flo, owner of the Big Banana Bar and see what she knew of the woman.

Flo was at the bar having her hair plaited when Winnie stopped by unannounced. Flo did not have any information to share about Myrna, as she had never met the woman. Winnie did not mention Festal, so no information was gained. She did question what interest Winnie had in her, and put a note in her memory to avoid any controversy with this woman, as she seemed to have an agenda in mind. Flo did not care to have her appointment with her hairdresser interrupted; this was her time to be pampered and catch up with the local news. She offered her visitor no drinks, and in a short time, Winnie left.

Winnie stopped by the Phiris' herself a month later. Neither of them was at home and she noticed a chameleon in the arbor. She could not reach it, but it was an animal her husband would like to have for his fetish medicine. She would drop by again and ask Myrna if she could have it. That would be a chance to form an opinion of the woman and make up her own mind about her worth. The community was so easily swayed; she was tired of hearing her neighbors sing the woman's praises when she had done nothing to earn them.

Winnie waited until Festal had left for work, then knocked at the Phiris' door. "Hello. I am Winnie Kafuma, wife of the local healer."

"I am Myrna. Come in."

"I see you have a chameleon that has climbed into your arbor," Winnie said, looking in the direction of where she had seen the lizard.

"Yes. She has been there since I arrived."

"My husband would like to have it for his medicine." As she was talking, the duiker bounced into the sitting area, and Winnie took note of this totem animal. What was it doing here? Did Myrna have special powers? It walked up to Myrna and she stroked it as she talked.

"I will have to ask Festal if it is all right with him."

"I thought you were an educated woman that could make up her own mind."

"I can, but I value the feelings of my husband. It may not be to his liking for me to give away a creature that is important to him."

"How can a chameleon be important to a cattleman?"

"I don't know. But I know I like to be included in decisions. Perhaps we can give you one of her offspring as she is ready to deliver."

"It is not important. My husband has many potent ingredients to use."

"Thank you for understanding. I enjoyed meeting your daughters very much. They are lively girls."

"Yes. That is a good description. I am going now."

"Be safe."

Myrna told her husband that evening about the visit. "I thought I warned you to stay clear of that woman. She is bad news."

"You did warn me. She dropped by unannounced and asked for the chameleon for her husband's medicine. I told her I would ask you."

"The answer is 'No'. We both enjoy the creature. Why should it be killed?"

"I agree. I like its chubby cheeks. I will not encourage her. I just wanted your advice."

"Well, you have it. Is dinner ready?"

They sat on their stools watching the sun melt into the tree line at the top of the ridge. Festal was put off by the request for something that he cared about, and by his denying the request when it was by a woman he knew wanted something from him that he didn't want to give her. Myrna was relieved that the mother chameleon, a comma in the trailing vines of the bougainvillea, would be spared. Her sides were bulging with the promise of young soon to be born. Myrna secretly called her Beatrice and saw her as a good omen.

Myrna was in nesting mode. She made small covers for their drinking cups with stones tied at the base so flies would stay out of their drinks and baskets that covered the food she was preparing. All the food scraps were saved and put in a heap for the chickens and goats to eat outside of her garden wall. The brooms and whisks for the household were held on one wall in the storeroom by loops of crocheted rags, which also had been used to make a rug in front of the washroom, the doorway, and the kitchen to keep rocks and debris out. For herself and Festal, Myrna made lotions and soaps, pumice for her heels, and a waxy hoof dressing she used on the calves' hooves during the dry season. Her husband enjoyed all the projects Myrna made to keep their home smelling fresh, and it saved on their expenses. He also liked to surprise her with materials to see what use she could make of them. One day, he carried home the branches of a tree worn smooth by the wind and the rubbing of animals. The following day she turned them into a set of clothes pegs for the wall beside their bed. Another piece of wood became a shoe scraper for the doorway.

One day Festal came home just as Myrna was returning from a trip to town. She had caught a ride with a neighbor and his wife, and returned with them. Festal arrived early and met her absence. His brow furrowed in anger and dismay.

Myrna thanked the driver and dismounted from the donkey cart. She walked into the house and put her scarf and bag down when Festal suddenly took her by the shoulders and shook her in rage. She let her body go limp and he shoved her to the bed in anger. She did not apologize for her absence, nor did she rush to prepare the dinner. Festal knew he was out of control, but he could not rid himself of the anger or the fear that her absence had raised in him. Myrna waited for him to calm down.

"Why did you leave the house and not tell me?"

"You were away. I did not know I was confined to the house. Am I a prisoner?"

He was silent as his face contorted with the pain of her words. She told him she had ordered something for him in town. She had asked him earlier about his childhood, and he had told her abruptly, "That is none of your business." She had wanted to surprise him with a birthday gift.

Ten days later the gift arrived and she handed it to him to open. It was the first birthday gift he had ever received and he wasn't sure what to do. She waited while he pulled the paper away from the box and pulled out a red harness for the donkeys. It was new and had no breaks or rough patches. The brass fittings were glistening and clean and the collars had clips for a string of bells that came with the set. The reins were long and supple with snaps for easy removal. Festal smoothed the leather over his fingers and explored every inch of the harness. His eyes were bright and he had a half smile on his face. Immediately, he left to gather his hobbled animals. That afternoon they drove around the hillside, stopping at houses and waving to their neighbors. The two hunting dogs coursed along beside them like proper coach dogs. Festal sat proud in the driver's seat guiding his team. That evening, after he had hobbled the donkeys and cleaned the harness, he brought it into the house and hung the red collection of straps on the wall to the side of the doorway, with the bells suspended from the door itself. From then on, the door made a pleasant ringing sound when it was opened. Both of them would learn to open the door silently, once the baby arrived.

There were many families in Copperfine. Myrna came to know the majority of them through her visits, and by inviting them to have tea at her house. She knew how to make chamomile tea, and red bush tea, as well as cinnamon. It was a pleasant break for women to come over and see what project she was working on, or how her duiker was doing. ! (Click) was a novelty in the village, as few people had a pet, and no one had thought of keeping a wild animal as one. Just before the baby was born, the chameleon had hatched out half a dozen young ones. Word spread through the village and soon Winnie came to claim one. She spotted the lizard and immediately asked for it.

"I asked you before for the chameleon. I know you would not want to stand in the way of someone's healing," Winnie said.

"What cure does the lizard provide?"

"I am not the healer. I do not delve into my husband's work."

"Nor do I. But it seems there is no urgent need at this time for chameleon cures. Keep in mind that the lizard is producing more of her kind. Should you need one for a definite healing, we can provide one."

"You said you were going to ask Festal's opinion. Has he made a decision?"

"I have. My decision is *No*. I did ask him about it and we are in agreement. Have you seen the new pattern that I am working on? I hope to make a cradle cover to protect infants from mosquitoes while they are sleeping," Myrna said. Winnie glanced at the sketch.

"I will have to send my girls over. Neither of them has learned to sew and perhaps you would be able to teach them."

"I am limited in what I can do, but what I know, I am happy to pass on."

With that, the two women parted and Myrna cleaned out the cups. Festal would soon be home and she had a meal to fix. She put away the patterns and watched Winnie pass through the yard, watching the chameleon on its perch above the melons.

Myrna made a meal of cabbage relish, tomatoes and peppers over rice. She added a pinch of cinnamon to the mugs of tea and had a small bowl of roasted groundnuts. When Festal was done, she brought up the topic of the lizard.

"Festal, Winnie, the fetish priest's wife came over today. She wants us to give her the chameleon for her husband's practice. I asked her what cure it provided and she couldn't say. I told her we could be approached if there was a definite cure that the lizard could provide, otherwise, the chameleon continues to have life."

"You would do better to stay away from her. She is a power in this community and I have always avoided her as I thought she wanted something from me."

"She is sending her daughters here to learn to sew."

"I don't want them in the house. Teach them somewhere else."

Myrna did not have the problem of telling the girls not to come, because neither of them was inclined to want to sew. They did not come and Myrna saw very little of their mother in the year to come.

Myrna did cultivate friendships among the other women.

Mrs. Mulengo watched the new wife walking down to the riverside where the women did their laundry. Most of them had been scrubbing away for the past two hours and had their clothes rolled up in the basket ready to take home and dry. They had been talking about the case of the missing child at the cattle station and what should be done to safeguard against further disappearances. Everyone had an opinion. The child was albino and some thought this was the reason for its going missing. One of the fetish sellers had probably seized the child, as they were considered powerful medicine. Mrs. Mulengo hissed a signal and everyone stopped talking. They were silent as Myrna approached and then spoke of more pleasant things.

Myrna had met the women on her first day at the cattle station and visited some of them in their homes. She was a welcome addition to the village as she had new stories to tell, and had married a man long a mystery. Festal had worked for years besides their husbands, his parents were from a village not far away, but he had never courted or showed any attention to them or their daughters. At forty-four, most had written him off as one of those men who did not prefer children or marriage. Apparently, they had been wrong. This wife was beautiful and pregnant. They would study her to see what it was about her that had attracted a man they thought unattainable.

Myrna put down her sack of clothes and pulled out the washbasin and board she brought from the house. She had a bar of lava soap and trousers that needed serious scrubbing, as well as a couple of pairs of socks that had not come clean. As she rolled up her sleeves and began to scrub the clothing, the women checked out her dress and the sandals she wore on her feet. One of them made a little sashay with her hips and sang a little ditty about laundry and how the scrubbing was like a man needing rubbing. Myrna couldn't understand the words, but the gist of the refrain was clear. She laughed out loud and rubbed the bubbles on her arm with a stiff finger, which made the other women roll in appreciation.

They began to dance a bit as they enhanced the story, assuring her that she was part of their group. Myrna could have done the wash at her rondavel, as hers was one of the few households that had storage for water, and a huge pot to boil enough for a laundry. But she wanted to join in and let the neighbors know she welcomed their company. Some of them pulled out a few *mopani* worms and a little sack of dried groundnuts to share. The morning passed pleasantly and the work was done before she knew it. As she walked back to her house, one of the women signaled her daughter to assist her with the wet laundry in her tub. When they reached the house and the girl set it down, Myrna gave her a ribbon from one of the wedding gifts. The girl smiled her thanks and bounded away with her prize.

Myrna made her way into the community with a certainty and purpose that surprised her husband. Festal had always held back from the communal gatherings. Although respected by the men he worked with, he was not popular. No one knew what set him off, or what pleased him. He worked hard, but he didn't play. After his marriage, this began to change. He attended more of the gatherings where food and news were exchanged, and work was done. Myrna did not make apologies or excuses for him when he did not come or join in. She had fun herself and liked being with the community.

When she started working with the women, Festal saw how the skills and confidence of the women increased. He welcomed her questions when she asked him for advice. She never asked when it wasn't necessary, and never to manipulate him into joining the work or doing it in her place.

CHAPTER 16

PLAYFUL

Festal enjoyed being grilled about the wedding he had just attended of Stephen and Esther. He didn't go into great description, but said the bride reminded him of a box chicken, all fluffed up and poufy white, unable to move on its own. Myrna asked him questions which only he could answer. Sometimes he teased her and told her things that could not possibly be so. He did it lovingly, but she would hit at his chest and say, "You are lying!"

Festal had never played, and now, in their little round house with the stupefying beauty of the pastures and the valley outside the door, and this wife inside who played with him, let him win, provoked him just a little, let him be the lion and the mouse, told him about the mouse and the elephant, and other stories of her village, and wanted to hear the tales he knew, and devised one game after another, he learned to laugh and to enjoy being with another person for no other reason than the fun of companionship. He learned to play and to be frivolous, in small doses. By the time the baby was apparent, Festal was in love with the woman and the girl. He couldn't wait to see the son they would have. In his evening hours he fashioned a small bull out of eucalyptus wood as a toy for the baby. Then he made a rattle of the cowboy whistle pod which he had polished smooth and made sure no sand remained in it.

Festal's herds were thriving. His companions were friendlier, and his orphaned calves grew into sleek heifers that would soon freshen with healthy calves. From the first crowing of the cock in the morning, to the last laughter at night, their home was his haven. But the fear of losing what he had built woke him at night, making him sweat with anxiety. For Myrna, this was a time of gestation, of going over what had been important in her life and what the arrival of their baby would mean and how it might change their lives. She did not worry about the delivery or the health of their baby. She had seen her mother pregnant. And saw how making a space for another child was all a natural part of life. She thought about what she would teach the baby and how she would dress it and care for it. It never occurred to her that a child would be a new thing for Festal.

CHAPTER 17

THE HONEYMOONERS

Stephen and Esther had spent their honeymoon at Uncle Dodge's apartment. His cupboard was full of tins of bacon, cheese, and semolina pudding that they added to the food they bought at the small kiosk below the apartment. The first few days, the couple pulled out treats from the cupboard like Christmas presents, and Esther would fix them a few eggs, a little bowl of fruit cocktail, or a can of sardines they could add to the fried yams, which were available at the bar below them at street level.

After a week, Stephen began to tire of the foods that had seemed so exotic. He was doing nothing, and wanted to get back to his job of setting a lesson plan for the students at the middle school where he had been hired as a math teacher. He had been desperate to marry Esther— afraid someone else would claim her. But he had never spent so much time alone with a woman. He learned several things about married life that were unexpected. Esther liked to stay up late in the evening and work on her stitchery or listen to the radio. She tended to sleep in mornings, and she liked all the windows closed and the room very dark. She piled covers of wool on the bed and tucked in the sheets tightly at the ends. Her nightdress was a chenille robe. Stephen liked a cool room with a loose sleeping cloth over him. He was used to sleeping naked.

The apartment was bright with lights from the streets below. There were no curtains or shades. It was noisy as soon as the workday started. Lorries, donkey carts and vendors working below made a steady racket which carried upward. While Stephen liked to sleep with few covers and went to bed early, he was wakened each night by Esther preparing her toilette, turning down the lamp, getting into bed and adjusting the covers. Sometimes she would want to talk to him long after he had fallen soundly asleep. He was not used to having the heat of another person next to him as he had slept in a dormitory room at school and in a separate small rondavel at home. Once she lay down to sleep, she had a niggling little cough and continued to clear her throat. She also smelled like chemicals and it made his nose run. It was something she used on her hair to relax the curls.

Stephen liked sports and was eager to stretch his muscles by doing physical work in the morning and enjoying the excitement of a soccer match with his friends in the afternoon. When he finished his morning jog or stretching, he was hungry, but Esther was still sleeping. While they lived above the Fat Chance Bar, it was easy to go below for a chat with Rubee, the Lebanese owner, and get a cup of tea or Nescafe, and a doughnut ball or hard boiled eggs. But he was not sure what there would be to eat in the morning when he had to teach classes at 7:00 a.m., and rise an hour earlier to bathe and prepare.

He tried to set a time to talk this over, but Esther would look pouty and hurt if he suggested that she needed to adjust her schedule. He enjoyed sex with her, but lately, it seemed to be at times when he had planned on going out with friends, or had a match he especially wanted to listen to at the sports bar.

Esther liked making new dishes for her husband at Uncle Dodge's apartment, but she had never cooked and had no idea how to put the available ingredients together. Stephen thought of buying a cookbook, so he asked Esther what they would have for their meals once they were living on the school compound. Esther looked at him in some puzzlement.

"We will have our cook prepare food for us, whatever you like."

"That's fine. But we have no cook. We will be living on the compound where the school is located, and we will not have the store so close. There will be a weekly market, of course, and we can pick up basics at the tuck shop and fresh vegetables from vendors. What do you like to cook?"

"I have never cooked anything before. My mother just told our cook what to make, and then I helped prepare the food."

"What do you mean, prepare the food?" Stephen asked.

"I would set the plates on the table and dish out food for everyone so it was divided equally. Otherwise my brothers would just have one thing. My father ate first, then my brothers, and we girls had what was left. We were three sisters, who you have met. We also had to save some for the cook and the watchman, but they usually just had the yams and the *nshima*."

"Do you know how to make *nshima*?"

"No, but I know how to pound it. At least, I have seen how it is done. My sisters did that for our house. I would do their hair and they would pound the corn."

"We are going to have to think how we can get you some help. I won't earn enough as a teacher for us to buy prepared food at the store. We will need to grow some, or figure out a way to buy staples and divide them, maybe with the faculty." Stephen could see that Esther was about to cry, so he soothed her, stroking her arm and holding her, while thinking he was going to have to figure out how a budget, and feeding the two of them, would work. They had plenty of time to come up with a plan, but she probably didn't do laundry or housework either. It had never occurred to him to ask about these things while courting her. He had mainly looked at how adorable she looked in her fresh tops and tight skirts. What would a servant cost, anyway? He would talk to Dodge and see if he had any suggestions. They had another week to stay in his second story apartment before

Dodge returned, and before moving to the school compound.

Stephen pushed back Esther's hair and nuzzled her neck, thinking how sweet she smelled and how feminine she was with her necklace and the patterned silk scarf tied around her hair. They would work it out. He loved it when he heard her singing while she pressed her clothes with the charcoal iron. She had not even had a chance to open all the gifts they received from the wedding guests. They would work things out.

At the wedding of Joseph and Violet, Dodge saw Esther and Stephen sitting next to each other, each talking to the person next to them. He had seen Esther briefly since lending them his apartment for their honeymoon. What an eye opener that had been. He had come back a little early from his ventures in Copperfine. His apartment was open, so he knocked as he walked in. Esther was still sleeping. Stephen was out and the kitchen was still strewn with dishes from the night before. It looked like bread and canned fruit had been the dinner of choice. Dodge glanced at the sleeping girl with her hair wrapped up in a scarf and then he left the apartment.

Stephen would need a helper for his new wife; he might be able to help him. She didn't appear to be the domestic type, and keeping a household when you didn't have a large salary took some planning. Beatrice would be upset if she were to see this mess. He wasn't exactly pleased, himself.

Dodge headed down the stairs and walked to the Fat Chance Bar, one of his favorite hangouts. The owner was an overweight man in his mid-forties who enjoyed music and gambling. He wore his hair in dreadlocks and an *abaya,* the traditional robe, to stay cool when he was barbecuing meat for the bar. Rubee had never married, but he attracted a clientele of all classes of people.

"Rubee, I am back. I see you are doing a good business," Dodge said when he entered the bar.

"Dodge, good to see you. I met your visitor. He seems like a serious young man."

"Thank you. He's my nephew, recently married. We are looking for a girl to help out with chores and who knows how to cook. You know, he will be working with the students at the middle school, so the girl would be close to your place. There wouldn't be room for her to live on the campus, but she might be able to work part time somewhere else, and still give them help. Keep me in mind if something comes up. You know, I need a little help myself sometime in that department. And I do have an extra room at my place."

"I can't think of anyone offhand, but I will keep my eyes open. We have a lot of new people moving into the area. It may work out. Anyway, I will let you know. You'll be around?"

"Yes. I am staying put until I get my niece married off in another month. She's marrying Joseph, who runs the mercantile where you probably get your supplies."

"I hear you. Yes, I will keep my eyes open. Thanks for thinking of me." Rubee refused payment for the beer, and pushed a plate of fried yams towards Dodge.

Dodge visited the couple again after they moved to the campus housing at the school where Stephen taught math. The parlor of the tutor's cottage on the Makeshaft Middle School compound was small, and the bedroom with its sloped roof even smaller. Too small for a regular bed, Stephen noticed with relief. That's one piece of furniture we can do without. The school had helped them out with a set of chairs for the sitting room, a table, and a chest of drawers. He didn't have the money at the moment to buy a standard bed and mattress. They could make do with a foam mat until he saved enough to get a bed.

Esther shopped for a clock, antimacassars, a kerosene lantern and a set of cutlery. She had no money but she told the store clerk to write up a bill and she would have her husband, who was the new tutor at the school, stop by and pay for them. She walked home, pleased with her purchases, and checked these items off the long list she had made of what was needed in their home.

Stephen returned home in the afternoon when his classes were finished. He came in the door and hugged Esther, then looked around and saw the new furnishings.

"Did the school provide these?" Stephen said as he glanced around at the items strewn here and there.

"Stephen, you haven't even said hello to me. I want you to see all the things I have found. Come and look and just put those papers in the drawer so they don't mess things up. I am so tired from shopping, you cannot imagine. I had no idea how much work it would be to get this place looking like a home."

Stephen noticed the new kerosene lamp and the wiglet on the dressing table. "Esther, we are just married. I do not even have my first paycheck, and I will have some expenses to cover. How did you pay for these?"

"Stephen, you are a tutor. The storeowners said it was no problem for me to have credit. You just need to go pay for these things when you have time. I have a list of the bills in my purse. Now, what should we eat for dinner?"

Stephen wanted the evening to go well. The house did look nice, and he liked the clock on the wall with its velvet red roses and the hour hand set with rhinestones. He hugged Esther again and sat down in his overstuffed chair, waiting for his dinner. After fifteen minutes, the clock chimed a song. He rose and went to the kitchen where Esther stood staring at a pot of what smelled like soup. She had added some vegetables and some meat to the water, but nothing was cooked. It was floating on the top and the fire had gone out some time before, but she continued to stir it intermittently, and to taste it. Then she put down the spoon and turned to the cupboard. She pulled out a tin of margarine and a loaf of bread. She opened a can of deviled ham and spread it over the bread, then made two mugs of Ovaltine. There was no milk, just hot water, so she added a little extra Ovaltine to each mug. They sat on their chairs and ate the meal.

They had just finished their sandwiches when the headmaster stopped by. He wanted to welcome them and meet Esther. "Hello and welcome to our compound. I am the headmaster. My name is Winston Phiri. I hope you will be comfortable here."

"Thank you."

"Did the furniture suit you? And are you finding the water sufficient?"

"We have not had a chance to check the water, as I have been shopping, but the furniture is fine. Can I get you something to drink?"

"A beer would be good," The headmaster said, wiping his forehead.

"I am sorry. We have not stocked up with provisions yet, but when we get a refrigerator, we will have a cold drink to offer you. I can offer you tea." She glanced at Stephen again to see if he could add to this, then excused herself to go and clean the dishes. She had noticed how the headmaster looked her over, and thought she would have to make sure Stephen was always home when he stopped by. Stephen did not seem to notice the man looking at her too long, and in the wrong places. She had been approached before by men in positions of power, and she did not want to confront behavior that was better avoided.

As she washed the plates and knives, she overheard Stephen and the headmaster discussing the curriculum and the soccer scores. He was asking Stephen what sports he had played, and would he be able to take on the coaching of a team? Stephen was stalling for time to see how his class schedule worked out. Then he asked how the faculty divided up study hall and after-hours activities for the students who boarded. In a few minutes, the men came into the kitchen area and Winston again checked Esther over, saying it had been a pleasure to meet her, and that his wife would be inviting them for dinner soon.

Esther nodded and looked to Stephen to acknowledge that he would be making any decisions regarding their social life. Winston reached out and gave her hand a squeeze, pressing his finger into the palm. Esther was repulsed at the gesture.

"Anything you need, you just let me know."

Uncle Dodge stopped by the house after school was over. He came to the back door with a load of provisions for them, and a letter from Myrna. He also had a chocolate bar for Esther. Esther was in the kitchen looking in the cupboard and asked him to come into the parlor and take a seat. Her husband was not yet back from the school sports.

"How are you finding the compound?"

"We are just getting settled in. I have done some shopping, but we still have several things we need. I am learning what the schedule is, and I am looking forward to meeting the other teachers and their wives. I met the headmaster last evening. He was most friendly."

"You know I am here for you. Anything you need, just let me know. Dodge looked Esther over slowly. She was wearing a tight melon colored skirt and a cardigan of white with melon colored flowers. The top buttons were open. Her breasts were magnificent and concealed just enough to make them enticing.

"Tell Stephen I stopped by and I will be at my apartment on Saturday. I am looking to get a housekeeper to help me with the chores."

"Good idea. I wish we could afford a person to help, but Stephen doesn't know what he will be making exactly. I am sure it will be enough to have a cook, but I need to wait until he sees what supplies he needs. I am counting on him to work it out."

Dodge listened to Esther and thought she must be a handful for Stephen. If she did not know how to work within a budget or to do housework or cook, things would only get worse. He had seen the soup, as it was still in the pot when he came through the kitchen. There were unwashed dishes in the dishpan, and no broom in sight. He hoped for Stephen's sake she would get a routine and learn some skills to make this work.

Dodge left before Stephen arrived home. It was almost 7:00 and no dinner was prepared. He headed back to his apartment and on the way bought a kebab and a serving of rice wrapped in a banana leaf to have with his beer. What kind of a servant would best suit this household? It would have to be a girl who had no better options or a young man with no chance at schooling, hoping that he could learn from this math tutor. That might be the best solution. But where could he find a young man who could cook and clean as well, and not be embarrassed doing women's work? He needed to be able to tolerate being driven by a woman who did not respect him? The refugee encampment near the border would be his best bet. Esther would need to overcome any reservations she had about hiring someone not of her background.

CHAPTER 18

JOSEPH, VIOLET, STEPHEN, ESTHER, DODGE AT BEATRICE'S

Sunday, Joseph and Violet went to church. Dodge attended and saw that Stephen and Esther had also joined them. Esther was looking very pretty in a light green skirt and matching top of a sparkling knit, with her wrap framing her ample bosom and her hair pulled up in a matching headscarf. She was smiling at the ushers and at Joseph and Violet. Beatrice invited them all to the Sunday meal, which they happily attended. Dodge included.

As they sat around enjoying the meal, everyone asked Stephen how things were going at the school.

"We are settled in our new bungalow and we would like you to come and visit us." He looked at Esther to have her encourage a visit.

"Stephen wants you to come and visit, but I would be embarrassed if I did not have a cold drink to offer you. So far, we have no refrigerator."

It was silent at the table as Beatrice and Bishop thought of their own situation, and how seldom they had drinks bought at the store to offer guests. Joseph asked what kind of refrigerator she thought they would buy, and did they have electricity at the house?

Stephen answered. "We are going to wait until I see what my salary will be and what expenses the school will have me pay. There is electricity on campus, but if it is too high, I will just use the study hall and we will make do with our lamps. We can go to the bar if we need a cold drink."

Esther tightened her mouth a little at this revelation and figured she could work something out. It would just take Stephen a little more time to realize that he could ask for what they needed. The headmaster would be reasonable. No one could live in such a tiny bungalow and not have a refrigerator or a hot plate. If he was expecting her to cook over the brazier in the rainy season, it was not going to happen. They would be living worse than refugees. He needed to realize that he was an educated man, and that people expected a little more professional way of behaving or they were going to see them as nothing but peasants. How did people manage? She would talk to him when he received his pay slip and the bills were paid and they would figure out how to come up with the money. Certainly this would not be in front of his mother and not in front of Violet and Joseph. Imagine, no cold drink to offer the headmaster. Yes, they would have to talk. She was quiet the rest of the evening as Joseph and Violet went over their plans for their wedding.

CHAPTER 19

WEDDING OF JOSEPH AND VIOLET

The wedding of Joseph and Violet was held in the Presbyterian Church, with the pastor who had known the Chitundu family all their lives officiating. There was a small music program for the wedding, with the members of the choir singing for them. Two of Joseph's brothers came to sing as well and Violet said she was looking forward to having them visit their home. One of Joseph's sisters was a junior bridesmaid. Joseph asked for Violet's brothers to be part of the ceremony, but Beatrice decided it would be best to just include the two oldest, as the younger ones might be too disruptive. Myrna and Festal had been invited as well as more distant friends. They did not send an invitation to Uncle Dodge, but they could not think how to prevent his coming.

Stephen and Esther were there. They were recalling their own wedding and honeymoon, and realized what a blur it had been. It seemed to have been months ago that Esther was all nerves planning for her bridesmaids and wondering if the flowers would hold up in the heat, and whether the caterer had planned food enough for the guests.

The day of the wedding, Bishop was pacing the narthex at the Presbyterian Church. He was reluctant to have his remaining daughter leave his home, his wife was worried over the health of Jethro once again, and the business had taken another downturn. When he saw his daughter enter the room, he forgot all his problems. Violet was dressed in a gown covered in tiny shells and as frothy as the waves of the sea when the tide is turning. She and Beatrice had designed it and it took more than a month to sew all of the tiny shells to it. She wore a small tiara on her head, with her hair swept up in a twist of ringlets. Pearl drop earrings hung down over the sweetheart neckline of her dress. She was a page from a fashion magazine. Bishop couldn't wait to see the look on Joseph's face when he saw his dreams come true. Together, father and daughter walked down the aisle of the sanctuary. The wedding party was waiting at the altar, dressed in fuchsia and deep pink dresses that went to their ankles. Each had a bouquet of plumeria and orchids that trailed from their clasped hands. The bride carried a bouquet of calla lilies and plumeria, which scented the entire area.

The audience began to ululate as the bride made her way down the aisle. Joseph felt tears well up as he watched this vision of a girl coming to claim him. His best man steadied him as he stepped down to meet her father and receive his bride. Beatrice also stood, her Jethro in her arms. The rest of the service, except for the tossing of the bouquet, was a blur. The music was excellent. Joseph's two brothers blended in an *acapella* song of joy and fruitfulness that was traditional wedding music for their region. The church choir began encircling the couple with their blend of feminine voices. The senior pastor, who had known Violet her entire life, intoned blessings, baptizing them into the family of Christ. Candles in stair-step candelabras framed the handsome couple at the altar. Jethro started to cry and then suddenly stopped when he saw his sister in her dress.

At the reception, Dodge was omnipresent. He claimed he had discovered Joseph, insisted on hugging the bride, then scouted the attendees for others in need of his services. Bishop and Beatrice took a seat further back from the main table, where they could observe and enjoy the hospitality. Valoo had surprised the family with a catering of samosas, and gold-covered tiny cakes. He also proposed an impromptu toast

"I want to congratulate the Chitundus on the marriage of their daughter Violet to Joseph Again Leibitsang. He has been like a son to me. Whenever a couple decides to join their lives together, the marriage must have three legs. It is like the traditional pot. There is the couple, the family, and values. None can be missing or the marriage will not hold up. And so I toast you, the family, the couple, and values."

There was polite applause, but also a buzz of talk. Several of the guests thought he had said Valoo, and were puzzled at his inclusion of himself in the wedding threesome. No one could understand what he meant because he gave the toast in English and spoke too rapidly. Valoo's wife was not present as their daughter in India was due any time.

Joseph and Violet ate with their guests, served out the tiny gold cakes, and greeted each of the tables of visitors. They had several pictures taken of themselves and all of the guests, with the flame trees providing a backdrop for their happiness.

Violet and Joseph drove to South Africa for their honeymoon, arriving the next morning at a small guest house. Joseph had been there several times on his travels and knew they would be welcome. The guest house was a stucco, half-timbered Tudor cottage near the base of Table Mountain. Violet was amazed at the height of the mountain, the clouds that would come rushing in, and the assortment of foods that were laid out each day on the buffet. She had never ridden in an elevator before, and this bungalow had a quaint wrought iron cage elevator that held two people. Joseph loved showing her the elevator, the neatly wrapped toiletries, and all the new things that this small town beauty had never been privy to.

The wedding night had one interruption. A South African official came and knocked on their door and demanded to see their passes. Both had their visa, and a passport, which they had left at the front desk and were just going to bed when the knock came. Joseph spoke politely to the officer and showed him the papers, then asked him to check with the hotel owner if he had further inquiries, as he was just married and had come here to show his new bride this beautiful country. The officer made a small joke, apologized, and in the morning the couple found a bottle of Johannesburg Riesling Reserve wine on their threshold. Violet had been frightened in the night, but Joseph comforted her. They made love for the first time in the small hours of the morning. Again in the late afternoon, they returned to their room to experience what they had waited for so long, and the wine was sweet and smoothed the way.

Violet remembered several things about her trip to South Africa. What stood out in her mind was how Joseph had handled the rudeness of the official barging in on them, and turned her fear into a good memory. She recalled the softness of the towels, and the number of them; the scent of the lemon soap, the full stream of water in the bathroom, instantly hot for her bath, and the tautness of her husband's slim body against her on top of the freshly pressed sheets. They had to be Egyptian cotton, she told Joseph, they were so dense and smooth. She brought back gifts for her brothers and her parents, and two bottles of the special wine to give to Myrna and Festal, and Stephen and Esther. She was glad to be back in Blancville, where the builders were clearing the lot for their new home.

CHAPTER 20

BIRTH OF LILY WONDER

It was late afternoon when the labor pains began. A storm had just drenched the area with much needed rain so the roads were slick with red mud. Festal hoisted Myrna into the donkey cart and headed the donkeys toward the hospital, eight kilometers away. He wiped sweat from his brow and whipped the donkeys in his haste to get there. Myrna had read about labor in her book, but the words did not come close to the pain she felt.

As they entered the clinic, Myrna's waters had broken and the baby's head was crowning. She heard someone moaning in pain, and looked at Festal to see who it was. He was squeezing her arm and tears were running down his weathered cheeks. The nurses rushed Myrna into the delivery room and scrubbed her down in record time.

They caught the baby and held it up for Festal to see. He was dumbfounded and groaned in his disbelief. The child had no testicles. It was a girl. Never had Festal imagined that he would not have a son. He put his hands in his pockets and walked out of the room while the nurses cajoled the mother and praised her for a healthy and full-weight girl. They made no comment about the absentee father, but instead concentrated on making sure Myrna knew how to care for the newborn. She bonded immediately with her precious little girl then overflowed with emotion for this new role of being a mother. She had a strong desire to share this joy with another woman, especially her sister, but she knew she would have to wait. Her body was absorbed with warming the child and making sure it was receiving enough milk, even as she flinched with every contraction— as the baby nursed and her body cleansed itself. She did not realize how devastated Festal was to not have a son.

They left the next day for home, the father walking beside the cart, and the mother contentedly nursing the baby. She named her Lily Wonder, although Festal was reluctant to give her a name. He left that afternoon for the fields where he told his fellow cattlemen that the labor was easy and they would have a boy the next time. Their neighbor Lottie said she would check in with Myrna during the day.

When Lottie came to see how Myrna was doing, she saw Myrna cuddling her baby. She had Lily wrapped from head to foot in a length of flannel, and a little knit cap pulled over her head, making the curls spill out at the sides and the forehead. Lily was a beauty. Lottie gave the mother the lunch she had made for her. Myrna let her friend hold the baby while she went and took a leisurely shower, sprayed herself with perfume, and put on a fresh blouse. Lily was asleep in her friend's arms when she returned. Myrna ate her lunch and Lottie talked about what lay ahead.

"I know you won't hear this, but I have to say it anyway."

"Why don't you think I will listen? I'm listening." Myrna nibbled at the bread her friend brought for her.

"You need to not get pregnant for the next two years so this baby will thrive and you will be strong."

"I can't even think about being pregnant. I am so happy with my Lily Wonder.

"Well, I spoke my piece. I am happy for you and don't forget to baby Festal."

Lottie left after an hour, with a good report of how the baby and mother were doing.

Lily was a placid baby with a big appetite, healthy and calm. Myrna wrote her sister about Lily, but did not send the letter until a couple of months had passed.

In December, when a full year had passed since she first met Festal, and nine months after she had married him, she sent out the announcement of her baby. Her mother was happy, her father wanted to see the child, and Uncle Dodge drove out to the cattle station immediately to visit his niece and the baby. Myrna warned Festal that the man could bring disease to the baby, so Dodge was only allowed to view her from the courtyard through the open doorway. Lily was bundled in blankets with a cap pulled over her head, leaving only a portion of her face visible. Festal was pleased at his wife's concern for the baby and said he would take Dodge to the local bar to show their hospitality since he had come so far. Myrna nodded her agreement.

It was late when Festal left the Big Banana Bar. The girls there were friendly and offered the father free drinks, then an additional one when they heard it was a girl. Dodge asked about the delivery, the size of the baby, and how everything was going. He wanted to see Myrna and the baby to make a better report to her family, he said, but Festal could tell him everything they needed to know. Festal drank his beer and told Dodge he wanted a son. He could not tell Dodge the weight of the baby, or the exact date it was born. There was no calendar at the house. Dodge said a girl was a good thing, boys could come soon. He put his arm around Festal.

"Waitress, bring us another round of beers. And if there is anything else this man needs, see he gets some, and send the bill to me."

They listened to the music while the girls flirted with them. Festal walked back to the ranch alone, leaving Dodge at the bar with one of the girls. Myrna was sleeping when he came in. Festal was calmer than he had been when he left the house. He walked over and looked at the baby. One arm had come out of her swaddling and when he touched her hand to put it back inside, she curled her fingers around his. He wrapped her up again, sighed, and stretched out on his mat.

When the baby was two months old, the neighbors in the cattle station came to see the child. They brought gifts—this time for the baby. Festal watched the procession and kept a close eye on his wife and child so no harm would come to them. He feared disease or any other kind of harm, and it was a time to protect them. Even when the hunting dogs got too near the baby, it resulted in an immediate punch from his fist. Myrna did not seem to notice his anxious protection of the family, and basked in the joy the baby brought her. The baby slept in the bed with her, and if she cried, Festal would waken to make sure Myrna nursed her and drank some tea.

On Violet's wedding day, Myrna took stock of her own marriage. They had a child and another on the way. What would be Festal's reaction if this one was also a girl? He had a hard time adjusting to the shock of one daughter; there was no guarantee that this would not be one as well. If her sister had a son, Festal would be reminded that he did not. Myrna let that thought pass and concentrated on having a healthy baby and making life good for her husband and the child. They made the storage room into a nursery, and that year they planted two more trees, a cashew and an almond. They also built a coop for chickens too high for predators and out of reach of the dogs. Festal made a pen that could keep Lily safe and would fold up against the wall when not in use. He bought her a small stool for her to sit on with cowry shells embedded in the base. He loved to watch how she imitated her mother and was learning to use cutlery. Sometimes in the evening, Lily would stand in the doorway with the last rays of the sun shining around her face, the tiny antelope leaning against her side, and Festal would try to memorize the scene, as it was so beautiful and so transitory. He had no camera to capture it, other than an uncluttered heart.

Suzanne Popp

CHAPTER 21
GROWING

A year later the second baby arrived. Festal and Myrna had made a small nursery next to the large room, clearing out the storage shed and taking it over for the children's room. They made it to the hospital before the waters broke, and were lucky to have the neighbor Lottie caring for Lily. This time, Festal was furious when the nurses announced, "It's a girl!"

Myrna had a more difficult labor this time and was not in a mood to have her husband belittle the baby they had made together. The nurses ordered him out of the room and Myrna took two days to leave the hospital. The baby was healthy and beautiful. Like her sister, she was born with a mop of curls on her head and lips like a bow. Her skin was light in color and her fingers were long and fine. Her amber eyes were surrounded with curling lashes, like Festal's.

All Festal noticed is what the baby was lacking. He now went to the Big Banana Bar on his own to be consoled. The girls were only too willing to hear about the birth of Pansy. When Festal complained about the baby being a girl, one of the barmaids informed him she thought the man had something to do with the sex of the child. He couldn't verify that one way or the other, but the girl's knowing about things he didn't was a total turnoff. He headed back to his home with the intention of talking to the village healer about remedies. He blamed the dark powers for not being able to produce a son, and wanted to fix this.

Within a year, the first son arrived to Violet and Joseph. Like clockwork, five healthy boys followed. Bishop relished the rough and tumble play of a houseful of grandsons, and Joseph hired a nanny to relieve his wife of some of the chores that came with such a full house. The two of them interviewed her together before deciding on her services.

Grandmother Beatrice made matching shirts for all of them from striped chambray and they had school jerseys with the letter "L" monogrammed on the front. Violet took them to the photography studio to have their portraits done, and their pictures sat in the window to advertise the photo shop. Each time a son arrived, a photo was mailed to Myrna and Festal. Festal would carve a small bull and have Myrna mail it to their father.

Once they were weaned, Joseph took one of his sons to the store each day and a small play area was erected for them. The customers stopped by to see which boy was at the front counter and remark how strong and handsome he was. When they grew older, they still bantered as to which one would be allowed to visit the store. Business increased, and more than one young woman came to the store to make a purchase just to see which brother she could meet.

Fifteen months after Pansy was born, Iris arrived. Festal did not want to even walk into the clinic. He was hexed, he was sure of it. Three girls. He was almost 50 and he would never have a son. He was consoled by more than beer at the Big Banana Bar, but never mentioned the child was another girl, because of the remarks of the bar girl following the last birth. His fellow workers began to heckle him once they realized how sensitive he was about not having a son, and only being able to produce daughters. Some volunteered to help him with his plowing to insure he had a son the following season.

A year later, Daisy arrived. She was slight in size but had powerful lungs that never stopped crying. Even the thick walls of the rondavel could not shut out her shrieks. The other girls would go out by the calves to avoid the sound. Iris, the one year old, who could not avoid the screams, would join in. Festal built a second small rondavel for himself a little distance away so he could escape the cries. In desperation, Festal visited the healer; he had been patient long enough.

CHAPTER 22

FESTAL VISITS FETISH PRIEST

Emmanuel Kafuma saw Festal approaching and donned his traditional robe. He waited for the man to state his problem.

"Hello. I am coming to you for medicines for my wife. She has been having only girls and she needs something so she can make sons," Festal blurted.

"How many children do you have?"

"Four girls."

"And how long have you been married?"

"Five years."

"And how old is your wife?"

"She is nineteen years."

"You have many years to make sons. You need to slow down. If you give her some time between children, you are more likely to have sons. I have no medicine for her. Just this advice. Get her some help with the children and wait before trying again. I am not charging you for that advice, but it is not easy medicine to take."

"I will try. Thank you."

Festal could not abstain more than he was. They had not had sex now for three months and the baby screamed on. Only when he carried Daisy against his chest with his shirt off would she stop her screams. It was a dry season, with not enough grass for the herds. The calves dropped weight, then died. The duiker that they had loved disappeared from their house.

Then Lily Wonder, the first born child, fell ill.

CHAPTER 23

LILY IS LATE

At first Lily had diarrhea and a fever. Then she could not eat and everyone advised them to cut back on her water, since it was going right through her. Myrna did not follow this advice, instead giving the child tea made with boiled milk. When Lily did not improve, Festal harnessed the donkeys, put Myrna and the child on the cart and galloped the five miles to the clinic. By the time they arrived, Lily was unconscious. Myrna was frantic. The doctor tried to give Lily fluids, but it was too late. Lily was gone. He asked Myrna to come into the examining room and be checked. She did not have dysentery, but she was pregnant. Within a few minutes of examining her, he reported to Festal.

"We could not save your daughter. This diarrhea is difficult to treat and you did all the right things. Only an antibiotic might have saved her. You will need to watch the other children and your wife. She is distraught with grief, but she is also pregnant with twins. She should stop nursing the baby and save her energy for the next children. We will watch her closely and she must come in for checkups. Even though she has had easy deliveries in the past, this is what we call a high risk pregnancy. Do you understand?"

"Yes. You mean I could lose my unborn children and my wife as well."

"Yes. Bring her in once a month so we can make sure everything is going well. I am so sorry you have lost your little girl. I know she was a happy and a healthy child until this illness. I would recommend you get some help for your wife as well, as she should do no heavy lifting and should avoid getting too exhausted."

"Thank you, Doctor. I will take care."

Festal suddenly leaned forward and hugged the doctor, then hid his face in his sleeve before going back inside to gather up his daughter and wife. It was a quiet drive back to the ranch.

When Dodge heard of Lily's death, he sent word that he was coming and offered to pay for the funeral. Festal told him not to come, the child was his, he had brought her into the world, and she would be sent out of it with his labor.

Festal spent the night digging the grave for Lily, and buried her next to the gate, and the wall on which she would sit to welcome him home every night. He regretted every harsh word he had said about having daughters, although he still thought there had been some spell cast on Lily. He hugged each of the girls and tucked them into bed, telling them that Lily would be in heaven and would hear their prayers each night. He then went in and took Myrna in his arms.

"I am sorry that I ever said I was disappointed in our girls. I hope both these babies are girls and I pray for God to forgive me for not being grateful for all my children. I pray that these children will both be girls."

"Both?"

"The doctor told me we are having twins. He wants to see you each month, and you need to stop nursing Daisy. You need to be strong for them to make it."

Festal was sure that his complaints about having girls was a curse coming back on him, and now with twins, he might even lose the mother. He was superstitious about having twins and was sure they would be sterile if they lived. This had been the case with cattle twins, as the government inspector of livestock had informed him when one of the heifers he purchased never produced a calf. Festal felt guilty that he had not abstained and given the mother more rest. Day and night he hovered around the rondavel. He did not sleep in the small hut he had built for himself. Instead, he lay outside the doorway, listening for the mother to call for him, hushing the children when they cried, and awaiting his fate. Life had been too perfect. All the old shame and guilt returned to him. It was all unraveling. He lost weight and became increasingly nervous and peevish at the slightest provocation. The children began avoiding him and even his hunting dogs would sleep out by the calves.

He comforted Daisy in the night when she wanted to nurse, and gave her small sips of boiled milk with sugar. She went back to sleep and Myrna was able to sleep through the night. He went to town to the nursery near the market and bought a plumeria seedling. The fragrant blossoms would remind him of his devotion to his family. Together with the girls, he planted it over Lily's grave and put a circle of stones around it.

That afternoon, he went to the pastor at the Full Gospel Church and took him a bull calf. He asked the pastor if he could baptize the children, and pray for Lily. The pastor assured him the child was in heaven, and that he would be happy to baptize all the children, and pray for the unborn twins. He also suggested that Myrna would need some help once the twins were born. Festal thanked him.

That night he asked Myrna to read him a verse from the Bible. She was tired and the kerosene lantern gave off a yellow beam that made the words hard to see. But she read him Psalm 16:6 that said, *boundary lines are laid for you in pleasant places, and indeed, you have a beautiful inheritance.* He had no idea what this meant, but as he tended his cattle the next day, and fed the calves that evening, he pondered the meaning. He had no fences on the range where he pastured his cattle. The lines must be a spiritual boundary that was laid down for him. A *boma* where he would be safe. The twins and all his children were his inheritance. If he could understand and believe this, he would have a beautiful inheritance. He let the idea rest in his mind, seeing what other meaning might come to him.

Each day, Festal and Myrna boiled water and milk for the children. They were careful to wash the dishes with the water from the boiling pot. None of the other children came down with the dysentery that was sweeping the village. Five other families that they knew also lost children, including Lottie. Death from diarrhea was an everyday occurrence and Festal was paralyzed with the fear that he would lose Myrna and all would be lost. Myrna was numbed by the loss of her daughter, and only the determination to have the other children survive, and to successfully deliver her twins kept her sane. She made herself follow a routine with her housework and childcare, so as to allow time to visit the women in her village and comfort them, as they had been so kind during her loss. It was difficult not to console herself by nursing Daisy, but she followed the doctor's instructions and in the heat of this dry season, her milk stopped flowing. When Myrna switched the baby to more solid foods and boiled milk, Daisy's screaming also ceased.

CHAPTER 24

TWINS

Six months later, Myrna began having contractions and Festal rushed her to the clinic, after taking their three daughters to Lottie's house for safekeeping. Festal was afraid to say anything to the nurses and paced the floor of the waiting room, only to hear the strong cries of one child, then the next. The doctor called him to come and hold his sons. Festal was faint at the sight of the blood and the cords, which the doctor had him cut. He could hardly glance down to see their maleness. When he did, they were huge. No one else remarked on this, so he was silent and let up a fervent prayer of thanksgiving. They were healthy. Maybe they would not be sterile as he had feared. The two boys were soon washed and placed on his chest for warming, while the doctor stitched Myrna's tears. Myrna asked him what he wanted to name them, and without hesitation, he called out, "Samuel and Reuben." Myrna gave them their character names, Self Control and Kindness, after the fruits of the spirit.

Within a week they headed home with the twins strapped to Myrna, and Festal walking beside the donkeys to keep them from bouncing the cart and its cargo around. Festal was very relieved to have Myrna safe after the delivery of the twins, and most grateful that both were healthy. He did not boast of having sons, but went immediately to the church and made the donation of a bull. The pastor welcomed him and said when he was ready, they could baptize the boys, and the other children as well. He asked if Festal had located someone to help his wife, as she would be exhausted continually nursing two babies and caring for the young girls. Festal told the pastor he had notified Uncle Dodge to find him a helper.

CHAPTER 25

DODGE PRICES GIFT

Dodge stopped in at The Big Banana Bar. The counter was covered with small bubbles of Omo where the barmaid scrubbed at the surface with her cloth—cleaning up the spills and food from the night before. Her hair was pulled back in a black knit bandana that framed her small, heart-shaped face. An indigo cross was tattooed between her eyes. She had a hesitant smile which she infrequently flashed, and when she did, it showed a gap between her front teeth. Her gums were also tattooed indigo. Between her full lips was a chewing stick, which she removed when she saw Dodge watching her.

"Do you want a beer?" she asked.

"What is your name?" he countered. "Do you have anything else to offer?"

"I am Gift. We have barbecue eggs and fried yam, but the chicken is finished."

"Give me a cold Mosi and a plate of yam. How much do I owe you?"

Gift wrote down a number on a slip of paper, put it on a saucer, and slid it across the wet counter.

She counted out the change from the bills he handed her and placed it on a plate, then reached to open the beer for him and pushed a plate of yam slices across to him, along with a small napkin. Her full breasts hardly cleared the counter. She was less than five feet in size.

Dodge watched her movements, noticing that she was not as slim in the midsection as her thin arms and long legs would indicate. It looked as though someone had already gotten to this one, was his ungarnished thought on the subject as he chewed on his makeshift lunch. Still, she was young and she might be a good second wife for someone. She might be a good worker. He would talk to her employers when they came back. She was not his type as she didn't seem to be one for conversation. He disliked a girl who didn't put herself out to please a man. He glanced at her again, and asked, "Do you have a husband?"

The girl jumped at the question. "No." she said. Full stop. No information offered. Well, he would get a better idea about her when he saw her with people she knew. Dodge knew how to bide his time. This might be the proper servant to help out his niece. Festal had been asking about getting a girl to help her. If this girl was pregnant, that might settle her down to spend time caring for the children. Who else was going to care for her or the child? Dodge took his time sipping his beer. He was in no hurry. He noted how the girl methodically counted the money in the till, made her note of the amount, closed the drawer, and then continued her cleaning tasks. She went over the counter with a dry towel, then buffed the hardwood with it and placed the napkins in their holder. The salt was low. She filled the small pedestal with more salt, placing a cracker inside to keep the moisture away. When she had gone over each of the items in the tiny bar, she pushed her hands in her apron pockets, then asked if he was finished with his glass.

He handed her the empty glass and watched her wash it, dry it, and return it to the row of six glasses on the shelf behind her. It didn't occur to her to encourage him to drink more, or spend more at the bar. He kept watching her, seeing the effect it had on her. She turned her back on him and stepped behind the curtain. No, she wasn't flirtatious and she wasn't shy in the least. Dodge prided himself on his ability to understand women. This one was clearly a methodical, conscientious girl from the country. She was here because she served a function, like the lantern on the hook at the entrance to the bar, or the kerosene refrigerator below the counter. She could be replaced by the owner of the bar by any of a hundred more personable young women. She was not an asset to what should be a pleasure setting. Dodge satisfied himself that his plans for her would benefit all of them.

It was over two hours before anyone came in. It was not a man. It was a middle-aged trim woman carrying a large purse covered with eye-catching grommets. Gift promptly relieved her of her bundles and poured a glass of tea with sugar for her. The woman did not ask Gift about the day, she could see things were as usual for the midmorning hours. Still, there was a good looking man sitting at the counter. Flo asked him if he needed anything.

"Is the owner of the bar about?" Dodge asked.

"Yes. Is there something I can do for you?"

"I want to talk to the owner of The Big Banana," Dodge repeated.

"You are."

"I see." Dodge was nonplussed for a moment. This woman did not resemble the girl in any way, but maybe this was the girl's sister, or worse, her mother. "I am interested in finding a girl to assist one of my relatives," he said. "What would it take for you to let Gift come and work for my mother?" he asked. He didn't want to indicate who the real party was, the price might go up.

"What kind of work are you proposing?"
"My mother needs some help with various chores, nothing too heavy, but more than she is able to do for herself. She has an extra room and it

would be full time work."

"I need the girl. She is indispensable to my business." Flo looked sideways at Dodge to see if he was buying this story. She had been worried about the girl's expense. If she was pregnant, this could be a good way to pass the problem on. Not that the girl wasn't a help, it's just that other girls could fill in with her duties, and with a baby coming, passing on the girl to an elderly parent could be the ideal situation.

She offered Dodge another beer. "Of course, I wouldn't want to stand in the way of the girl's advancing herself."

Now that Dodge saw that the owner had no real ties to the girl, the only thing to be determined was the price. "Are you going to be in tomorrow? I will need to make sure my mother has not found someone else to fill the position."

"I should be around in the afternoon. Let's say around 2:00?"

Dodge nodded in agreement and Flo refused payment for the beer. She collected his glass and he left to go and locate Festal.

Festal had been fretting about in the mercantile store for over two hours; waiting for Dodge to return. When he saw him coming, he dropped the clippers back in the bin and rushed towards him. Dodge could see his eagerness, and his attempt to conceal it.

"Did you have any luck finding a helper?" he asked.

Dodge nodded slowly, then began to bait the hook. "She is a little younger and a little smaller than you might want," he said. "I promised her guardian it would be light work, and she would be well cared for. I didn't discuss the cost, as I wanted her to see it would be an opportunity for the girl to get ahead. She is a pretty big help with the business at the shop as she runs it herself and has not had time or opportunity to become a town girl." Dodge tilted his head to see how this non-information affected the older man. He knew that Festal had probably been a little overwhelmed by the rapid growth of his family.

Five young children, including the set of twins, could be overwhelming, especially after being single for so long. Dodge wanted the man to picture a young and unspoiled woman joining their household. There was no mention of the bar or Dodge's suspicion that the girl had been serving Flo's customers upstairs in the evening hours or when business was slow.

"I can't go too high, you know I paid a ransom for Myrna. Not that she wasn't worth it," he quickly added.

"Oh, nothing like that. This is an orphan girl without family or expectations. She will consider herself very fortunate to have such a situation. We are talking housekeeper and maid here. I was going to have you suggest a price, but I may have to help you. I would say a bull, two goats and a barrel of beer should work to get the transaction started. Of course, her brothers or a relative may demand more if they get wind of this. How does that sound?"

Dodge was thinking that Flo would settle for a barrel of beer, but there was no point in wasting the profit that was to be made in these arrangements. He could feel his palms itch in anticipation of the trade. He had left some room for Festal to counter the offer. Festal did not ask to see the girl, but he wasn't willing to part with a bull. They settled on two goats and a barrel of beer. She would arrive at their compound the following morning, provided Flo would agree.

Flo did agree and Dodge spent a pleasant evening with her before delivering Gift to Festal.

When Festal returned home, he presented Myrna with a servant, a girl of thirteen named Gift.

"She is to do the heavy work and help you with the children," he explained. "Dodge located her for us."

Myrna looked at her husband in disbelief, then waited until he left to question the girl.

"Have a seat. Have you eaten? "

"Yes, my stomach is satisfied."

"What is your name?"

"I am Gift."

"Have you cared for children?"

"Yes. My mother had six."

"Where is your mother now?"

"She is late. All my brothers and sisters are late."

"Then you have come to find a home. You are welcome. You will help me care for the children and do chores. Are you able to read?"

"I was taken from my school when I was eight. I have only finished one form."

"If you would like to learn to read and do math, I can teach you. You will sleep with me in this room and you will be safe."

"What shall I call you?" Gift asked.

"You can call me Myrna, or you can call me sister, it is up to you."

"Thank you, Sister," Gift said looking down at her hands.

"Do you know how to prepare food?" Myrna asked glancing over at the sleeping twins.

"No. My older sister helped my mother with that. I can pound corn and carry water. I also can figure change."

"Those are good skills. Do you believe in God?"

"Yes, but I have lost him lately."

Myrna glanced at the girl's profile and saw that she was not as slim in the waist as her arms and long legs would suggest. Another baby, just what this house needed. She stifled the thought as she remembered Lily and what she would give to have that child back in the rondavel, and gave thanks immediately for her fortune in having healthy twins.

"Gift, do not go to the river alone, and do not leave the children alone. They are too little to be near the cattle, the fire, or by themselves. Do you understand?"

"Yes, Sister. I will be careful. I am grateful."

When Festal came in for the evening meal the house was peaceful. The twins were nursing, one on Myrna's lap, the second dandled and cuddled by Gift. Festal washed up and sat down to eat while the women took turns watching the children. It was a quiet meal, one of the first in months, and when they were done, Festal put the stools away. Then Myrna announced that Gift would be sleeping beside her, and that he could have the small rondavel for himself. "That way our caring for the children in the night will not wake you."

Festal looked at the two women and headed for the rondavel. It is not what he imagined, but he could not argue with the logic of the arrangement. In the morning, Myrna saw him talking to the girl. Gift was bringing the firewood from the storehouse.

"I am not married," Myrna heard Gift say to her husband.

That afternoon when Myrna was hanging out the washing, she saw Festal leave for town with the donkey cart. They needed supplies, so she didn't think anything of it. Gift had asked previously for the afternoon off to get the rest of her belongings from the Big Banana Bar.

CHAPTER 26

GIFT MARRIES FESTAL

When Festal returned that evening, he had Gift on the seat beside him. She was smiling and showed Myrna her wedding band. "We are now real sisters," she said. "Festal has made me the second wife."

Myrna dropped the sheet she was folding and went into the house. She had no words to describe the bitterness and the gall that percolated up into her chest. The twins were sleeping and it was relatively quiet. She walked back out the door and headed for the calf pen. She could still see the doorway of the house above her as she walked down the path, and Gift standing there beside Festal. Beside her husband. Myrna's eyes were red with rage. What remarks would her sister Violet make about her now? Replaced at twenty-one by a stunted teenager all of thirteen, who had worked in a bar, and who knows where else? Had she really believed that this girl would only be a serving maid to help her with the children?

She gave herself full rein to revile this girl, her husband, and Uncle Dodge. Oh, there were precedents, to be sure. Myrna knew her Bible. She thought of Tamar's rejection after being raped by her brother, of Laban's betrayal of Jacob, and his anger at finding the older sister under the veil, the disappointment of Sarah at having no children, and her disgust with Hagar once she was pregnant. All the stories of rape, of betrayal, of jealousy and deceit piled up in her mind like rotted corpses.

She stacked up her weapons then she took fire at Festal. He was ignorant, illiterate, old, and single minded. She had been sold to him, and she had cost him dearly. He was getting his money's worth with six children in six years. What had he bartered for this wench? Once she let the full weight of her anger and fury go from her, the balance began to restore itself. Was she better off without Festal? No. Did she want someone else to take her place? No. She knew she loved him. She knew he loved her. He had been good to her, as best he could. Like Joseph in the Bible, he had privately handled any questions he had on why their child had arrived so soon. He had not abused her or the children. She had never said she did not want another woman in the house. She had probably said more than once that she could use some help.

Now, here was a girl, dumb as a stick, to be sure, who had come into their lives and who needed love and protection. She knew nothing about this girl, but she knew what was right. The passages about the Shummanite woman who made room for Elijah and continued to show hospitality, even when her child was mortally ill, came to her. "All is well." It became a phrase she could use to clear her head. What thought could she use to displace her anger? Then she recalled Wellington Taylor and the advice he had given. *Be the Prince of Love.*

Wellington Taylor, her tutor, had once told the class they could write him and ask for advice. One student had asked for advice in love, and named Wellington the Prince of Love. While the message had been humorous, Myrna had often wished for more knowledge of how to love well. Here was her chance to practice love. This girl had obviously had some tough experiences. She was now part of the family. Could Myrna love her and have her feel loved? They would be raising their children together. The girl was legally married to her husband. If she could believe that what anyone intended for evil, God could make good. Myrna would be the love that this house needed. She would be the Doctor of Love and heal the wounds of herself and Gift. She would not allow her heart or her lips to condemn what this foolish girl had done, what this foolish husband had done. She would not hate Dodge, but she would never allow him to destroy the peace in her home. She would accept the gift that had been given to them both.

It was enough for now to remain silent and wait for understanding. She heard her twins wailing, but ignored them. Let this new wife figure out how to make peace in her household. She could feel her milk coming in. She looked back up at the house and saw Festal carrying both of the twins, trying to balance one on each arm. Myrna let him carry them down the steep path and come to the meadow where she was sitting. She took one twin from him and nursed him, then reached for the second. When they were both fed, Myrna handed them to her husband and followed him slowly up to the house. She sat on the bed while Festal tucked them into bed. He then left the room.

Myrna told Gift to go and bring her the box at the end of her bed. Then she gave Gift a nightgown to wear and put the impala necklace around her neck, spraying some of her floral perfume on the girl. She could not have said what possessed her to put the love amulet that Festal had made her on the girl, but she was compelled to do it. He had to know that love was not so easily shared, or it could be lost. At best, it was altered.

That night, Gift slept in the small rondavel with Festal. In the morning, the girl was up early. She came into the house. "Festal will not be at breakfast. He is going to town to straighten something out with Dodge." Gift picked up Samuel and rocked him in her arms. Myrna noticed bruises on her neck as the oversized night robe slipped off the girl's thin shoulder. The impala necklace was missing from her throat.

"Gift, we can talk. Or we can just do the chores and wait until we both are used to this new arrangement. Let me know if you need something from me."

Gift looked at her in disbelief. "I thought you arranged this. I know Dodge is your Uncle. Didn't you know they wanted me to marry Festal?"

"What is done is done. No one told me Festal was taking another wife. You are young. We have to be careful not to get pregnant too soon after the twins. Maybe he was thinking of me or the children. Maybe he thought he was helping you out." Neither of the women had mentioned that Gift was pregnant. Maybe the girl was like her, and didn't know. Myrna thought somehow that Gift had more experience with men than she had at that age. What was clear was the girl did not know how to manage Festal. She would talk to her about that once she was sure what she said would not be the topic of their nuptial conversations. She wanted to trust this girl, but she really knew nothing about her, other than Uncle Dodge had been involved.

Gift was silent and plunked herself down on a stool without being asked. Myrna made her a cup of tea, and waited for the girl to talk.

"I didn't want to leave here," she said. "I told him I couldn't sleep with him because we weren't married."

"So," he said "let's get married." We signed the papers and he gave me the ring. But when I tried to make him like me last night, he hit me and said I wasn't worth the thong on your sandal. She broke into sobs and Myrna poured her another cup of tea. The twins were both awake now and loud, so each woman picked up a soiled baby and started to laugh. Myrna thought she could tell the girl some things about what her husband liked, and what he didn't, but she might also learn a few things about men from this girl. She was not entirely sorry to see the girl had had a rough night. Myrna would be glad to have help with the children. They were going to have some bumps in the road ahead—that was becoming clear. Compared to the loss of Lily, the addition of this girl to their family was a small sacrifice. Maybe the two of them could make sure that all the remaining children were healthy.

After the girl finished cleaning her twin, she straightened her headscarf and looked in the mirror, laughing again at the mess her face was in. By the time Festal returned from the pastures, the house was tidy, all the children bathed and the wash was ironed and put away. Gift was wearing a fresh blouse and had her hair brushed and a clean skirt wrapped around her waist. She smelled of lavender and did not say a word as the man ate his dinner. After the plates were cleared, she asked if there was anything Myrna or Festal needed, and then excused herself to go and play with the children before bedtime. Festal looked at Myrna in amazement, and then kissed her fully on the lips for the first time, before going to his rondavel to sleep alone. The Prince of Love was tired.

Myrna had never been kissed before. What else would they learn from this girl?

Gift could not see well. Myrna discovered this when she set out some glasses for the girl to wash and dry. Gift couldn't tell which were clean and which were not. She did better with the pots, which only required a swipe with the fingertips to see if the food was still stuck on them. When she cleaned the babies, she placed her nose almost on the child to make sure she had done a thorough job. Myrna tried to explain to her about germs, but the girl thought she was telling her a folk story. She also confessed that she did not really think children were human.

Gift was a huge help with the laundry. It took two people to twist the towels and bedclothes to get most of the water out of them. Myrna's hands had been raw with the work of cleaning the nappies for the twins. As the days progressed, Gift occasionally was called to Festal's rondavel for the night. Myrna would then have the children to mind through the night, and the twins were relentless. Every two hours one of them needed to be fed. If she was not quick, the second one would be wakened and screaming and the first one would then start. Because there were two of them, they were not bowel trained as she had done with each of her girls. This required her to be constantly cleaning diaper cloths, which she now washed twice a day. Fortunately, the rains had not come, so the cloths dried quickly. Gift would iron the diapers when she took them down to kill the fly eggs so the boys would not get larva hatching on their bodies.

It always amazed Myrna how the other children could sleep through the uproar. Both boys together could not reach the pitch that Daisy had managed in her infancy. Festal could not sleep through the crying, as he had many years of living alone in the wilderness of the cattle station, with only the occasional howl of a hyena or the lowing of the cattle. His separate rondavel made it possible for him to endure the five young children without interruption of his sleep.

CHAPTER 27

GIFT DELIVERS

Six months had gone by and Gift's pregnancy was evident. Festal said nothing of this, but Dodge returned two goats that had been gone from the farm about the time the girl came to live with them. There was no sense of when the baby would come, as Gift had never had periods and no one in the house had a calendar to figure dates. It was well known that first babies could come anytime.

One afternoon when Festal was away, Gift suddenly experienced sharp pains while she was using the latrine and called out to Myrna. Myrna put a twin on each hip and went out to see what the matter was. She could see the girl was doubled over in pain and the waters had broken.

"Gift, this means the baby will come very soon. Stay put and do not move. I will hitch up the animals and come for you with the wagon. Festal is in the far pasture today."

After placing the large cook pot on the wagon, Myrna put the twins inside on top of a blanket, and then put a cloth over the top, fastening her makeshift pen to the wagon sides. Myrna rushed out to locate the hobbled donkeys to hitch them to the cart, something she had never done before. She sent the three girls to the neighbors' house, all of them holding the corner of a towel as they walked. Only when she saw Lottie wave, did she turn and lead the donkeys near the latrine and pull the howling Gift onto the wagon, on top of the clean sleeping cloths she had laid out. By this time, Gift and the twins were all making plenty of noise. Myrna grabbed a knife and a piece of string and a jug of boiled water from the pot in the outdoor kitchen, and then got up in the driver's seat. The donkeys set off at a trot for the hospital.

About halfway to the clinic, Gift shrieked, "It's coming! I can't hold back!" Myrna parked the wagon in the shade of a eucalyptus grove, hobbled the donkeys and spread out the sheet, fresh off the courtyard wall, on the wagon floor. As she saw the water flowing in the wagon bed, she had Gift spread her legs and the head was right there. The skin was taut and the child tore out of the mother like a fish at the end of a wet silken cord. Myrna caught the baby midair, a boy who was somewhat shriveled on one side. She dried him off with the edge of the sheet, wrapping him in fabric as she laid him on Gift's deflated abdomen. His legs were withered and curled up tight against his buttocks. His head was red and bruised with a tangle of wet thin tendrils glued to the top with a white, pasty substance. Myrna offered Gift a drink of water. Once the placenta was passed, she poured the remainder of the water over the girl's pelvis. She dropped the placenta into the earthen jar. As the blood cleared and the adrenalin left Myrna's system, she noticed that the girl had been excised. She had heard of this practice, but she had never seen the results.

When the baby came, everything had torn open, and there was a gaping opening that could not easily be closed. She wrapped the remainder of the sleeping cloths around the mother's hips, gave her a hug, then put another cloth under her head before heading to the clinic. Myrna felt the milk streaming down her chest as the twins cried out. She hoped the clinic would have the skill to patch this girl together.

Gift kissed the tiny boy on his head, still panting from pain and the effort of giving birth to him. She fell asleep and the child slid off her stomach. Myrna slowed the donkeys, reached back and pulled the baby to her, opening her blouse and letting him nurse. He latched on and began to suck. She let him nurse until he fell asleep, then put him back beside his mother in the wagon bed.

The fact that he was small and undernourished had probably saved the girl's life; the nurses told Myrna when they reached the hospital. They were praising Myrna for saving the girl and her baby. They said she had the skills that were needed to be a surgeon, or at least a midwife. To Gift, they presented a tiny knit cap and quickly wrapped the wizened baby in a gown to conceal his legs from the mother. The nurses placed the baby at Gift's breast and encouraged Gift to let him nurse as long as he could to get some energy. He latched onto his mother like a honey badger scenting honey.

Myrna was pleased at how they built Gift up, even as they discussed how to mend the fistula the birth had caused, and to make sure her excision was properly mended. It had been a struggle for Myrna to deal with the moaning, the blood, and the sight of torn flesh. For the first time, Myrna wondered if she would have had the aptitude to handle this each day as a doctor, or whether she would want to.

Festal came into the room and all three nurses said, "Another boy." Festal was worried at the news of the girl going into labor when she did, and how they had managed to get to the hospital. Myrna had never harnessed the donkeys before.

"I don't think she has ever been a midwife before, either," said Gift. "The nurses say she could be a surgeon, the way she saved our baby." Festal looked at the blood covering the cart, and the makeshift playpen the twins had shared, then thought he was going to be sick. He pulled his babies out of the pot and handed one to Myrna, cradling the second one against his chest. When Reuben was finished nursing, he passed Samuel to her, holding Reuben in one arm as he adjusted the blanket at the bottom of the pot. His head was pounding at the news of another son, and a wife that was so damaged. She would need a year's care before returning to her duties. He needed to get his life on track if these children were going to survive. When he saw the tiny boy with his shriveled side and pasted down hair, he felt an immediate and fierce love for this child that his mother had named Royal Festal.

A week later, his family was together again at the rondavel. Gift could not have relations for a year, and she was to report back to the hospital within a month to check on her fistula repair. She was flattened and tired looking; with great breasts that poured out milk whenever she looked at the tiny boy she named Royal Festal. Festal was afraid to pick him up as his skin looked so fragile. Neither of the wives remarked on how quick the baby had come, or that he looked nothing like the other children. It was enough that he was alive and that Festal had another son.

Joseph was most impressed by Myrna. On his travels to Copperfine to buy beef and hides, he had heard about the good wife from the villagers and learned they were talking about his sister-in-law, as the woman of virtue from the Bible. Myrna was living it out. Joseph asked himself how she could tolerate being uprooted from her schooling. Formal learning had never appealed to Violet, but Joseph had yearned for an education—and he could feel what a loss this must have been to the girl. Violet had said that Myrna was brilliant, and from the scholarship she received, the government had clearly identified her as one in a million.

What surprised Joseph the most was that Myrna was not bitter about her situation. No one in the family had ever heard her complain, even when she lost her first child, and later when Festal took a second wife half her age. How could she allow her husband to take in an orphan child and then allow him to marry her?

CHAPTER 28

UNDER THE MANGO TREE

Gift gathered the women into groups of four, handing each of them a slate and chalk. She brought the toddlers into the courtyard of the rondavel and pulled the gate shut. She had arranged small pots of water for the children to pour and cups to measure it with. There were drums and sticks for them to bang together. For the children who were able to walk, there was a small ladder and a hollow piece of wood that would one day be a bee's nest. Until then, it would serve as a toy they could squirm through or make into a see-saw. She watched the twins copy the older children, her little Royal swaying along on his bowed legs, laughing and clapping his hands. As they played, she wove her endurance baskets from the grasses she had gathered.

It had only been a year since Myrna and Gift started the women's co-op. They were now meeting weekly. Women were learning their letters and sums, and two work projects had been started. At first, the cattlemen were suspicious about their women gathering together at midday to attend the meetings. The women met once a month at the beginning, and the first order of business was to learn to write their husband's names and surnames. At each meeting, the women would bring a small gift, or food to share. At the end of the meeting, they would take home a simple recipe and a Bible text, neatly penned out to hang on the wall of their parlor. For many, these were the first written words they had ever had in their home.

Myrna and Gift then taught them to write the names of their children. They would mark the box with an "x" whether the child was a girl or a boy. The first lessons were spelled out in the sand underneath the mango tree that spread over 60 feet in width and provided deep shade from the noonday heat. Once the women could write their own names, they learned the alphabet in English, and each woman helped the others to learn letters she had mastered in her own name.

The government heard of their teaching and provided some small gifts to encourage the women to attend. Lessons were on basic health issues such as well-baby care, correct nutrition for toddlers, and simple first aid. Myrna would also share pictures from her biology book to let the women who were pregnant see what was going on in their bodies. She loaned the women her mirror so they could look at their genitals in the privacy of their home, then return it at the next meeting. It was the first time most women had seen themselves, or learned the names of their body parts. Myrna asked the health department to bring them a scale so they could weigh the babies and chart their progress. It was Violet's husband, Joseph, who first brought a scale for them to use. Two years later, the first government scale arrived.

Gift knew how to make baskets from the grasses that grew near the river bed, and taught the women the patterns to weave them into. Merchants from the larger town took the baskets to sell for the women. Women learned to make new recipes and how to dry fruits, as well as how to keep their food from spoiling. The biggest benefit of the co-op was the friendship and trust that built up between the women, and the knowledge of childcare the co-op provided. Women who had once left newborns alone the first day without nursing them, learned it was good to hold them and feed them breast milk right away. They were told how important it was to boil water for formula. With the Phiri twins, they learned that multiple births could result in healthy children. Sam and Reuben were robust and it was clear there was no demon stunting their growth. Some babies who had been sickly began to thrive as the women compared what worked. Royal Festal was disabled, but the community saw how he was loved and able to learn.

They learned from the new charts and scales the government health department had finally given them to verify that a child was thriving. Gift and Myrna learned to knit and taught the women this skill so they could make caps to put on the newborns. The men began to see the importance of the women coming together as they enjoyed each other's company, and consolation for the difficult job of raising a child through toddlerhood in cattle country.

When Lily died, Myrna was surrounded by women who had gone through loss. Festal held her but he could not listen to her weep. He was the one who dug the grave and placed a plumeria seedling above the mound. They never spoke of the child to each other, or their sorrow in losing her until their last daughter was born fifteen years later.

One of the things that Myrna learned was never to ask a woman why she stopped attending class. If a woman was absent for more than two weeks, either Myrna or Gift would go to her house, bringing a small gift and see for themselves what the problem was. Just as Myrna had seen bruises on Gift and knew that she was being hit, Gift would report back that she had seen that the woman not attending did not have sufficient food, or her child was not thriving. The group would then think of a strategy to combat this problem. Men who hit their wives soon learned that they would be shunned if the abuse did not stop. When a woman was treated well, that report flew through the village and a husband heard his praises sung out. Myrna had learned how important reputation is to a man. The husband was envied because his wife was quick to tell of his good qualities. His lapses were not overlooked, but neither were they exploited or gossiped about. Myrna and Gift also learned it was better for the women in the co-op to receive goods or foodstuffs because if they earned money, it was too often used by the husband to buy local brew or throw a party.

Gift was pregnant again and due in a month or two. She sat on the stool in the courtyard sorting over the groundnuts spread out in the roasting tin. Royal was playing with the other children on a teeter totter that Festal had rigged up from a hollowed out stump of a tree and a flat board he had planed. The women watched one child and then another go up in the air and the shrieks of laughter as they bumped at the top of their ascent, and then come down to earth. The twins were the most evenly balanced and could teeter-totter for hours, if they did not have to take turns with the others. The neighbor's children came by to share the amazing toy.

"Sister, what is it that you get from your books? You read them every day, but I want to know what is in them that satisfies you."

"Some of them are old friends. I read them and remember the first time I read them, and what they meant to me then. They have not changed, but I know I have because they have new meaning for me. Some I like because they allow me to see things from a different point of view. I may not agree with them, but the words are always the same, and different ideas are revealed to me, depending on what is going on in my life. That is how I read the Bible. Right now, I am thinking about the inheritance I have. I like to see myself as God's dream. Some books I read because they tell me how to do something, so I learn new skills; or how someone else does the same thing in another part of the world."

"I get that from people I meet or know," Gift said.

"Yes, that is firsthand, and it is the most direct. Usually. Except some people conceal what it is they think or know. In a book, the author wants you to get their point or their information."

"I don't believe what I read. I have to have someone explain it to me. Then I try to decide if it is true. After I hear it more than once, I will begin to think it might be true. Pretty soon, I think it is my own idea. Especially if other people are saying the same thing."

"I also like that a book can talk about the same thing, but you get to see many ways of saying the same thing, or slightly different ways of saying the same thing. Also, the book may have metaphors, where something difficult is told in a story. You can like the story for its direct telling, but you can apply it to other circumstances. Like our folk tales. Many of these are metaphors for what we know, and should do, but we make it into an easy telling so we can hold the truth in a nutshell, like groundnuts. A kernel of truth."

"Gift, tell me a story from your village."

"Let me think of one. Okay. Here is the story of the hungry mother. She lived in a small hut with her husband who beat her every day. She did not have enough food for her child, and only that child was left. Every day she would cry out as she hunted for something to feed her baby. One day, the elephant queen heard her cry. She came to the hut and asked the woman for a ground nut. The woman had no food, but she gave the elephant the last groundnut. The elephant told her, "Now I owe you a wish. Call on me when you need me the most."

"That very afternoon, the woman was carrying her winnowing basket but there was no grain to winnow. Her stomach hurt and she called to the elephant queen to hear her cry, and help her. As she leaned over her basket with her baby on her back, she saw her feet becoming larger and larger, and she could see her nose becoming a trunk. Her child was on her back and she felt the two of them becoming one as she turned into a powerful elephant with the voice of power. She could walk anywhere and when her husband came home that night, he saw only the marks of the winnowing baskets on the ground, and a path leading into the forest. There was a herd of elephants surrounding the young and feeding each other with limbs they had pulled down from the forest. No one walked alone, and no one went hungry."

"From that day forward, women knew that their strength lay in caring for each other, for the elephants revere women and give them their knowledge of how to endure. On their feet they bear the patterns of our winnowing baskets. And that is why we call the baskets we make the endurance baskets."

"That is a beautiful story, Gift. I am going to write it down so I do not forget it. I will tell it to the children tonight."

"Sister, I am your metaphor. I am Gift. You have never unwrapped me. I thought for a long time that you wanted me to leave. I do not think that any more. It takes me a long time to trust anyone, but when you called me Sister, it was the start of my happiness."

The two wives scraped up the groundnuts and put them into the mortar to make a paste to add to the evening meal. The children would be coming in soon, and there would be calves to feed and clothing to iron for the Sunday service tomorrow. The sun dropped like an orange being tossed into the trees and it was nightfall.

Festal had continued to fear for his family and sometimes could not sleep at night for worrying that something would come to destroy them. When Gift had tried her sexual skills on him, Festal told her, "A man should surround a woman. A woman should not surround a man." Gift learned to let him be the one who made the decisions, and to hold her tongue when she thought he was wrong. She found it very hard to trust a man after her early experiences, or to be clear about what she was thinking and feeling. She hid many of her feelings behind the routines that she developed to make her feel secure. As Myrna showed trust in her judgment and confidence in her skills, Gift began to be more sure of herself. Her teaching of the women taught her what she most desired to learn. As she learned to love herself, Festal began to treat her more kindly, and he doted on little Royal.

Royal was a child who commanded attention. He would clown for the other children and everyone loved his antics. When Festal came home from the pastures, the toddler would follow him, uncannily imitating his every move, even to the hiking up of his pants and the slight tilt of his head. He could imitate any body noise and gesture, even the limp of an old man with a cane. With Myrna, he would nestle in and hug her, then dart back to his mother, so that there was no jealousy. One day when it was the heat of the harmattan season, Gift asked

Myrna to cut her hair for her. The women sat in the courtyard with
Myrna plaiting Gift's hair after she had trimmed the ends. She told her
the story of the baobab tree. It was revered by her people, and Gift had
asked why they never planted one in the yard. Myrna gathered the hair
she had trimmed, then tossed it into the rubbish heap, poured them
each some tea, and sat to tell her tale.

The baobab is a mighty and powerful tree in the land, but it was not
satisfied with itself, and so it complained to the Great Spirit which ruled
the land, the sea and the winds that it wanted to be more. It wanted to
have flowers and fruits and to be even mightier. The Great Spirit
ignored the complaints. But when they continued day and night, the
Great Spirit lost patience. It reached down and pulled the tree out of
the earth, and rammed it down again, with its roots on top and its
branches shoved into the soil. All the animals and the birds saw the tree
with its roots exposed, and recognized the power of the Great Spirit.
From that day forth, the tree remained leafless nine months out of the
year, with its roots growing into the air.

It is believed that our ancestors hover in the branches of the baobab
tree and gather there. So we don't plant one in our yard because we do
not know how the ancestors would respond to such a thing, and the
tree takes more than our lifetime to mature. We use it for all kinds of
medicine, as you know, so it would be convenient to have one growing
close by, but sometimes we value something more when we have to go
far to harvest its benefits.

As Gift and Myrna gathered their work and went into the rondavel,
they thought they saw someone in the rubbish heap, but they were
tired, the children were now napping, and they did not investigate.

Gift became pregnant and gave birth to four more children over the
course of ten years, but none of them survived infancy. Only Royal
Festal endured. Myrna watched the care Gift gave the children and

could not see why they would begin to lose weight and eventually pass away. Myrna had suckled Royal when he was small because she had such a supply of milk. But this could not have been the reason for his survival.

Gift had been healed from her fistula, and went to the hospital each time before she gave birth, but Royal was to remain her only surviving child.

CHAPTER 29

MYRNA AND FESTAL VISIT JOSEPH AND VIOLET

Joseph and Violet could only speculate how Myrna had become such a wife and mother. "We need to have them come and spend a week with us and get to know their children," Joseph said. Violet agreed, and that Christmas, the families met together.

It was in the dry season that Myrna, Festal and Gift, along with their six children came to spend Christmas with the Leibitsang family, including their six sons. Seventeen made a very full house, even for the large home that Joseph and Violet now enjoyed. While Violet's boys were rowdy and often needed a diversion, Myrna's children were content to watch and participate quietly. They were easily amused with a story or a book, a picture or a small toy they could roll about the floors. Royal Festal was the comic, and loved by them all. He had captured the heart of Grandmother Beatrice as well. She held him and asked him tell her all about the trip coming to Blancville. She was so sorry Bishop was sick and not able to enjoy this little jester.

"Joseph has made our family very comfortable with all the things he has provided," Violet said to her sister.

"Yes, we have more than we need to get along. But you and Myrna seem to have captured the things of the spirit," Joseph said, and Violet had to agree. Festal was proud of his new found faith, content with his life, his wives and his children. Myrna was a large part of this. Gift praised her, and her children adored their mother. Myrna was aware of this praise, but she thought she fell short of her duty as a daughter. She had never really forgiven her mother, or gotten to know how her mother's life had been, and now, she wanted to give special honor to her mother Beatrice.

Myrna asked to hear details of how her life had been since she left. Beatrice was glad to have an audience for her reminiscing. Her life had become easier and more comfortable, she said, with her younger daughter living close to her. Jethro had been her last pregnancy, and the joy of grandsons gave her renewed energy. Myrna heard how she was missed. She was pleased at the love and respect her family showed to her and her family. Only the absence of her father Bishop saddened her during this all too short visit to her childhood home. He was sick with pneumonia and quarantined in the family house. No one was to visit him on doctor's orders.

One night as the girls were sprawled on the overstuffed sofa, the boys all bunked away upstairs, and only Myrna, Violet, Gift and Beatrice sitting out on the verandah, Violet asked Gift about her family. All of them were interested in hearing the account, as Myrna and Gift would be leaving for Copperfine in a couple of days, and no one had heard how Gift came to be married to Festal.

"Oh, this is a story I have never told anyone," Gift started. "It is a tale of long ago when I was living with my mother and father, and all my brothers and sisters, in another country. We grew small crops and made baskets from the grasses that grew along the river. It was a river filled with crocodiles, which were our totem. I was attending school at the Holy Sepulcher Primary in Form One. One day soldiers from the Lord's Resistance Army came and broke into our class right after we had finished our flag salute and prayers. They grabbed ten of us girls and told the Sister not to make a sound or they would shoot the rest of the class. We were forced to march with them into the forest, where I was given to one of the older soldiers to be his wife. The other girls were also given to the soldiers. We were told if we tried to run away, our families would be killed. I didn't know they had already killed all my family and burned our house."

"When my new husband went away, other soldiers would take me for their wife. I did not have enough food and we were tied up at night. By day, we had to work gathering firewood, preparing food, and washing the clothes. There were some very young soldiers there too, and they would sometimes cry at night for their mothers. If they were caught, the other young soldiers were made to shoot them, so they stopped that very soon."

"One day, I saw my chance when we were taken down to the river to bathe and wash clothes. I left my clothes scattered on the shore, made tracks to the water, then ran back using the clothes as stepping stones so there would be no tracks. I must have run for three days, but no one came after me. I had told none of the other girls what I was going to do, as I was afraid the soldiers would force them to tell, and then punish them for my disobedience. I thought if I left my clothes and the tracks to the river, they would think a crocodile had taken me. I was naked and bitten by insects, and very thin.

I finally found a house where they were willing to take me in. They gave me boy trousers and a big shirt to wear. I worked for them for two years without pay, until I left. I had heard there was a shelter for war orphans in the nearby town. There I was sent to a school, as they had found a sponsor for me. By that time, I was bigger than all the girls in Form 2. The teacher would taunt me and say, "Why don't you go and join your mother?"

"Of course, my mother was dead, so they were really telling me I should die. No one would be my friend and because the teacher referred to me as a rebel. I ran away because I couldn't stand the shaming. Somebody said that shame undresses us, and it is true. Flo at the Big Banana Bar gave me a job. She was like a mother to me. She washed my hair, got me girl's clothes, and she taught me how to make change and serve customers. Then Dodge came and arranged for me to come and take care of his mother. He received a bride price for me and gave it to Flo, so that is how I came to live with Festal and Myrna."

"Then Festal married me, and we are a family now. The best compliment was when Myrna told me I could call her sister. Now that I have met Violet, I see what a compliment that is. And that is my story." Gift reached for a glass of water.

Beatrice and Violet looked at each other with wide eyes and mouths wide open. Neither of them mentioned that Dodge's mother had been dead for twelve years and Dodge had lied to everyone involved.

"Gift, you never told me this story," Myrna said.

"No. I do not like to think about it because it makes me feel how much I have lost, and how I was nothing. When I try to remember things, I often can only remember the crying times, and so I would rather forget everything than have that fill my mind again."

"You have a family now," Myrna said.

"Yes. I cannot tell you how happy I was when I saw you in your beautiful house, surrounded by those babies. It was like my family had been given back to me. Festal reminded me of my father who worked with the U.N. Peacekeeping force in Zaire. He was a warrior who loved his family. He used to beg my mother to leave the country, but she loved her village and all the people and family she grew up with. She couldn't imagine war would come to them as they had never voted, or even carried weapons. She was a Christian and we were all baptized. Of course, you can tell that from the tattoo of the cross on my forehead. I think she thought we were protected. My father was killed crossing the border. The rest of the family was killed at night in our home and our village was burned. As far as I know, no one from our family survived." Violet and Myrna exchanged glances.

"Thank you for your story, Gift. We all need to get some sleep now.

We can share my bed and Mother can sleep on the other sofa," said Violet. The girls were already curled up on the one sofa, each of them cupped around each other with a blanket over the three. Festal was already asleep on his mat in the back parlor near the kitchen, with Royal curled up behind him. Joseph and the boys were in the dormitory upstairs. Beatrice went to check on her husband before turning in.

"Tomorrow, we will visit the mercantile warehouse Joseph is building." Violet said.

After they washed and cleaned their teeth, Violet sang a song of blessing to the family and their visitors; it was a song she had learned on the radio. "God Bless this House." Her contralto voice was even richer and more resonant than Myrna remembered. Myrna and Gift had tears in their eyes at the beauty of the music and the night. They slept well, the three sisters in the big bed, three little sisters on the sofa, and Beatrice on the mohair plush sofa.

In the morning, everyone ate sorghum porridge and sliced mangos, then followed Joseph to his new warehouse. The ground was a crisscross of white strings marking off the corners of the foundation. The children bounced across them as though they were jumping rope. Cement was being mixed in huge circles of gray on the ground as the trenches for the foundation were being excavated by workers. Violet stayed back from the dust and the melee of workers, holding her youngest son in her arms. He was named Bwalya, after Joseph's father, the first son given a traditional name.

Beatrice checked on her husband and took him some breakfast and Myrna insisted on going along. Bishop lay curled on his mattress. The room was dark and at first he didn't recognize Myrna. When he saw her, he said, "I must be dreaming. My angel is back. Don't come too close. I am so joyful to see you looking so well. I have prayed for you every night, and here you are. I am happy. This is the best medicine I could have. Now don't stay too long, the doctor was very strict about that. I guess I am catching." Myrna squeezed his hand and left to join the others outside.

During a lull in the conversation, when lunch was over and the women gathered on the verandah, Gift offered another story. The women looked on with anticipation, as Gift's stories were proving very interesting. Violet nursed the baby while the other women looked on.

"Did I ever tell you how Myrna saved my baby?" Gift began.

"No. Tell us," the women said in unison.

"I was just married to Festal and I didn't know exactly when the baby was due, as I had never had a period. One day, my waters broke and Myrna hitched up the donkeys, which she had never done before. She put her twins into the huge black pot with the three legs, and she hauled me to the doctor. Only my baby wouldn't wait. So Myrna parked the wagon and delivered Royal right there on the wagon under the eucalyptus trees. The doctors said Myrna had the skills of a surgeon, the way she had washed me and wrapped me up tight in the cloth she had packed. I had a fistula, and without her help, I would have bled to death, they said. That is my only baby that has survived, so far."

Beatrice was aghast at this story and praised her daughter for her courage. Violet said it just confirmed what a great doctor she might have been." Did you know, Myrna, how I coveted that big old pot with the three legs? I knew what it meant to Mother, and when she gave it to you, I was bitter for a long time. Funny, because I never had a daughter to pass it down to."

"I didn't know that, Violet. I will see that you have it one day. I don't think my girls will have any attachment to it, but it has been very useful to me."

"Myrna, why didn't you ever write and tell us that you did this? It is remarkable," her mother added.

"She has been an angel and an example to my boy and me," Gift said.

At the end of the week, Myrna was sorry to leave her sister and Joseph and the festive holiday they all enjoyed together. But she was glad to get back to her place, her women's co-op, her calves, and the serenity of their life in Copperfine. They were laden down with gifts from Joseph and Violet, including a clock with red velvet roses and rhinestones on the hour hand, a new kerosene lantern, a knitting machine for the women's cooperative, and half a dozen sewing shears.

Violet made a resolution to visit Myrna, once her latest baby was two and more resistant to disease. Gift, in her candid way, said, "In Copperfine, you could breathe flies if you weren't careful." That image disarmed Violet, so that she rarely found an opportunity to visit Copperfine.

One day when Joseph was in cattle country, he stopped by the Big Banana Bar to purchase baskets and sleeping mats from the women's co-op for his mercantile. He overheard Gift talking to Flo.

"You know, Myrna didn't know I was going to marry her husband. But when I did, she tried to help me stay in his good graces, even though I was jealous of her, because he told me I could never measure up to her. I can't, but she never makes me feel that way. She is my angel." The two women were sitting at the inside counter with Royal Festal pulling at their clothing. He didn't hear what response Flo made, but he wanted to understand how Myrna became such a paragon of virtue. He knew his family was lacking something that hers had. He would bring his family to visit their cousins in the country.

CHAPTER 30
COUNTRY COUSINS

Two years later, Violet visited the cattle country with her brood.

I visited Myrna and Festal when my boys were old enough to avoid the mud holes, the manure, and be strong enough to ward off diseases the flies carried. We arrived at midday when the heat was that dull, heavy white heat where the sun is so pervasive—it isn't even visible. The dust was settled, the birds were silent, and the cattle were standing in small groupings with their tails running like fans, trying to protect their udders and flanks. The calves hung under their mothers, never lifting their heads as they waited their turn to nurse. The cows sucked up water and you could see their sides fill.

Joseph was oblivious to the filth and the heat. He grasped Festal around the neck and held his hand all the way to the house. Our boys looked at each other in disbelief, then joined their cousins in one game after another. We had to corral them at night, they were so caught up in the expanse of the place, and the myriad of places where they could run and hide, fire slingshots, and capture locusts. The chameleon with her skittish brood of offspring was a huge hit, as were the calves that bucked around the corral, butting at the boys and chasing them.

Festal's hounds were ecstatic, slavering in their eagerness to give chase and play every game the boys dreamed up. Everyone had to have a turn at pumping water from the well. The girls were quick to engage their cousins in games of hide and seek, steal the flag, jump rope, and other chase games. The termite hills were their forts and castles. By nightfall, the entire group was exhausted, including the twins and Royal Festal. He fell asleep on the wall of the compound, his legs hanging down on either side, and had to be carried to the sleeping hut by his father.

Myrna and Gift and I caught up on the changes in our lives. While most of the women in her village of Copperfine still wore the traditional chitenge of patterned prints imported from Holland, our townspeople no longer sewed their own garments, nor were woven traditional fabrics readily available. The foot looms were now consigned to the cultural museum. We had graduated to wearing fashions from Europe. Some were current, but most came from the second hand clothing market. There was every conceivable fashion from the last twenty years, coming from all over the world, sold in the market place. Women wore pointed toe shoes, not a very good fit for feet used to open-toed sandals, or going barefoot on trails to get water or firewood. The town women were even starting to wear slacks, not in public, but at home. The hairstyles that imitated the afros of the civil rights movement – although none of us were too sure what that was about, other than hearing the names – had given way to wigs of every conceivable style and color. We had all heard of their King, Martin Luther, Jr..

When we looked at an Ebony Magazine, it was hard to see what they meant by a ghetto, since the buildings were better than what our wealthy magistrate owned. Women wore wigs to work, and long skirts and dresses of various styles. Many polyester leisure suits came our way, which were indestructible and of every hue, although burnt orange and baby blue seemed to be the most prevalent. Much later, Levis and sweatshirts, and printed tee shirts with a myriad of ads on them, flooded our market stalls. But in the early sixties, we were lucky to find sweaters and church wear in the dead-white-men's-clothing of the marketplace. We called them dead-white-men's-clothes because no one would abandon such good clothes unless he was dead, and only a white man could afford so many.

Most of the families had two sets of clothing, one for work, and one for church. Students often wore their school uniforms to church, and some churches even provided a gown or robe for church members, so the entire congregation could parade to church as one body. I could see that Myrna's family had two basic changes of clothing, and they hung them on the posts of their beds. She did not have electricity, but I gave her a new kerosene lantern with an adjustable wick. It gave off a brilliant glow, bright enough for her to sew or read in the evening. Festal took offense at it, and would mutter every time she lighted it, which she told me later, was every evening for the next thirty years. The children did their homework by it, and it allowed her more hours in her always long day.

Festal took excellent care of his family. His children were all in school, and his three rondavels comfortably housed, with simple, but traditional furnishings. They did not have any appliances or furniture other than the bed for Myrna, mats for the children, and a slatted crib Festal had built for the infants. The inside of the house was remarkably cool and free of flies. It was dark and smelled of floor polish and the candles that Myrna made from beeswax, and other scents such as lavender and cinnamon. When they would whitewash the inside, the whole room would smell like animal glue.

Myrna kept the bedclothes in hampers and the foodstuffs in clay canisters or tins. She had a water jug with a spigot that slowly leached through its red clay sides, the evaporation keeping the water as cool as if it was refrigerated. Only the kitchen table and single bed interrupted the circular symmetry of the house. While I was there I noted the small hole in the curtains and the worn-thin area on the table cloth. But Myrna was still meticulous about keeping them clean and ironed. I recognized the fabric we gave Festal so many years ago throughout the house.

There were no musical instruments in the house, but each of the children sang and the twins and Royal played the drums for school and church. When evening came, and the dishes were washed, the two families sat in the main house on the ledge that circled the room. They completely filled the circular step, and it was pleasing to see how the family had grown. There were stories to tell and verses to recite. Iris, Pansy, and Daisy sang a song they had memorized for this occasion. They wore satin dresses with a touch of lace at the neck and sleeves, and a contrasting sash their mother had sewn for them. Their voices blended perfectly. When they came to the lower part of the register, Festal joined in with a baritone voice to help them get through this part of the song. They looked up at him with admiration and he nodded at them to let them know he was proud of them. Reuben and Samuel cooked up a short skit with their cousins; performing it to much applause, much of it their own. It had more action than plot, and many rough and tumble battles. It was late when they sang their evening prayer with their Aunt Violet, and headed to bed, eager for the next day's play.

Violet and Joseph drove back to Blancville, encouraged by the order and peace of the Phiri family, and wondering if they should be doing something different with their own brood. They glossed over the differences. Violet reassured Joseph that he was an excellent provider and model for his sons, who were just very free-spirited young men; not to worry that they liked to wrestle and rough house rather than sing or recite. There was plenty of time for them to develop their minds and spirits

"Let them be kids," Violet said.

CHAPTER 31

VIOLET AND JOSEPH PROSPER

In Blancville, the population was increasing, and Violet and Joseph were contributing mightily. Every couple of years, another boy arrived. Each was cuddled and adored by their parents and the grandparents next door. They were handsome and healthy with full, thick hair, shining square teeth, and unblemished skin. They were taller and more energetic than many of the children at their school, and all of them were involved in soccer or cricket. Violet had the best medical care and assistance that Joseph could provide. Joseph's partner, Valoo, had remained in India, except for short visits every couple of years. He, too, had grandchildren arriving, and was doing his best to instill values in them, he told Joseph. Joseph had remarked how Myrna and Festal seemed to have a tight knit caring family, while his own were boisterous, more like a rambling vine than a tree giving shade.

Valoo encouraged Joseph in being a father, and reminded him that there was still time for him to introduce moral principles and discipline, but Joseph liked his rambunctious flock of sons. He indulged his wife with the latest fashions that he came across in the urban areas. When her boys were old enough to travel, they did the same. Benjamin was the oldest and the first to attend school in Joseph's family. Joseph was proud of his son, and would ask him to read a book to him in the evenings, — The Greatest Salesman. But the boy said he was tired, or needed to practice for his cricket league, and the book was never finished. When his cousins came to visit, Benjamin encouraged them to play sports with him. Then he would beat them mercilessly, as he was strong and trained. Taller than all the brothers. When they reached teenage years, however, some began to pass him in height and strength. At that time, he lost interest in wrestling or competing with them.

Bishop and Beatrice sat in the pew of the Full Gospel Presbyterian Church at the right of the support column. They observed families filing in, their own pew filled with their older children. The youngsters would soon be escorted to the Ark Sunday school for younger children.

Beatrice smoothed her wrap and looked over her children with a satisfied complacency. She and Bishop had been married noticeably longer than most of the others in their congregation, longer even than this church had been in existence—and it had been a fruitful joining. Seven children living, three now married, and the remainder getting schooling as finances allowed. Joseph had assured the Chitundus he could use more distributors, so they knew their boys would have gainful employment.

Bishop and Beatrice could have wished that Myrna was closer to them, but Violet with her throng of boys filled their days with anecdotes and adventures. Their own youngest child Jethro was a playful boy with a disarming smile and the tendency to make people laugh. He watched their faces and those of their guests for cues as to what would entertain and delight them. Neither parent had any idea of how Jethro's life would turn out. No child in their village had taken to performing, yet this seemed to be what fascinated Jethro. He was going to be in the Christmas pageant this year, the youngest child.

Beatrice pulled Jethro by his coat and motioned for him to sit down. The reflection time before the altar call was about to begin. She could hear small titters of laughter at her boy's antics.

Bishop's thoughts were on the dinner that would follow the service. He wondered if the kerosene in his refrigerator would hold out. They had guests coming over and he wanted the drinks to be cold.

Bishop sometimes wondered if he should have set some goals for his children. Stephen had finished his course at secondary school and become a math tutor. His wife Esther seldom visited their home, and had not invited them to theirs, saying it was too small to make them comfortable. Bishop did not know what the issues were between them, but he was not surprised when Stephen decided to stop teaching and start driving cab. He could make almost twice the money, now that the economy was good, and tourists and businessmen were coming to the area. Joseph helped him get a vehicle for the taxi, service, and within the first two years, Stephen had paid him back. Stephen and Esther now lived on the outskirts of Blancville, closer to Esther's parents. They had one child who spent more time at Esther's parents' house than she did in her parent's according to Beatrice. The girl was seldom brought to see the Chitundus, and this caused pain to Beatrice, so Bishop avoided mentioning the family as much as possible.

Bishop had set some goals for Myrna. The disappointment of having to take her from her schooling was almost as hard to bear as the death of their first child, Eunice. He had said this so often, the words came now without feeling or thought. These were peaceful times for Beatrice and Bishop, with letters from the country, telling how Myrna's family was growing, and occasional visits from their son Thomas, who was now in the prestigious Royal Academy boarding school that Myrna had attended.

Thomas was not a challenge to them, and seemed to be making his way in a sure, if uneventful course of study with no idea what he wanted to do when he finished. He did love being on the cricket team. What was the path that Violet's children would take? He knew that Joseph wanted them educated and spent time with them as they grew up. But Bishop wondered if they had been too scattered in their approach to the boys' education. None of them sustained an interest beyond what came easily. They didn't worry about their future, nor were they competitive if it wasn't comfortable.

Only Bwalya had shown a talent for any particular field. He had a desire to be an artist early on and would defend the illustrations he made in the margins of his exercise books. Joseph tried to understand Bwalya's art, and when he asked him about it, Bwalya would tell him, *if it doesn't tell a story with emotion and color, why bother?* He was a skilled artist, everyone said, but the grandparents had never seen him or his art since he returned from Europe. The other brothers would show up from far regions with tales of their travels, and gifts they brought back for their grandmother.

Beatrice was surrounded by her throng of grandchildren on the holidays, and sometimes on Sunday when they joined them for a special barbecue. No, Bishop certainly could not complain about the family they had raised together. The music started and Bishop felt his eyelids grow heavy with the peacefulness and familiarity of the sounds. He was asleep before the message on the Great Commission began.

Violet and Joseph spent Sunday morning in the warehouse. They led a circumscribed life with their business ventures drawing the circle. The assistant they hired to help had fallen ill, and the two of them were taking inventory of the stock. Buying, stocking, selling, and then repeating the cycle— occasionally choosing a new product to try— was Joseph's strategy. It was dark and cool in the building, a relief from the blast of heat outside on this November day.

When most of the goods had been accounted for, they took a break to eat some Welsh meat pies and take a drink of tea. By now, the tea was cold, but sweet to their taste.

The first years of Violet and Joseph's marriage had been a blur of infants, nannies, and visits to relatives to share the children. After they had passed the difficult times of infancy and childhood they had expected a release from the constant watchfulness over the health of their sons. The boys were in middle school, then secondary school, and vocational school when a cloud moved over the country. One by one, something was claiming the lives of young people, as surely as the cholera had taken the cattle from grandparents in days of old. This disease was not named, nor did anyone acknowledge that it had affected their families. The Leibitsangs attended the funerals of their sons' friends, crossing themselves in gratitude that it had not been one of theirs. Benjamin, now a senior in college, and the others were attending various vocational and secondary schools. They offered up a prayer for the safekeeping of all their boys and gave generously when the plate was passed.

CHAPTER 32

GRADUATION

Joseph watched the line of graduates go forward. He sat on a wooden folding chair next to Violet and felt the tightness of his breath against his chest. He had not attended school, and now a son of his, was receiving a degree from the University. As the music of the processional swelled, he wondered if others were feeling this overwhelming tightness in their chests. The tears welled up behind eyelids. He was swollen with happiness, his throat tight with emotion.

Nothing he had done in his work, or even his marrying his beautiful impala woman, compared with the pride he felt in having his son exceed his reach. Joseph knew he had made this success possible. For himself, employment and self-determination had been a quest. Could he rise to be a man of civility and of execution? It was not enough to have the ideas—could he make them tangible? As he had watched his employer strive for success, there had always been a doubt of the outcome, a fear that underlay the enterprise. Now, this son graduating gave him his answer. He was humbled to be a part of the tradition of education and the acknowledgement it brought.

Joseph glanced over at Violet to see if she was feeling a similar euphoria. She squeezed his arm at that moment, without looking away from her son. Benjamin alone was her focus and her joy at that moment. Later, she and Joseph would make love on the floor of their bedroom, celebrating what they had created and brought to fruition.

The crowd rose and cheered for the victory of a long concentration and discipline. Joseph would have a diploma to hang on the wall in his office, a reminder of this triumph.

Benjamin saw his parents in the crowd. His father was wearing his best pinstripe gabardine suit, too warm for this November afternoon, but he knew how proud they were. They could not know that his eyes were scanning the crowd for a girl forbidden to him. Benjamin's thoughts were on Henrietta, a girl he had met in the cafeteria at his college when he had been sweet-talking the cook into serving him a snack after hours. When Henrietta walked in with a basket of hot rolls balanced on her head, her small waist and tight breasts accented by the line her body made while she carried the basket on her head, Benjamin knew he had to learn all about this nymphet of a girl. Within the next few weeks, she was sneaking to his dorm room and making love in his bunk bed. They laughed at the danger of being discovered, or toppling off the narrow bunk.

He had also gone to her mother's flat on days when the mother was at the ovens, baking the rolls that supplied the greater part of the city. There he would join the girl on a mat on the floor, or behind the curtain that closed off the bedroom from the sitting room. She was a petite, athletic girl with a ready smile and eyes only for him. He did not doubt what his mother would say to this match. Henrietta had no family except for her mother, and her father had died from pneumonia when she was eight. She was not of Ben's tribe, nor did she have any intention of learning his mother tongue. So why was he so in love with her? He loved the adventure of his going to see her and planning how they would manage. She was not materialistic in the least. Her favorite gift was a page of music that he would sing to her, and she would transpose into a beautiful song. Whatever she heard, she could imitate. Her family had fled from the wars to the north, she never specified more than this, but he knew her childhood had been as unlike his as her music was to his wailings. She was a vision, that is how he pictured her.

Now that he was graduating from the University people would begin to ask when he would marry. He had already had Uncle Dodge making suggestions and trying to get him to share a drink and talk prospects. Uncle Dodge had no idea how much Benjamin loathed him.

Hen, for that was his pet name for Henrietta, knew that he had a hyena in the family, that is how he described the character of this uncle. Sometimes they would play a game and try to guess how many cows, goats and chickens Uncle Dodge could negotiate for Hen. Benjamin would make a tiny offer and Hen would pounce on him in mock fury. One day, her mother had come in just as Hen had pounced. Both of them came out with the identical lie, they had seen a mamba and were looking for it under the bed. They did not know if the mother believed them, but she looked terrified and went rushing to get her broom to protect her child.

When they called the names of the graduates, Benjamin heard the name Leibitsang, and walked jauntily up to the platform, saluting his father before he took the rolled up diploma, then shook hands with the dean. He saw his parents snap a picture at that moment, and it was over. He was a graduate.

Benjamin's graduation party was riotous. More and more people showed up and his father realized that he had no way to keep party crashers from wining and dining off the sumptuous spread he had laid out to celebrate the occasion. At 8:00 Joseph announced he was closing the gates. By this time, the party tent was a shambles and the drinks and food were gone, along with many of the plates and cutlery, the cushions, and the decorations. Joseph tried not to let the rampage of the guests spill over on his mood. But Violet echoed his concerns and his lament at the behavior of the guests who had been drinking. Many just couldn't handle such an excess of meat and drink after their normal restrictive diet. Some came to be rowdy—it was a party, wasn't it? They wanted to forget their work-a-day lives. The pent-up frustrations boiled over in raucous laughter, dancing, drinking, and eating. Some seemed to be high on the amount of beef they had consumed. The barbecued beef had been a full sized steer, now it was a ribcage and less. A child in the corner of the garden chewed contentedly on one of the ears.

Joseph's other sons looked dazed at the carnage of the back yard and the piles of rubbish left behind. A lone rooster wandered into the suburban backyard and started to crow. After Benjamin left, Joseph and Violet headed to their room, arm in arm; they would clean up the tomorrow, determined not to let the aftermath destroy their jubilee.

It was Sunday. Benjamin normally went to church with his parents and family. He liked the lively youth group, the music, and the big screens where he could see every portion of the large cathedral hall. The music was alive with rhythm. Today, however, Benjamin was missing. His mother thought he was probably sleeping in after the excitement of yesterday. His father didn't want to be irritated, as he was basking in the congratulations of the congregation for the graduates and their families.

Not until late afternoon did Joseph ask where Benjamin had gone. Dodge who had stayed at the Leibitsangs for the party offered to go and look for the boy. He said he had seen him looking around the party last night and thought he might have an idea where he was. It wasn't like Benjamin to not be at a family gathering, which they had planned for this evening.

Henrietta spent the weekend at the hospital. Her mother had collapsed at the communal ovens where they were baking hundreds of special rolls for the graduation weekend. By the time Henrietta located her at the hospital, her mother was asleep and the nurses advised her to let the woman rest. They told Henrietta her mother was suffering from heat exhaustion from exertion and the heat of the baking. Henrietta sat in the chair beside the gurney. There was not a private room for her mother, but the nurses had kindly placed her in a side hallway near the cafeteria. Henrietta waited for her to wake up.

When evening came and she was still not awake, Henrietta went looking for food for them. She returned to the hospital around 9:00. By this time, visiting hours were over and she could not get in. She waited outside the doorway, and when a doctor came in for a late shift, he let the shapely young girl through the doorway, signaling her to be quiet and stay low. She did. She found her way down the hallway where her mother had been sleeping, but there was no gurney there. In a panic, she traced her way down each hallway, then again. Her mother was nowhere to be found. In the morning, she located the nurse that had helped her mother the night before. The woman had to think for a moment, then she smiled.

"Your mother has been put in a private room. The patient there died, not of anything contagious, so we just moved her right in. It will take a few days before the paperwork sorts it out, by then, she may be feeling much better." The nurse hugged the girl around her thin shoulders and guided her into the room. There lay her mother, surrounded by a filmy cloud of mosquito netting with a large drink of guava juice with a straw sitting next to her bed. She opened her eyes when Henrietta came in, and patted the bed for the girl to lie next to her. Henrietta pulled the sheet over herself and lay beside her mother. She felt the warm net of security settle over her tired body.

It was late afternoon before Henrietta woke, wondering where she was with the white clouds of curtain surrounding her. Amnesty smiled at her daughter when she saw her awake. "I am feeling much better, Henrietta," she said, reaching for her breakfast. "Have some eggs. I didn't want to wake you, you were sleeping so soundly."

Henrietta could hear her mother's breathing as she lay beside her and wondered if her mother was really better. She didn't let herself think what she would have done had her mother passed away while she was searching for some food. She hoped her mother had not been worried about her. With everything that had happened to Henrietta's mother, she hadn't thought about Benjamin's graduation and party. She knew he would be worried since he had no way of knowing what had become of her.

She had to find him and let him know she cared and that she had not wanted to miss his big day. She hugged her mother again and told her she would be back that evening. The nurse smiled at her as she let her out of the room and Henrietta turned to note the number. E 126.

Henrietta knew approximately where Benjamin lived. She did not have cab fare, but she had some leftover rolls, so she spent half an hour selling them at a discount to raise money for her fare. Within an hour, she was at the wrought iron gate of the Leibitsangs'. The guard asked who she was seeking and when she said Benjamin, he immediately let her in.

The family was gathered in the sitting room discussing where Benjamin might be. Uncle Dodge recognized the girl as the one he had seen near the University.

"This is the girl that knows Benjamin. Ask her where he is," Dodge said.

Henrietta looked at the family. She could recognize the mother immediately. Benjamin resembled her. The brothers less so. In their midst sat the father Joseph. By his stern look she knew right away he was upset by the disappearance of his son, and her arrival.

"How do you know my son?" he asked.

"I bring rolls to the University, that is how we met," Hen explained. "Where is Benjamin? Is he missing?" Her gaze went from one face to another and anyone could see she was shaken. Henrietta saw Dodge looking at her. This was the hyena uncle Benjamin had described.

Dodge was appraising the girl and he immediately summed her up as a poor girl who was no marriage prospect at all. She would be lucky to bring two goats for her dowry unless someone worked on her appearance. He liked the bones of her face and her graceful movements as she entered the sitting room. Still, the boy was throwing himself away on such a twit. She had no substance. As he was sizing her up, he missed his brother-in-law's question.

"Dodge, are you listening? The girl just told us Benjamin is probably out looking for her. Her mother is at the hospital, and he may have heard this from the bakery people and gone there to locate her. Can you follow up on that?" Joseph asked. It was more of a command then a question. Uncle Dodge said he would go immediately, and Henrietta said she would go with him to show him to her mother's room. Violet stood up and announced she was going as well.

"You stay here, Joseph, in case he comes here first."

At the hospital, the nurse ushered the three of them into Amnesty's room. She had combed Amnesty's hair, spruced up her bed, and was talking to the young man sitting beside the woman. Benjamin rose as they came into the room. "Mother, Hen, Uncle Dodge,"

Henrietta walked over and took her mother's hand, while Violet hugged Benjamin. Uncle Dodge sized up the nurse and the deluxe private room and wondered if he might have misjudged the girl. Ben was so relieved to see them all in this space; he even gave Uncle Dodge a brief embrace. The nurse said she was glad to see them all united, but now her private patient needed a little privacy to get her rest. Henrietta could come back in the evening if she arrived before eight o'clock.

Violet was happy that her son was safe, and she had met the girl he was pursuing. Details could be ironed out over a cup of tea when she had Joseph close by to help her think everything through. She looked the girl over carefully and could see that Benjamin had an eye for beauty. She hoped the girl had character and some backing as well. She would need it to get through this gamut. Uncle Dodge wasted no time in investigating the bun girl, as he nicknamed her. She lived in a flat with her mother, who was a master baker. Amnesty's husband had been in the U.N. Peacekeeping Force in Zaire, and died later of malaria. There were no brothers or sisters, nor could he quiz the mother as the nurse kept him out of the room. She was almost militant in her misplaced guardianship of this family, Dodge thought. Well, they weren't going to foil him. This girl was not going to trap Benjamin. He would see to that.

On Tuesday, Dodge waited outside the girl's flat. He had knocked on the door, but there was no answer. At nine o'clock, Henrietta came out, dressed in a pleated jumper and a school jersey. Her hair was covered with a scarf and she carried a small basket. No purse, no phone, no magazine. She walked to the bakery area, filled her basket with scones and rolls, and sold them rapidly, then took a taxi to the hospital. Dodge had not anticipated her having transport, and by the time he arrived, visiting hours for the morning were over. Or at least Captain Nurse told him they were. He did not see the girl leave, nor did he see Ben arrive. He had nothing to report to the family. Nevertheless, he allowed them to invite him for luncheon, anticipating fresh news. He acted surprised when they asked him for information. "These things take time and some delicacy,' Dodge said. "Pass the rolls."

Nurse Busia was taking a liking to the bun girl and her mother. She enjoyed seeing Amnesty gain weight and strength. The girl brought fresh hot rolls each day, and a change of clothing for her mother. The boy talked of faraway places and ideas the nurse had never thought about. He was in love with the girl, and Nurse Busia had never seen such a fanciful pair of young people, without guile and without greed. That is what had impressed her from the beginning. They came to represent love to her, how life could be if sickness and greed were suddenly dismissed and kindness prevailed. It had been only a week since they came into her life, but she had begun to see herself as they saw her; the angel of E126.

It was Friday when the flak hit the fan. Dodge had been making his investigations into the mother's situation. Something didn't add up. The mother was living in a small dark flat with intermittent electricity and water, but she afforded an expensive private room. He learned from the front desk that a private room cost over $200 dollars a day.

On the following Monday, Dodge went to the hospital ward and asked if he could view room E126. Nurse Busia showed him the room and asked if he was going to be a patient there. She reported her patient had been dismissed. She could give no details. Patient confidentiality. Dodge said he was not sick and Nurse Busia asked, "Then why are you wasting the time of staff at this hospital? I should make a report." Dodge scuttled out of the room and down the corridor, fuming at being dismissed so abruptly.

Dodge began investigating the bun girl and her connections. Her mother was friendly to him, and would share her baked goods, asking his opinion on whether the croissants had proofed long enough, or whether the palmiers were sweet enough. After a few trips to Amnesty's place of business, and never seeing the girl, Dodge realized the girl had disappeared. He checked in with Joseph and learned Benjamin was now on the road on buying trips, and he figured the girl had joined up with Benjamin. Dodge was frustrated at being outmaneuvered by the young people and vowed he would get even.

CHAPTER 33
DODGE'S INQUIRY

The boys were busy with their lives, trade was going well, and Joseph and Violet heard that Bwalya their youngest son, who had been studying art in Paris had married a woman from Europe. He was now teaching at the Burrisfuro Academy only a few hours away, and they expected to hear from him at any time. Then their son, Calvin became ill. He was tired all the time, his skin had eruptions, and his breathing became labored with pneumonia. He developed a high fever. Before they could determine what was wrong with Calvin, his wife and children had fled back to her village. Although Calvin took quinine, it had no effect, and he died of malaria. A second son then became sick. He was traveling, and his illness might be food related, his mother thought. But the hospital could not help and he died three months after Calvin. In the next six months, two more sons died, each of a different disease. One of pneumonia, another of leukemia. Each time, the wife made no contact with the Leibitsangs, but returned to her people taking the grandchildren with her.

The family took extra precautions, using the bed nets that had been prescribed, and avoiding drinking water unless it had been boiled or made into tea. After the death of four sons, and the wives going back to their villages, Bishop could no longer ignore what was happening. He talked to Joseph and asked him to bring the sons together and see if they could tackle this plague that was robbing them of their future.

Joseph in turn, talked to Violet. She agreed that something was terribly wrong in their family. She dismissed the servants, reduced the diet to what was traditional, and even called the fetish priest. She was still surrounded by her remaining five sons. They did not dwell on what had claimed their brothers' lives. It could be explained. Probably they had picked up a disease traveling so much and eating foreign foods. She talked to the pastor about this epidemic of *the thins* that she had heard about. He told her that if he heard of anyone in his congregation having *the thins*, he would ban them and their children from attending the services. He said that this disease was a punishment from God, and people who contracted it deserved to die. It was the disease of homosexuals and profligates. Violet went home, not sure of what her sons had been accused, and told her husband. The two of them stopped attending the church. They also stopped attending any funerals. Violet urged her boys to stay home, but their business and her husband's, was in commerce. They hugged their mother and told her not to worry. They were not going to be catching anything at the road stops or in the guest houses where they stayed. They were hopeful a cure would be found.

Within the next five years, twenty percent of the congregation of the Full Gospel Church had died. Another third stopped attending. The funerals had to be confined to the weekends as the number of services was interrupting the business of the city. But no one admitted to having the disease, or having anyone in their family die of it. It was other countries, other tribes, other groups of people who had that disease. Not the decent folk that taught in the schools, did commerce in the cities, or cared for the sick. The number of funerals kept climbing. The schools, hospitals, and businesses, such as banks and the trucking industry, were especially hard hit with the loss of skilled employees. Families that normally could have absorbed an orphan were now stretched to the limit with caring for their own orphaned nieces and nephews, grandsons, and granddaughters.

Not until the sixth son had suddenly come down with pneumonia, and was rapidly losing weight, did Violet panic. She and Joseph decided they must contact Bwalya and the other two sons, and see if something could be done. Joseph was no longer able to sleep at night for the memory of his strong and beautiful throng of young men wasting away. There was fungus on their skin, thrush in their mouths, and the torment of the virus that robbed them of energy and vitality before they succumbed to some disease. Hospitals overflowed, with three to a bed, but the government insisted that HIV was not a threat. Condoms were not allowed by Christian religious teachings, and the wives fled, afraid they would no longer be able to return to their villages should the rumors spread that their husbands had died of AIDS.

Joseph and Violet asked for Dodge's expertise for their second son, who was dating a girl in South Africa he had met while marketing. The parents wanted to know who her people were, and whether he was becoming serious.

It was the end of the rainy season before Uncle Dodge made his way to Cape Town to check on his young nephew. Orin had been a more reserved son than Benjamin, and welcomed the independence of being a long distance trucker. Orin would pop in a tape for music, pile a few cold weather items in the cab of his truck, and head for the border, barely taking time to say goodbye to his mother and siblings. Orin loved returning just as much, although by now, the family had learned to give him some space before asking about his adventures. He liked to orchestrate the telling of his tales, which poured out of him like wine from the palm tree, after a long road trip. Like his Uncle Dodge when he recounted a successful brokerage, it wasn't enough to merely give the facts of how he had arranged a marriage, or broken one up that was going to cost the parents. He wanted them to hang on his every word and see him as the master manipulator of relationships. He could make or break a couple, he boasted, when he was before a worried set of parents or relatives. He was indispensable.

Orin would be quiet for a while when he returned from a marketing trip. Then he would open up, explaining the business and the customers and his skill in obtaining what no one else could.

This liaison between Orin and Lady X played right into Dodge's favorite scenario. A bold but naïve young man and a calculating woman, thinking she was going to snare a real catch. Or it could be an alluring young woman for whom an older man had the hots, and must have, and no price was too great to extract to make his fantasies reality. What worried Uncle Dodge about Orin was the boy didn't operate out of sheer lust or greed. He tended to be a romantic. It was hard to figure what would lead the younger brother to fall into the trap of seduction. His father, Joseph had been straightforward when he was seeking a wife. He had to have stability, an unspotted family tree, and social status. Bingo. Violet was the woman for him. He won her with his honesty and drive and Dodge had been left out of the financial arrangements. Dodge had counted on recouping that loss with the successful pairings of their nine sons.

With Orin, other elements played into his love of women. They had to interest him. Orin watched cinema and there were scenes and dialogues that captivated his imagination. The most stunning women who lacked this star quality, as he called it, didn't interest him in the least. He did not care for women who were too compliant. He liked a woman with a little edge. Also, Orin was in no hurry. For Festal, time had been of the utmost importance. He could not delay what had already been delayed for too long. Fortunately, Dodge had helped Festal net a woman who was worth all he had given for her. No one argued his good fortune or her worth. So the bar was set high to find such a catch for Orin. Who or what he had found on his own would have to be investigated. That was how Dodge saw his commission. He was ready to track the couple down and pass his judgment regarding the match.

His excitement for his journey tomorrow kept him from being tired. Dodge decided to stop by the Big Banana Bar to check in on Flo and see how her new girl was working out; as well as catch up on the news of the region.

Flo watched as Dodge sauntered to the counter. She gave the bar maid a signal and the girl disappeared into the kitchen.
"What can I get for you, Dodge?" Flo asked.

"How is your new girl working out?" Dodge said, trying to catch a glimpse of her through the gap in the curtains.

"She's taking her break. Do you need a beer?"

"Give me a glass. I stopped by to see if you've heard anything from Gift."

Flo handed him a beer and a glass. "No," Flo said. "How is your mother getting along with her?"

Dodge had forgotten he had told Flo that it was his mother needing an assistant. He gulped the beer.

"She had to let her go," he said. "I didn't catch what the problem was."

"Really?"

Just then the bar girl came out with a tray of glasses. She was near-sighted from the way she studied each of the glasses, but her smile was engaging. Dodge couldn't help but watch her until Flo told her sharply to go and tend to the cooking. She bobbed her head in compliance and headed back to the kitchen.

Flo asked if there was anything else Dodge needed, because if there was not, she had some work to tend to. Dodge finished his drink and left, knowing that he was not going to get the information he wanted from Flo tonight. He should have spent a little time warming her up; he would remember this in future.

At sunrise, Dodge climbed into the Toyota and headed for South Africa. It was a small car and it handled well on the highways and the laterite tracks that went to the small villages. Orin was all the way in

Cape Town. Either his phone was not working, or he wasn't accepting calls, so Dodge would have to stop at the major truck stops to catch up with him. He would drive during the day and check out the guest houses at night. With luck, he would find the boy within two weeks.

Meanwhile, he would watch for something unusual to take back to Flo. She was put out with him and he didn't like to burn bridges. At least, not those he thought he would be using in future.

Dodge located Orin in Cape Town and the two went out drinking together at a small highlife bar. Orin wanted to know how Dodge started his matchmaking business. Dodge was pleased to regale him with the history.

"I was like yourself. I had wanted to find a woman that intrigued me, and that I wouldn't grow tired of. Well, when I was sixteen, I found her. The problem was, she had parents that wanted her to marry one of her father's friends, an older man, since he was rich and could give her a comfortable life—not to mention a hefty *lobola* for the family. She wanted me, but he had the bride price to offer her parents, so I never stood a chance. I came across her years later, after he had found an even younger and more choice girl. By this time, she was living in a slum area, and no one would touch her, because even though her ex-husband didn't want her, no one else dared to have her either. I was not about to take anyone's leftovers anyway. I let her know that she had missed out on my love." Dodge glanced over at the dancer gyrating on the small lighted stage. She was whipping her hair in circles as she slowly removed her clothes.

"I started to see there could be a profit for me in lining up marriage partners. I began to understand the feelings of regret and of being overlooked, and I could use them in creating urgency for mates to step up to the plate or miss out. It also gave me first crack at any of the girls I wanted." Dodge took a sip of his scotch. "Not that I ever would take advantage of that privilege, you understand. I developed a pretty accurate eye for what was under the wraps, and how to merchandise a girl who someone had overlooked. Or I could bring one down a few pegs if she thought she was too good for marriage. Some men can hunt, but they don't have the balls to dress out their prey."

Orin did understand. He wasn't worried that Dodge was going to mess up his relationship with Lady X, as Dodge called her. She was divorced and her prospects were limited. Orin cared for her but he also liked the excitement of being the undercover man in the relationship. He liked showing up, and her excitement at seeing him. Most of all, he liked the long conversations they had when they discussed the changes that were taking place in society, and how they would affect the future.

Orin learned that Lady X seldom saw her ex-husband because he traveled overseas. Orin's business trips gave him opportunity to visit her during the man's absence. Orin was careful because he heard the man was jealous and possessive. Even though he had divorced the woman, no one else could have her. Let Dodge investigate all he wanted. The worst he could do was get himself shot.

They finished their drinks. When Dodge went to use the restroom, Orin put a tip down, then slipped out into the night. Dodge returned to an empty table. He pocketed the tip and went back to his car. He needed to get back to Blancville to report to the family. His nephew would pay for ditching him when he was only trying to help.

As Dodge passed through the suburbs of Johannesburg he happened upon Benjamin and Hen. They were beside the road purchasing a wood carving of a colonial with a baker's hat on his head. Dodge stopped and greeted them, telling Hen he had seen her mother. He would have something to share with the family, at least. This girl was no catch, in his opinion, as she had no family other than her mother, and could bring nothing substantial to the table. This would be his recommendation. As for Orin, he would say there was no girl in sight.

With his stories sorted out, he cruised back to Blancville, Dolly Parton singing her heart out on the tape player. He had a colonial bartender carving that he had purchased for Flo, with a white tray in his hands, all wrapped up in butcher paper and tied with twine. He couldn't wait to see her again.

CHAPTER 34
THE THINS

Royal attended primary and middle school, following his success in the community school that the women had organized in the cattle station. For him, the pastoral life was good, especially the long evenings around the campfire when he would regale his listeners with his stories.

Royal knew he would one day write his mother's story, as he was proud of her for her courage. From time to time, he would ask her about a particular person or incident, and then record her answers in his notebook before he went to sleep. He now had four completed notebooks of her stories and her history.

Royal loved to cook. This was unusual for a man in the country, but Festal learned from Joseph that baking and cooking could be a good trade. He allowed Royal to enroll in a culinary school in Blancville, once he had completed middle school, and paid to have Royal board there.

It was at this school that Royal met Henrietta, the chief baker. The teacher noticed this lovable and funny student with a heart as big as the savannah he came from.

In Blancville, Violet's sons were marrying and starting their families. Benjamin had graduated and gone off to pursue business opportunities with the trade in South Africa. After a short time on the road, he had dropped his girlfriend Hen. Uncle Dodge had influenced Benjamin, discouraging him from marrying an immigrant. Women found Benjamin attractive; he was in no rush to tie himself down, as Dodge advised.

His brothers followed a similar path. At first, they were infatuated and wanted to marry, but after making the commitment, they would stray to the more exciting life of sales, liaisons, appointments. *Networking*, Dodge called it, with a wink. Uncle Dodge tried to help Violet know of their whereabouts, but soon lost track of them. He was getting older now and no longer had the energy to rein in boys who only wanted to elude him. He had recently been pursuing a woman himself, Florencia, owner of the Big Banana Bar. She had everything he wanted in a life partner. Dodge was oblivious to her deficits and won over by her assets, as he liked to say. Violet had no idea that Dodge himself was the influence that corrupted her sons, and continued urging him to contact them.

The youngest son of Violet, Bwalya, married a woman from Holland. They met while stranded in London when British Airlines went on strike. By the time they reached Nairobi, they were planning marriage and a life together. They married at the Karen Blixen estate and continued on to Burrisfuro where both were hired by the same school. Bwalya would teach fine arts and Karin would teach math. Their life was a whirl of students, travel, colleagues and campus intrigues.

When Karin started to have leg cramps and blurred vision, they traveled to London to have it checked out. She could not travel to South Africa where the hospitals were excellent, as it was illegal for the races to integrate, much less marry, and a mixed-race couple was guilty of the crime of miscegeny.

Karin had been diagnosed with MS and she was pregnant. She never hesitated to have the baby; and actually felt better while pregnant, than she had before. After Lily Wonder was born, Karin's health deteriorated   and Karin was confined to a wheelchair. With her husband and a caring faculty at the school where they taught, she managed to raise her baby. She also raised the scores of her students on their math tests. The headmaster, Mr. Kerala, respected her and

Bwalya, and would often have them over to his house, where he would drink scotch and regale them with stories of how he was discriminated against at a boys' boarding school in Australia. Both Bwalya and Karin knew that racism was prevalent in many countries. For them, Africa would always be where their daughter Lily Wonder belonged. They worked hard to make a better life for her and a secure one where she would be able to choose her path. Bwalya was gaining recognition for his painting and was invited to several art shows in Europe. He declined, because his family came first. They were his inspiration, and he pursued his passion and taught his students to do likewise.

Bwalya wanted to see his art students learn to think for themselves and express their point of view through their paintings and sculptures. He was aware of the devastating swath HIV, or *the thins*, was taking on the lives of young people in Africa. As a way of opening the channels of communication, and overcoming the fear of this disease, Bwalya decided to have himself tested. At this time, three of his brothers had died of pneumonia, and unknown to him, the other five were having recurrent bouts of illness and fatigue. Bwalya felt invincible because he had been faithful to his wife. She was the one who was in a precarious medical condition that they were handling together.

Bwalya sat in the HIV/AIDS clinic waiting his turn to be tested. There were benches along the walls where patients sat looking studiously at their hands, the upper seams of the stucco wall, or at their feet. He wished he could talk to a few people to find out what had motivated them to be tested, but this was not going to happen. He, too, began to avoid looking directly at anyone's face. He checked his watch. He was due at soccer practice in 20 minutes. If he wasn't called soon, he would have to leave.

"Bwalya L.?" a clear voice called out. He stood and walked to the small room where a sample of blood was taken. His hand was stamped then he was told to check back in one week's time. His card would be marked with either a plus or a minus, indicating his status.

Bwalya whistled as he headed for the practice field. He would do a brief research on the history of HIV, then present it to his class when he had his results. He'd show them the card and tell them how important it was to be tested. Maybe making a poster showing stigmatization would be a good project, with possible interest from the government in printing and distributing it. No one was ahead of this curve, and art students should learn how to be current with their ideas and illustrations if they wanted to benefit their community and be commercially successful.

On the practice field, students were jostling each other, dressed in the red and blue of Bessbro Academy. They had such energy, he would have them go out full force and play a few quarters before working on drills and plays. The ball was soon flying from one end of the field to the other, and he loved the movement of the legs in their flashing red color with the stripes at the cuffs of the socks. They moved so fast, they reminded Bwalya of bicycle wheels. Maybe this would be a winning season for Bessbro.

A week later, Bwalya dropped by the clinic to pick up his card with the results. He noted the plus sign, and was relieved for a second, until he realized what it meant. Then it struck him like a blow in the gut. It was not a positive result for him—it meant he had the disease. Bwalya's head dropped to his chest, his arms were leaden, and he felt the weight of disaster. There was a flood of memories racing through his head and he thought he would be sick to his stomach. What had he done? He was overwhelmed with the message he would have to deliver to his wife and the school.

How could he be positive? He had never cheated on his wife. They had been together almost six years. She needed him, and he had never disappointed her. His unsullied marriage was now tainted. Bwalya thought back to the girls he had known. Most of them were girls in middle school, young girls who had scarcely known what was going on as he coaxed them to part with their innocence in his dormitory room, or behind the bushes while on school break. There had been a couple of encounters with women in France when he was attending art school. The models had made him lustful, but he couldn't imagine them being diseased. The list was not long, and he had avoided the women his Uncle Dodge had provided for his nephews. Bwalya had an aversion to the control his uncle exerted over the boys in return for these favors. In his body, there was no sign of any sickness or disorder, no nausea, or coughing, no fevers, no fungal infections.

Bwalya had seen his brothers when they were infected, and they had no energy or beauty in their bodies. They were listless and their skin was drawn. His was radiant with health and he had never been more physically fit. He thought he was pure and would be an example to his family and his students, of how a man should live. This ended with a blue index card with his name at the top and a plus sign in black below. Bwalya looked at the paper with the test results again, staring in disbelief. He was feeling strong and at his most creative. The headmaster at school had just rewarded him with a grant to expand his teaching of the arts to the college in Blancville. His paintings from the last school break had won the prestigious Cultural Award given by the President. And now, his life was over. How could he tell his wife Karin or face his family? He wouldn't. He would pack up and leave the area, not to be seen again.

Bwalya recalled how appalled he had been when he learned his oldest brother had the *thins*. Almost before he could absorb this news, a second brother was struck with the telltale pneumonia and recurring infections that accompanied the diagnosis of HIV. He had never suspected he would also fall prey to the epidemic that was winnowing the young men of southern Africa. How could his parents endure the continuing loss of their children?

As he walked home from the clinic, Bwalya saw his daughter sitting on the swing. He could hear her singing as he got nearer, her magical curls blowing in her mouth as she swung back and forth under the gigantic mango tree. She was singing a ditty about how many kisses she would give or get, while he thought of how he might have contracted this disease. He had put away his materials, written down his wishes, and briefly considered taking his life then and there. Karin came through the door.

She could tell from his face something terrible had happened.

"I am HIV positive, Karin," he sobbed.

"Oh my God! We will get you medications. We will let the school know so they can help you make a schedule that will not be too strenuous, just as they did when I had the MS setback. Let me call the clinic and see what medications are available for you. If not here, we will get them from Holland." Karin wrapped her husband in her arms and pulled him to her. Lily came running in to hug him and they sat on the sofa and saw how brilliant the setting sun was against the plantings in their yard.

Bwalya arrived at the teachers' lounge early for the weekly meeting. He knocked on the door of the headmaster, and Mr. Kerala welcomed him in. "I came early to share some information with you before anyone else got here." Bwalya started.

Mr. Kerala saw that Bwalya was upset by the way his hands shook. "What is wrong Bwalya? Are you ill? Is something wrong with Karin or Lily Wonder?"

"I went to the HIV clinic and had myself tested. I am positive."

Mr. Kerala said nothing. His mouth opened and he sucked in his breath, flattening his nostrils. "Have you told anyone?"

"Just Karin. She suggested I tell you immediately so we could adjust my schedule and make sure I get enough rest and the medications I will need. I feel fine, but so little is known about this disease."

"Yes. We will have to make some adjustments. Let me think about this, and I will see you in the meeting."

The morning assembling of the faculty began as usual with Reverend Joseph offering a prayer and passing out the agenda. Bwalya looked it over as Karin rolled her chair to the end of the long table next to the headmaster. There was a buzz of small talk between colleagues, most of it centering around food and extra-curricular activities. The subject matter had changed in the last few years since Karin joined the staff, but it was mostly sexual innuendoes that those not interested in dating ignored and glossed over. Today, there was no conversation with Bwalya, and Karin too was left out of the teasing. Headmaster Kerala concentrated on the papers in front of him and after taking roll call, he moved to the first action item. There would be a general cleaning of the school as the Ministry of Education would make their annual visit in a week's time.

"I know you will all prepare your best students with something to present," the headmaster said. Mr. Kerala was a tall, slightly paunchy man with an imposing face that suggested he could be much harsher than his quiet voice indicated. He had spent several years in boarding school in Australia, getting his education and paying for it with his spontaneity and his humor. Now, at 46, he had reached the pinnacle of what he would be. He was keenly aware that more might have been expected of him and of what it had cost him to achieve this security. Nothing was going to disrupt his path to order, security and a retirement. His wife stood behind him, never seeking to socialize with the other wives at the college compound, never venturing to attempt more than meeting her obligations to be a ready hostess to his visitors, the guardian of his appearance, and the mother of his children.

He was thinking of her this morning, knowing he would have to dismiss this promising young tutor. His wife would question him about it because she had always liked Bwalya. How could the man have not seen that he would not brook a member of his faculty being HIV positive? What had possessed the man to get himself tested? Now, he was in the awkward position of having to remove him from the faculty.

The students had progressed well under Bwalya's teaching. Kerala only hoped Bwalya would have the good grace to go quietly. He would not tolerate his reputation or that of his college being put at risk of censure. Imagine parents turning away to another school because of this stigma of a tutor known to be HIV positive? And now, with the Ministry of Education coming to call, this was the worst timing. Awkward was too simple a word. This was the stigma he had spent a lifetime avoiding.

"Bwalya, you will be relieved of preparing your students. I have an assignment that I will need you to work on immediately. And Karin, I will need to speak with you after the faculty meeting. We are going to have to relocate you from the school compound. I know that may prove difficult for you to maintain your schedule. We are going to go to a divided schedule for the remainder of the week. You will teach your first classes, then return in the late afternoon for study period and tutoring."

Karin looked at the headmaster in disbelief. She already had difficulty getting to the classrooms from their bungalow on the campus. The paths were not paved and without Bwalya's assistance, she could not wheel her chair to the classrooms. With a divided shift, she would have to repeat this process four times. If Bwalya was away on an assignment, how would she manage to get to class at all, or pick up her daughter at the preschool in town?

Mr. Kerala continued with the agenda. There was a lot of discussion about the upcoming Ministry visit, the need for improved test standards, and who would be monitoring the students as they took their exams. Karin tuned out as she tried to figure out how she could fulfill her teaching duties.

After the meeting was over, Mr. Kerala waited for Karin in his office. He closed the door behind her, then pressed his hands together in front of his chest, the long fingers bending from the pressure. "Karin. I am sorry you will have to leave the faculty. Unfortunately, my hands are tied. We need to be professional about this. We cannot have one bad apple spoiling the barrel." Karin mentally rang up the clichés, one after the other. Mr. Kerala was on automatic pilot, or should she say, bureaucratic overdrive. Next, he would be recounting again how he had suffered as the only black student in his boarding school who survived the racism of the sixties in Australia. But she was not going to let her dismissal go unchallenged.

"On what grounds do you believe you should dismiss me?" she asked. Mr. Kerala was taken aback.

"You know I am having to let Bwalya go," he said.

"No. I did not hear that in the faculty meeting. What I heard you say was that he would not be assisting with the Ministry of Education program this year and that you had a special assignment for him."

"Do I need to be blunt? The man has stabbed himself in the foot. He has burned his bridges."

"You are not being blunt. You are not being candid. You are not being honest. But what offense have I committed?" she asked.

"Surely you don't expect to be working when your husband is no longer welcome here?"

"Why not? Am I not performing well in the math department? Don't my students need my tutoring to do well on their "O" level exams? What is the cause for dismissing a teacher who has done excellent teaching for this college?" Karin could feel the heat in her cheeks at the indignation she felt.

"Our discussion is over. Please plan on leaving the campus by the end of the week as I am having your bungalow renovated and need it vacated." Mr. Kerala rose to open the door but Karin had already opened it and was on her way out.

She headed for their home to console Bwalya and help plan what they could do to survive in this emergency. She would need to take Lily

Wonder out of her preschool if there was no immediate work for her to do. She could always tutor students. They would think of something. She would write a formal letter to Mr. Kerala asking for an explanation of her untimely dismissal. With a push of the wheels, she launched her chair through the pea gravel, sweating in the midmorning heat of December. It was a day she would not forget.

Karin wasn't the kind of woman who saw the dark side of life. She had been with her husband when he told the faculty he had been tested and found positive. She noticed that no one looked at him after that. Karin and Bwalya were asked to move off the school compound to a flat in town. Within the month, Bwalya was laid off. Karin had to wheel herself along the sandy road to the school compound each day, while Bwalya remained at home with their child.

The students who had been so eager to take lessons in drawing and painting now made excuses why they could not come to the house. The housekeeper no longer showed up, and when Karin went to the grocer, he laid her change on the counter, not in her hand.

Karin applied for anti-retrovirals for Bwalya, but she was refused. She was told her husband would have to come to the clinic himself and explain why he needed them. There was never a convenient time for this appointment, and the pharmacy told Karin that it was not their policy to stock what were not proven medications. Next Karin tried to get the pills from Holland, but the government would not allow them to be issued without seeing the person directly to determine the need for them. Bwalya found himself ostracized from even the beer hall in town. People stopped their conversation when he entered, and if he put his hand out to shake hands, they withdrew theirs. He concentrated on his art and on his child, but depression set in as the illness took its toll.

For a brief period, Bwalya attended the Full Gospel Evangelical meeting, but when he confessed that he was positive for HIV, the pastors said they could not accept a person with HIV, nor want them in their midst contaminating others. Karin too was singled out and asked if it wasn't HIV that made it necessary for her to be in the wheelchair. Her daughter was denied admittance into the preschool that Karin herself had founded in the village. Now, the family fiber was stretched as the two parents struggled to provide for their child and shield her from stigmatization.

The newspapers began to carry a few articles on this mystery disease, but it was seen as a visitation of punishment on those who fornicated or committed sodomy, and the best advice was to avoid anyone who tested positive. As a result, few people went to be tested. There was a growing consensus that those with the disease should be shunned, and this led to fewer people willing to admit that they had the disease, or had lost family members to HIV. Some suggested those infected should even be denied a funeral, if they were known to carry the virus.

Bwalya's first encounter with a positive HIV message of hope came from a group of gay men who were traveling in Africa. They shared their medications and reported that HIV was also in other parts of the world. For a brief time, Bwalya felt hope and opportunity, and felt better after taking the medications. He could not overcome the fact that he was now the last of his brothers alive, and that his parents might learn of his illness. He had already shirked having them meet his wife, who was not only white, but handicapped. He didn't want to face the criticism or questioning. He was losing everything he had worked to attain, and finally, even his creative spark no longer kindled as he retreated into the world of the outcast.

Joseph called his wife, Violet, out of the house and took her by the arm. "Violet, I have heard from Bwalya. He is not well and he does not want us to come and see him. He says the school where he works is letting him go at the end of the month and that he will need someone to care for their daughter. Do you know anything about this?"

Violet could see the anger and the pain in her husband's face. He had never confronted her like this, and she felt all her frustrations and fears run together like the whitewash on a freshly painted hut in an unexpected rain.

She answered him in a voice she did not recognize. "Why are you telling me this now? It has been five, no, almost six years since the boy has visited us. He went to University, we heard he had married and had a child, and suddenly, you are concerned. Have you heard anything else?"

Joseph shook his head but said nothing more. He left for the gathering at the Rotary club. He had heard rumors that his son was ill, rumors he could not face. This was his last son out of nine. All the others had started out well, pushing their way into the business world, going to far places with big dreams. One by one, they had come home and each had passed away. There was no explanation for the wasting, the coughs, then the sudden catching of every disorder. One son had gone to hospital to try the new medicines, but it was too late and he died of pneumonia. Just before he was gone, his wife had hurried back to her village, outrunning the rumors of what had become of her husband. One had claimed her husband was killed as a peacekeeper in Congo, but no one had ever seen him in uniform, or heard of this position being available.

Bwalya was the only surviving son. And he had not come to see them. It was more than Joseph could bear. He found himself arguing with the men at his club, daring them to challenge him. Later that same night, he stepped into his Toyota and drove home at breakneck speed, determined to take his wife and go visit the village of Burrisfuro where Bwalya lived. Joseph's mind was on his sorrows and what lay ahead of them on this journey. He did not see the rocks that had rolled into his path. When they found his body, the map of Southern Africa lay spread across his lap.

Bwalya's paintings hung in the National Gallery and in the home of private collectors, but his depiction of life as it was, had altered. He was no longer sought out. Only his wife and his daughter reminded him of his youth, his travels, and the celebrity he had enjoyed. Bwalya could see how his sickness had hemmed them in from their friends and activities and taken away their freedom. He passed away at his home two days short of his 33rd birthday.

Karin arranged for his funeral, which was attended by half a dozen students and no faculty members. Clair and Blessing were beside her along with his daughter Lily Wonder to see his casket lowered into the red earth. His family was notified by mail of his passing, and by that time, his grandfather Bishop had passed away, as well as the sudden death of his father Joseph. Three generations of men were gone from the family within the month.

Violet no longer went into town. She remained in her house, occasionally writing a letter or reading a newspaper, and taking Valium to calm her nerves. She had seen the ward at the hospital filled with young patients dying of this new plague called AIDS, but she didn't understand how the disease was spread, nor could she admit that AIDS was what was taking her remaining sons; now all nine were dead.

CHAPTER 35

KARIN PREPARES TO RETURN TO HOLLAND

Karin prepared the boxes for shipping. She would be taking one set of Bwalya's paintings to Holland, along with her personal journal and a single set of clothes. The remainder of her belongings would remain in Zambia.

"Claire, pick out some things you like." Claire looked with longing at the tape player and the cell phone, but she could not ask for these.

"I would like a bracelet that will remind me of you, Karin that one made of copper from Copperfine. I would like to have a picture of you both."

Claire wanted to ask for the picture Bwalya had painted of her, but she was unsure what Karin might make of this. She and Bwalya had spent so many hours together when he was finishing her portrait. Bwalya had called this painting of herself a masterpiece. She had not known before that a man could be a friend without taking something from you. They had talked of art, of God, of the world outside this small village. She cherished the respect he had given her, and the trust Karin had shown in letting her spend these hours with her husband. Now, he was gone and no one wanted to admit how much he was missed.

Karin gave Claire the photo and the bracelet immediately, and filed away that it would be good for Claire to have a camera. Karin also planned to leave Claire her comforter and all of the cooking pots in their kitchen. Violet would not need these as her husband had been a supplier in the hardware business, and all these necessities would be in her household. Claire had never shown an interest in Bwalya's art, so it didn't occur to Karin to ask if she would like the portrait he had made of her. She had packed it to take with her to Holland.

Karin was not an art critic, but the painting was unforgettable. At the last moment, she decided to leave it for the grandmother to sell, along with two other paintings of landscapes of the area.

The packing was very quick, the tickets were purchased, and within a week, Karin was headed for Amsterdam. She left two letters behind, explaining her departure from the school, her appreciation for the faculty, and her desire to have her child raised by her mother-in-law. She also requested that Blessings Sikala be made guardian, in the event the grandmother could not fulfill her obligations, or chose not to accept the child and her estate. This woman had worked with her in forming the preschool and had loved Lily Wonder since the day she was born.

Then Karin was off, without a party, gifts, or prolonged farewells. She had given their cat to Elise, her neighbor and consultant, and told her to take anything from the garden she could use, including the much coveted garden hose. Karin was focused on breaking away quickly and without loose ends. She did not see the pain she caused her friend Claire, who was grieving a double loss. As she sat waiting for the flight to arrive, Karin recalled the conversation she had had with Claire.

CHAPTER 36

PREPARATION TO LEAVE

Claire looked at her friend in amazement. "How can you give up the child you and Bwalya had, in spite of everything the doctors warned?"

Karin wanted to agree with her friend in what she was saying. She and Bwalya had been so eager to see the birth of their child. The village and the school had been so welcoming when Lily Wonder was born, and concerned that the mother would not survive the birth. It had been a time of challenge to give birth in the basic little clinic of this village, without anesthetics, ultra-sound, or even an x-ray machine. Karin had been proud of her ability to endure the pain and to deliver their child. Bwalya was the ideal father, never indicating that he would have preferred a son, as so many men do.

When Bwalya learned he was HIV positive, he and Karin bonded even closer. Biology and medical issues were foreign to both of them, but they studied up on the disease and did their best to support each other. Bwalya refused any intimacy with her once he learned he was positive, so the closeness they had shared physically, and which had been so healing to her as her MS progressed, was over. She had accepted that this was the only way he knew to protect her and their child. Now, she had to decide what would benefit their child. She also needed to get medical help for her MS that was steadily worsening, and explain to her parents how her life had altered.

Karin knew Claire could not understand what this small village in

Africa had to offer. She had heard about Europe and it was like Disneyland to her, a magical kingdom where all children have enough to eat, they enjoy life, and they grow up. She could not know the undercurrents of being a minority child, much less a child orphaned by her father, and with a disabled mother. Karin didn't explain.

"Trust me, Claire. I know what is best for my child. Bwalya has always honored his mother by telling of how she cared for the children. There was no animosity towards her. I think he was just selfish in not taking the time to travel and see her. His art consumed his passion and his spare hours. You know how intense he was about teaching his students the essence of being creative. There were so many other brothers and cousins; he didn't really think his mother missed him that much. We were busy with our teaching and our personal issues. We forgot that his family—and mine as well—would be there for us. And we were selfish about our lives as a couple. We loved the privacy and the freedom to be ourselves. By the time we realized we needed them, Bwalya was in a state where he did not want them to see his condition. He did not communicate with his parents. I think he may have talked to one of his older brothers, but anything having to do with sex was taboo. I doubt any of them confided what illness had been stalking them."

"Now, there are no brothers surviving and the wives deny anything that could cause them to be stigmatized. My best recourse is what I am doing. Violet should live a long time and my daughter will have the benefit of her love and full devotion. That is what I anticipate. I will need you and Elise to assure that the woman does attach to this child." Claire nodded to show she understood.

"Karin, I will be your eyes. If there is any hesitation on the part of the grandmother, I will call you immediately." Claire wondered if she could have parted with any of her children in this way. She stopped herself from thinking whether more of them would have survived had she been able to get more help from her family. It was water under the bridge.

She and Karin continued packing until all the paintings were wrapped and sealed, all the clothing sorted and packed into containers for taking, dispersing, or leaving behind for the grandmother and child. They hugged when the taxicab arrived and Karin handed Claire a key to the house. Then she was off.

CHAPTER 37

HOLLAND

Karin watched her mother prepare ginger tea, crushing the slices of ginger root, pouring boiling water over them, adding lemons. Her mother was twice her age, but athletic and flexible as she bent over and pulled cups from below the counter. She stored her cups and breakable china beneath the counter, unlike so many women who stored the pots there and the cups and china in a more visible upper cupboard.

"I have never asked you why you put your best cups down below where no one can see them." she said.

"They could drop if they are overhead and would shatter on the stone counter. I have never lost a cup in thirty years. The pots are durable." She looked at her daughter, thinking of all the questions she had for her. Maybe after a couple of days, a few cups of tea, she would begin to ask them. How could this mother have left her child behind, her only grandchild? Did she have any idea how much a grandmother would want to see her grandbaby?

Karin sipped the tea and looked at her mother closely. She could tell her mother was feeling strong emotions, the way her neck became rosy and her cheeks flushed. She didn't really want to know what it was, she had enough to deal with, just getting used to Dutch culture again after so many years away. Her mother had always found it easy to share her feelings, so much so that Karin didn't want to risk the rush of emotions and avoided opening the spigot. She was thirsty to know what her mother thought of her return, and the death of Bwalya, and the absence of Lily Wonder, but for now, she just wanted the comfort of tea, a crisp newspaper, and the Valium of morning television. Soon enough she would sort out what she was going to do with the rest of her life.

"Karin, I want to see my grandchild." Whoa! Karin saw she was going to have to answer some questions. It had been two days since she returned to her old home in Nijmegen. Karin looked at her mother and put down the paper.

"I have given custody to Bwalya's mother, Violet. I have not heard from her yet."

"Call her on the phone and see how she is doing. Tell her she is welcome to come here with the child. I will send tickets for the two of them and they can stay here."

Karin took a gulp of tea. "Ma, I didn't expect this. It is so far for them to come."

"I have waited six years for this visit. I have lost my son-in-law. I do not want to lose my granddaughter."

Karin was taken aback by the passion of her mother for this child she had never met. She felt her own bottled up love choke her and wondered what had she done to leave her child? Then she recalled how she and Bwalya had talked about what would come of the child should he pass away. He had endured life in France as an art student and had a clear picture of the abuse and ridicule his daughter would have if she lived in Europe. He had never been to Holland, but his experience made him insist that the child remain in Africa where she would enjoy status and acceptance. Now, with his dying of HIV, that future came into question.

In the few days she had been back, Karin had seen the diversity of people on television and on the streets. This was a changing country.

Maybe her mother had a point. If she was willing to pay for the tickets, how could such a journey hurt the child?

"Ma, you will love the child. She is bright and loving. She reminds me so much of you."

"I don't care if she is short, ugly, and blind. This is my granddaughter. What were you thinking to never bring her to see us? Your father could not even mention her name because he knew how emotional I would become. You contact her other grandmother and bring her here before it is too late. I am not even going to mention it to your father until she is at the airport. Do you know how that man has wanted to see her and Bwalya as well? Enough. Let me know how much the tickets are and when they can come."

Violet read the letter written by the school headmaster. She had been a widow for nearly two months when the letter came, and she decided immediately that she would travel to where Bwalya had lived and worked. She needed to make some sense of what had come of her family. Her grandchildren were as scattered as free-range chickens. There was the possibility that Bwalya's child, her granddaughter would need a guardian. She didn't know what to expect, but she would travel to the region and straighten out her thinking. She tossed the remaining Valium into a drawer and pulled out a map.

Violet was not a traveler. The world of commerce was for her husband and sons, all of whom took long journeys to various countries. Two had been long distance haulers, some had been merchants and wholesalers like her husband. She had expected something far different for her later years. It had included the two of them surrounded by a band of grandchildren, the wives and sons laughing and enjoying hospitality at the ample homestead they had built up over the years Violet was alone in the seven room house near Blancville with the view of the city out her kitchen window. Alone, except for the guard and the housekeeper, who kept a grandchild in her one- room house behind the main house. These were the companions of her days, ignored by her, and she living in dread that they pitied her or talked about her losses. The church and her friends kept her from pitying herself. She had a sister and brother that she could visit. She had been able to raise her children to adulthood, all nine of them, and this is something most of her friends had not been able to do. She was free to follow her dreams, but Violet had never been a dreamer. She had been content to obey Joseph and to keep track of the household, making sure the meals were on time and the place was always furnished nicely, and clean when Joseph brought friends over. Violet enjoyed good health and basked in her worship at the church where she was one of the best singers. She no longer traveled with the choir, or thought about reaching out to anyone beyond her circle of friends. She had a narrow circle of influence which she saw as her strength and her lot in life, and maintained her daily routine of checking the supplies, folding the laundry, and making sure the garden was watered and pruned. Beyond this, she read little, worried little, and thought less about things each day. Until this letter. Now, her world was about to be tested. She could no longer ignore the fact that she had a grandchild and the grandchild needed her.

What would Joseph have said? It had been irresponsible of him to be driving so fast so late at night, and in the rainy season. He had a driver, George. He could have waited a few days until the man had recovered from his fever. Violet cut off this uncharacteristic judgment of the man, and crossed herself once to purify her spirit of uncharity. She recalled the verse that Myrna used to see her through the most difficult time. *Light will overcome the darkness*, or something to that effect. She would make a small list of questions, get a bus ticket, and go and see this place where Bwalya had lived his adult life. Her planning was interrupted by a knock at the door.

"Who is it?"

"George, the driver. I am seeing if you need me to drive you somewhere. I am well now."

"You are an angel sent to me. I need to go to Burrisfuro tomorrow. Can you take me? I will pay you."

"Just provide the petrol. This trip is one I was planning to make with the two of you. It will be my pleasure to take you. Shall I come at 9:00 o'clock in the morning?"

"Yes. I will be ready. And George, thank you for the card. Joseph valued you so much." Violet dreaded the thought of travel, of confusion, dust, and contact with so many people she did not know, and did not want to know. She could think no further about it, nor did she want to share this sense of new openings with anyone. They might disturb the peace she was feeling now that she had determined her action. They would leave tomorrow. She would stay a week or until she understood what was going on and how to deal with it. Then she would return to her large house and her plants, and her life would continue in tranquility and acceptance of what was her lot. *Wife, Mother, Grandmother, Widow*. Progression that was normal. Yes, very normal.

She needed to get together with her sister Myrna and her husband Festal. Together, they could make a plan for how to care for the granddaughter Lily Wonder that had suddenly been thrust into her life. Their mother, Beatrice, was 82 and could only shake her head at the mystery of young lives being mowed down. Beatrice still had her children and her brother Dodge, but her legacy of grandchildren from this ideal love marriage was gone. She, too, was a widow wanting to find peace and comfort in her old age, alongside thousands of other women who were losing their children and raising grandchildren without the extended family, or support they needed.

Violet sat in the backseat of the Toyota, watching the road ahead for unexpected ruts and potholes. George played music by artists she no longer recognized, but that soothed her nerves. She was taking action. Regardless of how this interview with the child turned out, it was a chance to have her life back. She would be needed and could help make one life better by showing up. She had read those words in a self-help pamphlet at the doctor's office when she went to get her Valium. Now, she had stopped taking it. They would soon be in Burrisfuro, and George would help her find the house. It was Number 9 on Black Rhino Drive. That was an easy address, Bwalya had been her ninth son. Nine lives. She still had one left. And that was Lily Wonder.

While pumping petrol, the attendant peeked in the window and saw Violet in the back seat. "Aren't you the mother of Bwalya Leibitsang? I've seen your picture at their home and recognized you. Welcome."

"He was a good man."

Violet was surprised, and pleased to be greeted in such a way. He pointed out to George the way to their home. "It's the fifth house on the right, just after you make your way on Rhino Drive. No, I can't take a payment for the petrol. Not from Bwalya's mother. Have a nice day."

Minutes later, Violet and George pulled up in front of what once was a tidy bungalow. In front was a rampant hedge of lilies. A small face peeked out the front window. The child bounded out to greet them, a mass of curls highlighted in the late afternoon sun.

"You are my Grandmother, Mother of Bwalya. You are not as old as I hoped."

"You must be Lily. You are every bit as beautiful and bright as I imagined. How are you?"

"I am waiting to see if you want me. Until I know that, I am just waiting."

"Let's go inside. I have been waiting too. I did not know what to expect."

"Well, I have been praying and expecting you. No one else is here as Claire had to go and teach today, and my neighbor Alicia is cooking dinner. Come in."

George raised his eyebrows and looked at Violet. This child was going to give this widow a run for her money. She was radiant with her tendrils of golden brown hair floating in the breeze and the energy of a child of five receiving what she had been waiting for for days. She plopped herself down next to her grandmother on the sofa and pulled her shawl off her shoulders, then she got up to get her a cup of water from the kitchen. Alicia came over, having seen the Toyota pull into the driveway. She had two cups of tea and milk on a tray. "Welcome. I see you have met Lily. She has probably filled you in on the history of the family. I am Alicia and I have known them just a year, since they moved here from the school compound. Karin and I worked on the preschool in town, where Lily and my daughter attended. Now, I am watching her until something permanent takes place. I want you to be very direct in telling me your feelings about the child, as Karin asked me to be her ears and eyes. She wants Lily to be where she is loved and not passed around. I am going to leave you two to get acquainted. I will bring dinner over in an hour, unless you have other plans."

Violet nodded her agreement and drank the cup of water Lily had brought her. She had put a little flower in the cup.

"My mother couldn't walk. She had to roll around in a chair which we called the Gollichair."

"I didn't know that. What was wrong with her?"

"She had MS. My Dad pushed her to the school and home again. She couldn't make it through the gravel by herself and I am not strong enough to push her, so I think that is why she went to Holland. They have everything paved over there."

"Well, we will find out why she went. I think she just went to get well. She never wanted to leave you, she just thought it would be best to get better first." What am I telling this child? I have no idea why her mother would leave such a precious little girl alone. I had better find out from Alicia or Claire what had happened and what they have told the child.

"Tomorrow I want to take you to town and see some of your Daddy's art. I have not seen it and they say he was such a good artist."

"He is. His paintings are in the Museum. And I am an artist too. My daddy said you used to draw."

"He did? That was so long ago. I used to make sketches of the boys and illustrate little stories for them. I can't believe he remembered that."

"He said it is in our blood. We are all artists, even Uncle Dodge. He is a con artist, Dad used to say, then laugh."

"He had something there, all right. Well, I am going to learn so many things from you. You can ask me questions."

"Do you believe in keeping promises?"

"Well, yes. We all want to keep our promises. But sometimes we are unable."

"Grandma, you know what I mean. Are you going to keep me? I need to know."

"That is why I am here. Look, here comes our dinner. Now, we need to go and wash, and I am going to freshen up my hair. It looks like yours could use a little picking as well."

"My Mom used to make me braids and poufs. Claire doesn't know how to plait my hair, so she just pulls it up into a knot."

"Come here. I can make you poufs."

Violet pulled the child between her knees and ran her hands through the luxuriant curls. It was a soft and silky as feathers. With a few cuts with the pick, she had organized the mass of tendrils into two poufs, then took the slippery hairs around the hairline and plaited them into a slim braid, which she pinned back with a clip she pulled from her bag. She handed the child a mirror and watched her eyes light up as she saw her new hairstyle.

"Grandma, you are an artist! I knew it." Violet felt her throat close a little at the words. She couldn't remember the last time she had felt more capable and ready to take on the future. When Alicia brought in the nshima and relish, she waited to hear what else this child would have to say. She reminded Violet of Myrna, the way she jumped from one imaginative idea to the next, and you had to pay attention to catch the progression. They had their dinner and talked, then it was time to sleep. Violet was tired, the night was cool, and when the child asked permission to sleep at her back, Violet nodded.

Now it was morning, and she had never had a better night's rest. There would be new stories to learn about, but where was Lily Wonder?

Lily was gone. Violet jumped to her feet and looked out the door and there was Lily, feeding the chickens. They circled her and she doled out the grain to them like a schoolmistress giving out papers. Her hair was a halo of light around her head as the morning sun highlighted the tendrils that had loosened in the night. They would go to town today and see the pictures Bwalya had painted. Violet looked forward to hearing how Lily would comment on them. She would call George and they would have breakfast in town then go to the bank where the paintings were being stored. It would be a chance to see the campus where Bwalya and his wife had worked, and she could then report to Karin any greetings or news. Yes, it would be a full day. She drank the remainder of her water with the flower still floating in it, and called to George.

In town, everyone knew Lily. Violet thought she would be showing the child around, but she was the one being featured, as Lily introduced her to the postman, the baker, the policeman, and everyone else they came across. Violet was enjoying being a celebrity and seeing her granddaughter shine. Karin must have been quite the mother to raise a child so friendly and social. She heard many kind things about her son as well, and couldn't wait to see his art.

The banker was most solicitous, taking the two of them to the enormous vault and opening the storeroom for them. It was air-conditioned, climate controlled, and highly secure. He lowered his voice and spoke of the paintings in a hushed tone that had always signaled money to Violet.

"Take your time, we are honored to have the mother of such a renowned artist paying a call." She quit listening to the man as he to unveiled one painting after another. The first one was a valley of incredible beauty. She recognized it as Copperfine and wondered when Bwalya had seen that place. There was no mistaking the portrait of his daughter, his wife Karin, and a beautiful woman with a smile that hovered but never really opened up.

"That is Claire. She is my Mom's best friend."

Another landscape was eerie in its isolation and the sheer despondency. She turned to the next. They were not chronological. Some were from places she had never seen—the atmosphere, sky, and colors were not those of southern Africa. They were cooler and more ephemeral. She could experience where he had been through his works. His paintings exposed an inner world that she could not interpret, but just feel. In an hour, she was exhausted. They thanked the banker, assured him they appreciated his concern for the works, and they would be back again.

Back on the street, Violet shook off the coldness of the air-conditioning and the humidity controlled air. She signaled to George to pick them up then asked Lily if she was hungry. She was. Violet took her to the bakery where she ate a Welsh pie, and continued on their adventure.

At the college, Mr. Kerala welcomed Violet Leibitsang with a great show of sorrow and consolation. He wrung his long fingers in a display of condolence, then looked down at Lily and asked her if she would like a treat.

"No thank you. My family gives me all the treats I need. My grandmother wants to meet some of the people who were kind to my father and thank them."

Mr. Kerala knew better than to ask who she considered these to be, as he was sure from the way she had phrased her request, he was not numbered among them. He invited them to feel free to go anywhere on campus, as classes were not in session, and they were most welcome.

The first house they decided to try was that of Mr. Kerala. His wife was in, and she embraced Violet and began to weep. "Of all the tutors at this school, your son was the only one who showed respect to me. And Karin as well. They were a beautiful couple and we learned from them, just as the students did. I am so sorry he is gone. I would never have made him leave."

She stopped speaking immediately when she realized what she had said. "I am an ignorant woman who knows nothing of protocols or procedures. But I did love your son."

Violet hugged her and thanked her, then decided they would go elsewhere. They did. For the first time in her sixty-two years, Violet went on a mini safari. She and her granddaughter climbed in the vehicle and jaunted around a small game park on the edge of Burrisfuro. They drank Fanta and she laughed until her sides hurt at the animals, the bumps, the dust and the roller coaster ride the vehicle was making over the white dusty tracks. When they dismounted, her mind was made up. This girl was for keeps.

Lily saw the fun of having a grandmother who could take some chances, and they made their commitment to each other, before returning to visit Claire and Alicia to announce the decision. George was delighted to hear he would be taking a load of paintings back to Blancville, along with an energized Violet and her granddaughter Lily.

Karin had the flu for the following week, followed by a bout of pain with her MS. It was the following month before she received word back from Violet that they were now living in Blancville, but would be returning to Copperfine to stay for a few weeks with her sister Myrna. The letter said Violet was receiving help from the Myrna's son in law to handle the paperwork and the inventory of Leibitsang Provisioners. There was an invitation for Karin and her parents to come and visit. Violet and her sister wanted to know what they should send for Karin and her mother and father. Enclosed in the letter was a drawing that Lily Wonder had made of what she thought Holland looked like. There was a dyke, a windmill, a small round house with a palm tree in the yard. She had also included a cooking fire in the front yard with a prominent three legged black cooking pot. Steam was rising up in a spiral of blue blending into the azure sky. Karin felt tears coming down her cheeks as she handed the drawing to her mother.

"Our Lily is also an artist. She has the eyes," her mother said.

Garrett, Karin's father, came into the room and reached down to give his daughter a hug. He took the picture they handed him and said, "I wonder what she's cooking up in her Dutch oven?" Karin laughed, thinking that the child was winning over these grandparents without even having met them. By morning, they had decided that they could make the flight to go and see the child, and the rest of the family. Karin was not sure she could travel that long by plane, but she was silent as they planned this reunion.

It was good to know her child was loved and that the family was gathering to make her life secure. As she climbed into her bed that night, she glanced up at the picture of Clair she had hung on the wall. She needed to let her friend know there would be visitors soon.

A week later, all plans changed. Karin had a spell of being unable to breathe and having small seizures. She was taken to the hospital and the prognosis was that she was in serious condition. Her MS was flaring out of control and pneumonia had attacked her lungs. Her parents were beside her and sent a telegram to Violet. They would wire her the money to come to Holland immediately. Their travel agent would help cut through the red tape, as time was of the essence. Violet should phone them and let them know her flight numbers and when she would arrive. They made it clear that Karin was not expected to live.

CHAPTER 38

VIOLET FLIES TO HOLLAND

Violet reached into her pocket for the fourth time to feel the tickets. She was sweating from the nervousness of never having traveled, as well as meeting people of another country. She was also tasked with the additional pressure of doing right by her granddaughter, who trusted that she could navigate across the world and arrive at the right place at the right time. Again, she felt for the tickets and the passport which she had wrapped in a small cloth to keep it clean and safe. She was wearing it around her waist, along with her large pile of bills and her smaller pile of kroner.

She had a cell phone in her handbag, a sack of food to keep the child healthy, and a bottle of water for the journey. Lily Wonder carried a book, a stuffed toy, and a small drawing pad and pencils, along with her comb, and two bands in a small backpack to help hold her curls away from her face.

The taxi was waiting for them as Violet locked up the house. The servants would be watching the property; the night guard, the cook, and the gardener. There was no need for them to go into the house, as she had distributed the perishable food and turned off the water inside. Violet had no pets, no houseplants, and no electrical appliances that needed attention. She was ready to go, with one suitcase for the two of them, and a small carry-on with gifts. She had packed a second crate with paintings for Karin to sell. The market for such things in Blancville had been very slow. Only one painting had sold in the six months since Bwalya's death.

The airport was busy with passengers from all over. Violet could recognize those from India and Malawi. Some, she thought, might be from Holland, England, America, or France. She looked down at Lily Wonder and thought these people could also be from her country. It was more mixed than she had been aware. She knew there were so many other countries, but these were ones she was familiar with. There were also a number of Asian people at the airport. Black suits, shining black leather shoes, and always with a flat case that had a keyboard like a typewriter. What these were, she did not know. Something like a large cell phone made into a television, she thought. They did not have to press very hard on the keys and there was no paper in them and no sound of a bell when they finished a line. She concentrated on finding the queue for Holland. Before she went very far, a solid bodied sister in a crisp white habit took her by the arm and asked where she was bound. "I am a Christian. I am going to heaven."

"No, I mean now. Where are you flying?"

"We are going to Holland. This is my granddaughter. She is Half Holland." Violet could see her granddaughter roll her eyes and hear her puff of embarrassment.

"I am Sister Bernadette. I will help you locate your flight. Where is your ticket?" Violet pulled the tickets from her pocket. Some of the bills she had stuck there dropped out. Lily Wonder dived down to hand them back to her. Another puff.

Sister Bernadette maneuvered the two of them through the customs line, filled out their forms for them, and put them in the right waiting room for KLM Flight 262. They had a three hour wait before boarding. Violet settled into the plastic chair and put her remaining suitcase between her knees. She had been reluctant to check the bags that held the paintings and their clothing. Now, it was just a matter of waiting. She sighed with relief and was soon nodding off to a brief nap.

Lily Wonder drank some water, checked the drawers of the vending machine, and found money in the return slot. She pocketed it and looked around the waiting room. A few boys from India were climbing over their brother's stroller as their mother struggled with the latches on her carryon. Her headscarf dropped into her work, and she would push it back, then try again to get the overstuffed satchel to close and latch. The boys tormented the younger brother until he set up a howl that raised even his mother's attention. Further down the row, a group of men sat in a queue with briefcases. They were all dressed in black. Lily Wonder thought they looked like undertakers she had seen at her father's funeral.

When an announcement came on, they all looked around turning their heads back and forth like a pup grabbing at flies around its head. Lily Wonder took out her sketchpad and recorded the gestures. A family of white people poured into the waiting room. The baby was enormous and smelly. His mother plumped him down on a row of seats and proceeded to change his nappies. He was soiled and when she pulled away his diaper, Lily saw him splayed out and laughed at his freedom. He had red hair and white yam-like legs with a pointer in the middle. It was the first time she had seen white boy parts, and she wanted to ask Violet about it. Her grandmother was sleeping, her mouth slightly ajar, and her purse held high on her chest, like she was offering it to someone. Lily Wonder stopped watching the baby as the parents bundled him up again and dropped his diaper into a trash bin. The whole family ate continuously, chips, biscuits, meat rolls, and small circles of something. They laughed and poked at each other. Lily Wonder hoped her Holland family would be like them, they seemed to like each other and be having fun.

On the ramp to the plane, the two travelers tried to remember how many steps, how many windows, how many pilots, how many lights. They weren't sure what was important or necessary to their surviving this flight in the belly of the 747. At last they were strapped into their seats and it was no longer up to them. Both of them prayed. It was enough that they were in the air. *Everything is up in the air*, Violet thought. She looked across the aisle at the young couple pulling the magazine out of the rack. She would wait a few minutes, then pull hers out as well. She could learn how to do this traveling. She glanced down at Lily and saw that the child was putting a pretend seat belt around her stuffed dog. She did not seem upset or fidgety, just following the pattern of the other passengers on the flight. Violet let out a deep breath she had been holding since she left the house that morning. *All is well*, she repeated to herself. *All is well.*

The airport in Amsterdam was crowded as two airlines from Europe had flights cancelled and KLM had to make up the difference. As Violet and her granddaughter debarked, they looked around anxiously for Karin. There were customs to clear and lines to go through. Violet was confused by the cards she had to fill out, and struggled to recall what the surname was, and where the information went in the blanks. She had filled out that she had products to claim, so she was shunted off to a line and all her pictures and luggage was examined.

At last, she was released to the waiting room where Lily spotted an older couple holding up their pictures. They made their way to the couple, who assured them Karin was fine, she just wanted to leave room for the four of them and their luggage. Violet could not stop the rapid beating of her heart as they whizzed through the parking area, the turnstiles, and along the highway to Nijmegen where they lived. She wanted to answer their questions, but it was difficult to understand their English, and she spoke no Dutch. At last, they arrived at the home. It was a two story stucco building , and dazzling white. Violet noticed the neat plantings of bulbs, the clean shutters, and the odd blue sky that her son had portrayed in his paintings. She asked the Kroners if she should remove her shoes as they entered the doorway. No one answered, they were so eager to speak with the child and see her united with her mother.

Karin wheeled forward to greet her daughter. The child pulled back and hugged the skirt of her grandmother Violet. Everyone turned to Violet to greet her and ask how the journey had been. "It was my first. I cannot say how it was. I am here and I am greeting you for your kindness." Violet had rehearsed this welcoming greeting, but she knew it was coming out wrong. She felt little Lily squeeze her hand and she could breathe again. They had made it. She was now a 'been to'.

Karin wheeled her chair close to Violet and asked her in perfect Bemba to have a seat on the sofa. She did. Then she directed her mother to bring them some tea with sugar and to slow down with the questions. Garrett came and sat near her and asked if he could take her coat. She shook her head "No." It was cooler for her than she had imagined, and she wanted the security of her wool wrap. Lily Wonder now reached out to her mother and hugged her, smoothing her hair and holding her face in her hands, studying any changes. She seemed satisfied that her mother was all right, and went into the kitchen to see how Cora made the tea.

The kitchen floor was wide planks of polished wood with pegs holding the planks. Lily got down on her knees to trace the grain and feel the joining of the wood and the pegs. Then she stood up and asked if she could bring the sugar into the parlor. Cora looked at her and nodded yes.

Garrett listened to the conversation between Violet and Karin. As he watched the two women, one in her sixties, the other barely thirty, he thought of the bond they shared. He had wanted to meet Bwalya. Violet was comfortable with them as she told of her desire to meet Karin, and now, she was meeting her most valuable people as well.

Bwalya been a good husband and father, Karin told her, and he had often spoken of how he loved his mother.

"He was afraid he had disappointed his family by marrying outside his tribe," Karin said. "He didn't want to face your disapproval, so he stayed away; involved in his work, his child, and in me. I was not in this wheelchair when we met. We actually got to know each other in London and my life changed when I met him. I miss him so much," she added.

Violet looked at the grandparents. "I do not want to keep this child from her family. I have lost all my children and when she came to me, my life returned to me. How shall we share her?"

This question had been on everyone's mind, especially once they knew the child would be visiting them. Cora spoke first. "Bwalya and Karin wanted you to have the child because your country has so much to offer her. I hope you see when you are here that our country, too, is a good place. You both will always be welcome here. I have spoken with Garrett and we would like to come and visit you in your home as well. Karin is getting medical treatment and the flight may not be possible for her, but we want all of us to be a part of your lives."

Garrett grunted as Lily piled into his lap and handed him a book. She wasn't sure of all that her family was planning, but she felt the love and the connection of her mother and these old adults. She was tired, a little hungry, and content.

The next morning, Lily was up at six o'clock asking Garrett where were his chickens? He took her on a tour of his yard. In the street, women were washing the curbs and sweeping down the sidewalks. The two of them walked to the park at the end of the street and climbed into the swings. Garrett's long legs swept the sand and he felt the dizzying motion as he swung his head back into the cool morning breeze. Lily lifted her feet high to pump the swing into the air. She sang a little song that Garrett could not understand. Then it was time to eat and she let him know she was very hungry. They headed back to the house.

Two weeks later, Violet and Lily returned to Africa to start their lives together and prepare for the visit of the Kroners.

CHAPTER 39

KINDNESS

Copperfine was changing. Groups from the north and the west were converging with their herds into the fertile, if dry, valleys of this region. Festal had seen small bands of people he did not recognize camping on the hillsides, their evening fires each night in the same location showing that they were not nomads, but settlers looking for a place to settle. He was not concerned as the weather had been generous. For the last few years, the grasses had come in the proper season. Calves were born to robust cows, the water was clean, and the river basins provided an ample supply, even in the dry season. Festal had taken in Mpala, who was orphaned by some disaster, man-made or natural, to the West. There had always been groups that had fallen on hard times in the region; his own family had struggled during an earlier famine and his twin sister had been indentured to a foreign family to bring in money for food which allowed the rest of them to survive the hungry period. He had been placed with the cattle herders to earn his livelihood with only a blanket and a pair of sandals between him and the elements. He had endured.

Festal did not read the newspaper, and there was only one radio in the village, so it was months after the droughts in Ethiopia and the Horn of Africa had reached even the insulated countries of Europe and America that he realized that a more severe time of hunger was pushing in upon Copperfine. The emaciated faces of the women coming into the area, and the absence of male children suddenly became apparent. There was no way to stop this influx of people. Like the locusts that appeared every fifteen years or so, the problem had remained hidden in the soils of Africa. Each family and village absorbed its difficulty until the fabric was too thin and too worn to hold up. Then the rents in the social fabric were obvious. Families shunned those who were not their blood. Communities could no longer take in the hungry or the homeless. They began to see the stranger as intruders and interlopers and hospitality, so important a concept, disappeared. They turned a blind eye to those who were not born in the area. Rumors of killings and genocide emanated around the campfires and the face of hunger was an abomination that pulled people away from their generosity or the impulse to share. Suddenly, sharing meant getting less. Men who had left a portion of the animal for the gleaners or left behind a little grain now pulled each kernel into the sack and slept with the bags in their sleeping chamber.

There were no animals kept who could not earn their livelihood. Only the dogs remained fat, and no one asked why they wandered in packs at night and came home bloated. The villagers were more insulated, as the poorest, or those ostracized through war or disease or widowhood poured into the cities, which now had children sleeping on their walkways and in the alleys. Every restaurant had its contingency of beggars hoping for a handout when the patrons were finished with their meals. Babies were abandoned and no one picked them up to try to save them, or heard their cries. Those who had gone through warfare and seen the specter of hunger and genocide were terrified, but no one named what the fear was that stalked their environs.

The fetish priests were frequented by even the staunchest of Christians, as they were desperate to find how they or their country had offended the gods. For Festal, it was a time of drawing in his energy and his resources. He did not want his wife to venture beyond the pastures or the road that passed behind their rondavel. These were desperate times, and she could be taken or robbed for the basket of food she was carrying to the house. Festal warned Gift against visiting the refugee camps which sprung up on the rockier bluffs. He told his children to only play with the children of the neighbors closest to them, and questioned them what they had seen and where they had gone during the hours they played. It was a relief when they were in school, as they could go and come as a group, protected by their uniforms and their numbers.

The political climate of the country was changing. There were parties that sought the vote, and others who wanted the farmers to side with them. Festal avoided making a commitment to one party or the other. He did not wear the hats or the scarves they passed out to encourage solidarity, and stayed with the worn clothing that herdsman wore. He did not get into discussions with the agitators who came in cars with megaphones and then with loudspeakers to unite the countryside, nor did he put his name to resolutions or strikes. He remained with his land and his family, and circled them more tightly in as the boundaries and the names of what he had known gave way to new configurations, ideas, and titles.

The railroad, the discovery and upswing in prices for copper, and the influx of money from countries such as China had no bearing on what he wanted for his life, and that of his family. Festal thought that if he could limit his freedom, and subdue his fear, he would come out of the changes intact. He wore his cross, had his Bible read to him each night, and guided his children to believe in integrity and standing firm for what they believed. His wives were loyal to him, as he showed that he was working for the betterment of all their lives.

Festal did not buy into the paranoia of the general population towards the thousands of refugees that were streaming in across the borders or the displaced persons within the country. When the police and border patrol tried to gather information about who was a part of the community, and who should be removed, he conveniently forgot the names and the location of those who had newly arrived. He referred the officials to the refugee camps, where they had already rounded up too many newcomers, and asked if they had checked there. He was judged to be simple in his understanding, and no one he knew was turned over to the government forces. Mpala, Hen, Gift, and others breathed easier, seeing that he would protect them.

In time, the forces who were in power were out of favor, and more patrols, more soldiers, and more warring occurred. It was a time of great stress for Gift, who had experienced the trauma of being captured and uprooted, her family and her childhood destroyed. She learned she could rely on Festal, and that Myrna valued her and would tell anyone they were sisters.

CHAPTER 40
ROSE

"Festal , I am going to have a baby." Festal reached around Myrna and planted a kiss on her neck. She had been ironing the clothes for the twins who were going back to school that afternoon.

"Is it one, or more?"

"I think it is just one. I must be about 4 months along. I wanted to tell you on your birthday, but I wanted to make sure you knew before anyone else." Festal needed to go outside and catch some air. He was elated. It was a good time, since most of his children were out of school, the girls had suitors they liked, and there would be a double wedding for the twins once they finished their seminary training. But was his wife too old to have a baby?

It had been many years since the twins came. He could still recall the nights of worry when he thought they would die and he would lose the mother as well. He had turned to God and now both of his sons had decided to be pastors. They explained to their father that he had always been a pastor caring for his herd, they would be a pastor to the community. Samuel was taking over the pulpit at the Full Gospel Church while Reuben elected to serve the immigrant population in the area. They would share the facility and that would leave funds for feeding programs. Festal was proud of his sons. They had a deep love for the Copperfine region, and each had found a future mate at their college. Festal had met their prospective wives and approved their choices.

From the moment he knew she was pregnant, Festal was fixated on the coming child. He brought vitamins and herbal potions from the local market, and liniments to make sure there was no stretching of the skin. Myrna was baffled by his attention, since the twins had been so healthy, and her body had accommodated them, she had no fear of this single birth. It had been some years since she had last given birth, that was true, but she had stayed physically active and she had never felt better.

For Festal, this coming birth was an epiphany. Festal had attended church with Myrna and she had always known he was a believer. Now that she was pregnant, he donated a steer to the congregation, and he was never absent from the service or the prayer meetings. Each of his children was to be blessed by the new head pastor; just to be sure they had the best protection. Festal took to wearing a cross, not a small discrete one made of wood or bone, but a metallic ornate one the size of his hand that he had the smithy forge for him out of remnant metals. He refused to drink beer or wine, although he had been steadily increasing the amounts of sorghum beer he consumed as the ache of his bones set in, especially in the cold season.

After the passing of Lily, all of the children had been dosed with a nightly reading from the Bible, which Festal would then give his own interpretation. He had especially liked to reflect on the story of Job, and the chapters from Leviticus that spelled out the rules for right living. It fell upon Myrna to read him these chapters. In the evening, she was often tired and her eyes would start to blur as she looked at the small print of the Gideon Bible they had been given by one of the elders. They did not have electricity at the house, and the kerosene lantern with its flickering flame made the print difficult to see.

Myrna soon let the twins take over the reading, spelled by the older girls. Each of the family members came to enjoy these sessions, as they never knew what interpretation their father would give to the words. He had always been fonder of the Old Testament than the New, and he had seen himself in the role of Moses, herding his family through treacherous times and places. Gift was moved by these stories and said they had helped her deal with her losses. She seldom spoke of her past, but when the Seder was discussed, and how the families repeated what had happened through the generations, the bitter herbs and the salt reminded them of their sorrow and their tears. She told Royal she saw her difficult times as knots that had occupied her emotions for so long, and she couldn't see how to untie, but now they were being unraveled and she was seeing them as places where she had been tied to God. Royal told her he was writing down her memories as they interested him and inspired him. He thought others would like to read or hear them as well and his wife Henrietta agreed. She said she found herself and her mother in the struggles Gift had overcome.

When Gift and Myrna first started the women's co-op, Gift had tried to learn, but remembering one thing would bring back the terrors of what she had endured, and she would lie awake at night recalling and unable to forget how her life had been enslaved by the soldiers. She would be afraid to leave the rondavel in the daytime without someone with her. She decided it was better for her to shut down her thinking and recalling. With the scriptures that Myrna and the children read, Gift could coat her history with a new balm. Gift now saw herself as part of a legacy of women and men who had endured, and were remembered because of it, not shamed. She was no longer the outsider, but part of the history of her family and her place. Her valuing of herself increased, and she began to take a new interest in her life, her son, and her future.

As Myrna's pregnancy progressed, Festal took on a new direction in his Bible readings. He had the family read from the New Testament. Each of the stories was familiar to them, but Festal had new insights on what they meant because his life was now shining forth. The old fears seemed to have gone away. For Gift, these were good times. She had located a living relative among the refugees that had poured into the border camp as she was helping Reuben set up his ministry. She spoke the tribal dialect of the refugees and could translate the scripture and the responses. She was also able to learn more about her family that had been lost to her. The new immigrants welcomed her sharing and empathy and sought her out as a mentor. Many were pouring into Copperfine and Gift encouraged them to record and share their experiences because people wanted to know. At least Royal did.

He had been through hardships of his own, and was a responsive son. He also found himself in the stories. He liked the story of the Shummanite woman, and how she had repeated, "All is well." He related to the son, overcome and then brought back to life. "All is well" became his mantra. He loved David for not forgetting the maimed descendant of Saul, and that King David would have the crippled son eat with him at the table.

Gift and Myrna became closer in the way they saw their lives, and Festal was an important part of this. Royal once called him the Angel of the Seventh Seal, with his foot on the land and the other on the sea. Festal was straddling a changing landscape as the pastoral life gave way to commerce, his family grew, education became more widespread, and Copperfine was swollen with new residents, mines, and businesses. Festal had internalized the struggle between standing out, and fading away. Those of his fellow men who had once laughed at him for his antique ways were gone. But here he was, virile at 70, with wives and children who respected him. He was learning to conquer the fear and superstition that had controlled so much of his life, and accept that no disaster would overcome this child that was about to arrive. And so he took the Word and made it his. Each verse and story was translated into the life he led, or intended to lead.

With the birth of Rose, his faith was confirmed. He thought of calling the child Lily, but Myrna vetoed that. "We have loved our Lily; we can love this child as much wearing her own name. You give it to her, Festal."

Myrna was undergoing a time of reflection. She was watering the plumeria, the nut trees, and the hedge of lilies along the front of the adobe wall that surrounded the front courtyard.

How is my life with Festal? I think about it more now that I have time to sit and write. I saw myself when I was very young as a sacrifice for my family, and not a very willing one I was a Christian girl, called to deny myself and my worldly pleasures and desires to go into the wilderness and take up my cross. In fact, when I got to Copperfine, it was more pleasant than I expected. The land was spectacular with its fertile river valley and the hues of light on the grasses and hillsides, the colors of the cattle and the softness of calves. I loved the adoration of the powerful hunting dogs, and how Festal made love to me. I felt more powerful and alive in my femaleness than I ever dreamed. Even before I discovered my husband, and came to admire his courage and tenacity, I had determined I would be happy.

I hoped for a beautiful inheritance. I didn't want my sister to feel sorry for me or my-sister-in-law to despise the way I lived. Violet disparaged my husband and thought my life would be a total waste. I wanted to be somebody, and I claimed that. I would be the mother in a family that was a beacon to this community. We lived in a clean, simple home that my husband had built with his own hands. He had prized me; I would be a prize. He would know each day when he went out to the fields that no man was loved or respected more. He would be eager to return each night, and my education would be applied, not wasted. Otherwise, why had I been allowed to go so far in school? Of course, I knew I would teach my children. I also thought I would teach my husband. Not so. He was a new creature to me. I had never read about anyone like him, and I had no knowledge of him before we climbed on that oxcart together. I began to study him.

As I learned more about him, I began to respect him, then to love him. We had joy in our lives. I also learned about my inside self as I had never experienced it before. I learned I was capable of intense passion in love, and equally intense jealousy and rage; that I could covet and despise, and reject. I could also be passionately alive, fiercely nurturing, and domineering. Not all at once, nor did I admit to any of these until I saw my children and the second wife reflect these back to me.

I had little experience of men. Festal was unlike any I had known. My father was docile. He catered to my mother, provided for our family, and loved me. Bishop did what society expected of him. I think he would sometimes have liked to be more resolute, or go against the practical, such as refusing to marry me off to a stranger, but he complied and put economic security above everything else. He knew Dodge was a predator, but he never chased him off. Festal was not tamed. He took what he needed, and what he thought he had earned, but he remained an outsider. He never forgot that he had been raised in a wilderness where the forces of cruelty and violence were held back by taking a stand. Gift referred to him as a warrior, and she was right. He knew that he could easily be driven away again out of the circle that society drew and have to retreat to the wilderness.

Festal did not back off when he needed to protect us, and he was willing to sacrifice himself for his freedom to choose. He had chosen me and I came to know him and seek to become the woman he imagined me to be. As surely as the sun dries the pottery placed beneath it, my life solidified to Festal's vision of me. He worshipped me, he feared me, and he loved me passionately. I don't know if that is enough for any woman, but it was for me. Oh, I might have liked a few better manners out in public, but not when it was just the two of us and our children. They knew and adored us, and we raised them. Our best times were when we were fighting for their future, building a home for them, and seeing them exceed what we had hoped for in their lives. Our worst times were when we succumbed to what others wanted from us, and we recognized they did not value one of us. Maybe that is why Gift came to be part of our lives.

Gift was a woman who survived by her instincts. She was not bitter about what she had endured. She did not dwell on the might-have-beens. She had lost her father and mother, her brothers and sisters, her country, and her sexuality and her innocence. Her children, except for Royal Festal, died in infancy. She tried to have more. She also formed instant alliances with little consideration She cherished the woman who sold her for a barrel of beer into our lives. She admired Dodge for making it possible for her to join our family, even though he had lied about where she would be going.

Our children were our treasure. We coveted their safety, our connection with them in the future, and the bonds they were building between themselves and our community. Each of them was an individual, but they also bore the stamp of our family. They were true to their word. They spoke less than other children, but I think they thought more about what they said. They protected and were loyal to each other. If a team could not include Royal, they did not want to play that game. They loved me and they respected their father because I demanded it of them. In time, they loved him for himself. Festal had integrity. It might not be the same as yours or mine, but he held himself to a relentless standard of endurance and courage, in spite of his continuing fears of the spirit world and what he stood to lose.

Festal had been separated from his twin sister. He believed that he was cursed for this loss because he should have been the one sacrificed. This guilt controlled his inner voice for many years. He wanted control of his destiny, and to be justified for this failure to protect his sister. He did not flinch at protecting his family or his cattle from wild animals, the harsh environment, the soldiers, or the political winds that were blowing around the country. He was a warrior. Sometimes I defined myself in terms of his hardness. That was the literary student I was meant to be coming out in me. Because he was a rock, I could be a stream and nourish those around me. Because he was a wall, I could be a garden. Festal did not join me in my teaching, my ministering, or my speaking, but he was the source of what I knew and could do. My life was not shallow, nor was it pointless. Survival alone was satisfying at the cattle station. I was grateful that I had clear boundaries and a path to my future, even if I was unclear what that future would hold. And so we grew to respect and balance each other.

My sister Violet pitied me for the marriage I had entered. She had been the younger sister and that position kept her from expressing in words to me what she felt. Her absence and the way she would talk about her Joseph let me know what she thought I was missing. I did not like being patronized. When Lily died, this was the worst. The whole family would be sorry, and never realize that Lily had the best life a child could have. Yes, it was too bad that her life passed before she reached adulthood, but her life was sweet. She died without them ever knowing her, and what a loss her passing was to us all. This is what I would have told Violet, if she had been willing to hear me out. I listened to her condolences and did not share this insight with her.

I did not visit Joseph and Violet as often as I should have because she was never open to the idea that Festal and I could have something of value between us. I regretted this lack of correspondence between us when Violet's own children began to die. I had to check my own responses and make sure that I was genuinely grieving for her losses, and not thinking of my own vindication. When I was grieving and inconsolable, I went back to the verses about the Shummanite woman of the Old Testament, who realized the significance of hospitality, and is able through her faith to stand on the belief that "All is well," even when all evidence is to the contrary. I wanted to get to know the children of Violet and Joseph, especially Bwalya and Benjamin, but seldom saw them. I do not know if they thought of me, or what they were told about Festal and me. I did not want to have to explain ourselves and risk being pitied or judged.

Festal found his way through the Bible and reflected what it spoke to him. We never really directed our children in what paths they should take as adults, but they were taught the principles from the Bible and by our example. We were learning about faith by living it and searching for God. The twins were a unit unto themselves as children, and the girls doted on them, but recognized their unity. How will this new child fit into the Phiri plan?

CHAPTER 41

LIVING WATERS

I am sitting on my small courtyard wall looking at the melons crowding each other under the arbor. Gift has lost another child, and I am not mourning, or even thinking about it. My life is a series of small gestures to prove I am even here. We, that is, Festal, Gift and I, have been battling a drought that does not seem to stop. The cattle drank from a watering hole because they couldn't wait for us to purify water for them or put some iodine in it, and the cholera took about half of them. The heat and the lack of feed will probably take the younger ones in another week, if there is no change.

I am 40 years old, and pregnant, after a long spell of not being. My body tells me it is ready to have this child soon, but I am not ready. I just want something to change in my life. Gift and I have been working with the women and the well-baby project, but without enough clean water and food, what we do is give hope to women who know that they will not make it through this hungry time unless someone or something steps in to help. Why have the rains not come? We talk about nothing else. We no longer ask if Bwene's baby is getting better. If someone doesn't show up at our meeting, it usually means they have lost a child, or at least a cow.

Festal withdraws more and more from us, but I know he is not able to deal with pain in the same way Gift can, or I try to. He just shuts off, like the old buffalo that go off to the riverbed and just lie down waiting for the hyena or the lion to take them. I want to give my children a better picture of what it is to be an adult because they are watching to see how we manage. When I first came here to be a wife, I thought it just meant losing my dreams and hope. Being a parent meant always being at someone's beck and call. Always being needed and tired to death. Now, I am not sure what I see myself as. I am a shadow at noon, looking for a person to attach myself to, I am a first wife, an over-paid bride price who no longer nurtures her family or can even tell you for sure where they are or what they need at this time of their lives.

Reuben and Samuel have gone into the ministry. Each of them has a fiancée and they are planning on getting married when the rains come and the drought is over. What happens if rain never comes? Do they wait on hold for weather that is changing? Is that what we did when the country was becoming independent and we did not know which group we owed loyalty to? I am afraid we did go on with our lives, disconnected with the larger picture as the politicians called it, but knowing that our function was to raise a family and stay close with our neighbors. We functioned in the way we knew we should and assumed the bigger picture of changing borders, governments, and parties would work itself out. What has put me in this mood of seeing myself as such a piece of clay?

I am a three legged cook pot that burns the food because the holes in me are getting too large to patch. I am a wilting zebra plant that needs water, and no one seems to notice my leaves are dropping. Can I not move and change my lot?

"Myrna, you are leaking. Has your labor started?" Gift asked.

"Oh. I was sitting here feeling that I was losing something, and I was. I will get to the doctor."

"You are not going to make it to the doctor. I will go and get Lottie."

Gift took off for the neighbor's house. It seemed some time had passed and Myrna went into the house to lie on the bed. She could feel the contractions, but it was as though she was thinking about them, rather than experiencing them. She fell asleep and wakened with Festal leaning over her. Gift was nowhere in sight. Together, they delivered the baby, who was born with a flap of skin over her face. Festal trimmed it away, and cut and tied the cord, holding the wet baby girl in his arms and raising her up for Myrna to see. He was delighted in the child and that he had been there to save her and the mother. They spent the night in each other's arms, none of the children being at home. That night, the rains poured down and the explosion of thunder, and water hitting the parched earth, could be heard even inside the rondavel. Both the hunting dogs whined to come inside, but Festal ordered them out. It was morning when Gift came back. She had spent the night at Lottie's, she said, once she saw Festal approaching the house.

Myrna recalled how she had felt nothing before the baby came, and the pain of her delivery was a relief from the emptiness of not being present. Of course, she wanted this child to survive, as she nursed her and cleaned her. Festal took the flap of skin and the afterbirth and buried them in the garden, saying a prayer for another child who had been born with this same strange feature, his sister Whenny. He had not thought of her for some time, but this portent of the caul made him aware that all lives are connected, and his had been richly blessed with this birth.

Festal did more than he ever had with an infant. He carried the baby that he named Rose on his chest, and kept her clean so her mother could rest. He emptied the wash basin and cleaned it with boiling water, then cooled it and bathed the child, being careful to keep her naval dry and coated with charcoal. He would rub her forehead, which was healing. He put salve on it and covered it with a leaf and then the knit wool stocking cap to keep the flies away. His fellow cattlemen came to check on him and he had no embarrassment to have them see him with his hands scrubbing out the soiled nappies. No one laughed at him—they were celebrating the rain and the end of this season of dying.

The child seemed a portent that things would improve. Gift took to the child and was relieved to have another child that needed care. She still had milk from her recent stillborn, and Myrna did not press her to help with the chores, instead let her mother the child as much as Gift wanted, even nursing the lusty little girl.

They started new projects that they had talked about, but never gotten around to doing. Myrna had Gift take some letters to the post office and asked her to bring back a photographer. She posed all of the children and herself, Gift and Festal, Hen and Royal, in a picture, then asked the photographer to make copies so she could send them to Festal's family and to Violet and Stephen, as well as her mother Beatrice. When the baby was a month old, they took her to the church to be baptized. Everyone agreed that she was the most beautiful baby ever, and Festal held her as the sign of the cross was made on her forehead. Royal, Hen and Gift were the god-parents. Myrna loved her but from a distance that was more objective and less anxious than she had been with any of the other children. She would sew her simple dresses and watch Gift put them on her, or let Hen take her for a walk in the morning. After Myrna bathed and dressed herself, she would pull a book from the shelf to read, or write in her diary. She had a row of books she had written, and when there was a question of what had gone on in the village, she could pull up the information.

She recalled when the soldiers had come to the door, demanding that the men come and join them. She had shown them Royal, and they had left her alone. Gift had gone to hide in the cistern which was empty when she heard the troops approaching. All this was noted in her daily messages to herself. She had no plan to do anything with these writings, but they kept her grateful for the days that she had lived, and the changes that had occurred in the village. She noted the arrivals, the passings, and get-togethers. She also interspersed the letters from Violet in the pages, and knew one day, the sisters would compare their paths.

Economics were always a part of her life, but Myrna had learned to budget for the things that mattered or brought her joy. She was a woman who looked attractive in simple dresses and plain fabrics, and she could sew dresses for herself if need be. She had made clothing for Gift as well, because the woman was small boned and busty, and it was hard to find clothing in the markets that fit her figure.

As the years passed, fewer people wore the traditional clothing, or at least the embroidered tops. They bought the dead-white-man's clothes the traders brought to the market, and mixed the knitted tops with the traditional wrapped skirts. Sometimes Myrna would see a shirt being worn by a man that said Barbara down the sleeve and wondered if they were meant for a woman. No one paid attention to this, as gender was part of their lifestyle and activities, more so than a color or choice of a garment.

When Myrna married, Violet had given her a brassiere. It remained the only one she had ever owned, and it was patched and repaired over the years until little of the original material remained. Other clothing also was vintage, such as the Dutch wax prints that she had maintained for her twenty years of married life. She wore the traditional petticoat with lace at the bottom that had been the fashion in the sixties, and continued to serve her to keep her legs covered from the insects. Myrna took pride in her figure, which had thickened some with the number of children she had birthed, but was still shapely and trim. She had never tried on or owned a pair of trousers. She walked and lifted constantly, and her muscles were firm and smooth.

Festal too, aged well. He had never developed a big belly and his legs were strong and muscled, while his chest was thin but muscular with the work of walking, herding, and carrying new calves, milk, water, and wood. They ate the foods they grew and seldom had sweets. Their tea was the only indulgence, except for an occasional biscuit when they went to church suppers or weddings—until Hen taught Royal to bake. Now, life was sweet.

CHAPTER 42
SAMUEL AND REUBEN MARRIED

Two years later, Samuel and Reuben had their weddings. Each of them had met wives at the seminary they attended. They were neighboring pastors in Copperfine, one at the traditional church, and one at the Blessings Healing Center, a tent church that helped refugees and displaced persons from the wars going on in the north. The brothers had always worked together on their dreams, and their father did not worry about their future, as it was clear they were getting guidance directly from the God he had always feared. He waited for a confirmation that they would bear him grandchildren, but his focus was his daughter Rose, the child he felt was his blessing for turning his life around.

Rose would be the flower girl at their joint wedding, and she could hardly contain her excitement. She had informed her father of what she would require for the ceremony, and he had listened to her make the list and check off each item as he provided it for her. Gift was going to sing at the wedding and had been practicing her songs each morning when she thought no one was listening.

CHAPTER 43

BABY ROSE

From the moment Festal saw his daughter Rose, he was bonded to her by a tenderness and care he had not known before. She was chubby and mellow, and both of them said how much she reminded them of their Lily. What made this child different to her father was a mystery to Myrna. He seemed to celebrate her arrival, and would even carry her around when she was a newborn, resting on his now thin chest. Myrna would come into the house after her classes and see him on his mat with the child sleeping on him. All of the children adored Rose as well, especially Royal. He was twenty, in love, and a graduate of the culinary school. When he visited home, he couldn't wait to pick Rose up, often carrying her on his back, or holding her while Myrna and his mother prepared food or did chores. Henrietta also loved her, and would make special treats for the child, including roses of sugar.

When Rose was four, she was able to read. Festal was so proud, he would bring her a book from the store in Copperfine and give it to her. She would tell the story and put her father to sleep with the lilting words. Myrna and Gift would laugh to see the effect this child had on the man. Rose even went to the near fields with her father carrying a slim stick and driving the cattle. If she was made to stay at home, she would sit on the wall of the compound, under the plumeria tree, writing her letters in charcoal on the red clay of the wall, waiting for Festal to come home. She named all the cows and would tell Festal stories about them, if he would not tell her a story first. Each story he told her, she remembered and could repeat. Rose learned the fables of her country and those of Aesop as well. She could see the connection between the behavior of the animals and that of people, and liked to cite the moral at the end.

As she approached five, Festal began to have panic attacks concerning Rose's health. He had Myrna keep the curtains drawn across the entrance way. Every dish had to be sanitized in the boiling water, and no one was welcome to come into the house during the fly season before the rains came. Myrna and Gift guessed it was his memory of Lily that made him so cautious. When Dodge said he wanted to come and pay a visit, Festal was adamant that the man stay away. Gift liked Dodge and did not understand this restriction, but she accepted it. She had come to see that Festal had his reasons.

The Phiri family was growing by leaps and bounds. By the time Rose was finishing middle school, her brothers had each produced a child. She was Aunt Rose. She was a good student and her early interest was to run an academy for girls, as she saw many improvements that could be made in her own school. Her father cautioned her to be respectful, but Rose did not like traditional rote methods and automatic approval of everything the headmaster said, whether it was right or wrong. She was learning how to check out facts in her encyclopedia from the library, and let her father know each time her teacher was in error.

Festal was now almost 85 and he listened to all his child's beefs about the teaching methods and the lack of correct information. He had been afraid that his child would be taken, and she was not. He was afraid his wives would abandon him, and they did not. He was afraid his sons would be sterile, as they were twins, but both had produced grandchildren for him. His life was blessed, and he was humble in his thankfulness and gratitude. He had feared getting old, but the young men helped him with the more difficult tasks, and the calves he had raised listened to his commands like his dogs. In short, his life was sweet, satisfying, and longer than he had ever imagined. He chose to be happy, just as Myrna had done when she came to live with him in Copperfine. Theirs was a house of love.

Not all Festal's children wanted to continue their schooling, but they were all content to live in Copperfine and remain close to their parents. Iris liked making pottery. Daisy was set on running an orphan school, as the number of children needing assistance had increased with the influx of refugees and displaced persons. Pansy enjoyed drawing and making models of the animals which she would use to dramatize her stories to the young students. She would start an animal out of clay, then get her father to help her refine it. She did not carve them from wood, but molded them in her hands.

Royal enjoyed storytelling, but he also had the desire to become a baker. He struggled to do things sequentially, to know which thing came first and how to do them in order. Only cooking seemed to hold his interest so that he could focus on following directions through from beginning to end. He knew from his Uncle Joseph that people would pay for baked goods, and his mother Gift was not a cook. This way, he would be able to care for her if they were ever on their own without the family to support them. When Festal did not know if this was a worthwhile occupation, Joseph brought him some of the meat pies and the small breads that were around and so popular and Festal saw this could be a good business. Myrna had applied for a scholarship for the boy, and he enrolled at the vocational school in Blancville.

Royal was 16 when he started at the culinary school and there he came across a master baker named Henrietta. They formed a friendship and she began to teach Royal how to make pies and other desserts in addition to the Welsh meat pies and bread that were now a staple in the bigger towns. Royal was fascinated by this little woman who had traveled all over southern Africa, and once dated his cousin Benjamin. He wanted to know her story. It intrigued him how they were already connected. She was a girl who had supported her mother, and managed to be independent, but who longed for what he had, a family that was there for each other.

While he learned about kneading the dough, and techniques of heating the oven, he also connected with her as a person. They were different in age and background, she was petite and limber while Royal was a young man with withered legs, and had never been anywhere, but he had big dreams of what he would be doing in the future. He was funny and he adored women. He loved to read, and in his reading, he had tried different ideas, but always returned to his respect and devotion to home.

Hen had traveled and enjoyed the clubs and restaurants during her time with Benjamin, but her desire had been to settle down and make a life for herself and care for her mother. Her mother had passed away, and her first love and fiancé had left her. He was now dying of AIDS, she had heard, and she sometimes wondered if she might have it as well. She would have to be tested sometime, but for now, she was loving her work and teaching this young man. In Royal, she recognized a loving spirit that was deeper and more pure than she knew from her twenty six years of making a way for herself.

Hen enjoyed her position at the vocational school where she was respected by the staff and her colleagues. She was strangely attracted to this student, and wondered if he thought her incredibly old and out of his range. Day old bread, that's what she was. And he was orange Danish, waiting to cool.

When Royal came home during the Christmas break, he brought a box of baked goods for his family. He had grown a couple of inches taller, was clean shaven and dressed in a white jacket that the school had awarded those passing the bakers' program in the culinary school. Uncle Dodge had brought him out to Copperfine to visit. Royal was glad to see his uncle and discuss what opportunities Dodge saw for employment. Dodge had many contacts, but his real interest was in the four lovely daughters of Myrna. Any one of them could be promoted for marriage on the basis of their mother's reputation, even if they had not been physically beautiful.

Iris had the height and the willowy body with the taut breasts that reminded Dodge of protea blossoms. Pansy was curvaceous, chatty, and liked people. She would suit anyone, especially a politician. Daisy was petite and her waist was tiny, with an hourglass figure and a spirited personality that bubbled over when she liked something. She had the singing voice of her Aunt Violet, and a gift for language. She was very positive and friendly to this Great Uncle Dodge she did not even remember. And Rose. The girl was stunning. She looked like her mother, had the mane of glossy ringlets, the long neck, and the elegance of a girl who has never had to compromise, and is beloved. If he was younger...

Dodge recalled how Myrna had been revealed to him in her bath. If only an artist could capture that sheer sensuality, innocence and beauty. He thought of Bwalya and wondered if he ever needed a model for his studio. Festal was watching his daughter and caught a glimpse of Dodge gazing at her. "Rose, leave the room." The girl looked at him in surprise at the tone she had never heard before. She did as he said, but he could see her eyes brim with tears. The old fury and fear was back again and rose in his throat. This time it had a name.

"Uncle Dodge, I am asking you to leave. You are disturbing the peace of my house. We do not have anything that can be of value to you, and I will help my son find a position. Thank you for your concern and take some of the beignets with you. You will find them sweet."

Uncle Dodge glanced at the two women, standing together near the doorway, expecting a reprieve. Neither of them moved an eyelash. He turned and walked out of the house, feeling like an unwanted cur. They owed everything to him. Everything.

For Festal's sons, this was a time to determine what they needed to do to become men. For the twins, they served the community by feeding the poor, and ministering to the refugees. In time, they saw this as their life's work, and went to the seminary to be trained as counselors and as ministers. They had never really taken to the life of raising cattle, but they respected their father and told him they were also herdsman and warriors, but it was men that they would care for and protect.

In the case of Royal, he was protective of his mother, of Myrna, and of Hen. He loved Festal, and he asked his permission and his advice before choosing his profession. His physical difficulties made too strenuous a life impossible for him, but he accepted this, and never saw himself as less a man for it. He wanted to honor his mother and have her life be known, although he knew that it was too new and too common a story in their area to be revered. He would keep his notes, and one day, she would be seen as one of the heroes of the emerging country. He would make it so. When he met Hen, there was an immediate identification with her background and her struggle. All of it had contributed to the love Royal felt for her, and he let her know that she was somebody to him, and would always be. She wished her mother Amnesty could have lived to meet this Prince of Love, as Myrna called him. She would have loved him too.

CHAPTER 44
THE STILL

Whenny was seventy when she immigrated into the Copperfine area from the West. She bought her first sack of sugar with the money she had made selling the beans she had been given by the Copperfine women's cooperative. She had shown up one day when Gift was telling the women her story, and she could relate to the isolation and enslavement the girl had endured. Her life was a collage of broken promises and crushed dreams. She didn't dwell on these, as she now had three grandchildren to support. She needed to make money fast. She did not own a building or a way to protect any supplies, but she could use a portion of her younger brother's house and start a still.

Within weeks, she was able to feed her grandchildren and her younger brother. He was lying in the front room on a mat of foam rubber, trying to stay clean and clear his head of the constant pain and the infection that made his nostrils and his bones ache. Lamont had been a trucker on the coast route for the past ten years. He had a wife, but she had long since returned to her village with their children, once Lamont was unable to support them. Whenny's husband, who was several years older than she was, had died a year ago from pneumonia and they had no money for a proper funeral, so the family did not claim his body at the hospital. This lack of decorum was becoming the norm as the fabric of society broke down from the pandemic of HIV.

Whenny was happy for the first time in months. As the customers came into the bar and she poured the brew into their containers, she counted up the money she had made and sent one of the girls to the butcher's to get half a kilo of ground beef and six eggs. When the girl returned, Whenny cooked up the meat and took it to her brother. He raised himself up on one elbow and she could see that his eyes were coated and draining. He had bumps on his almost hairless scalp. He smiled at her, seeing the meal she had prepared for him, but he was too weak to eat it. Instead, he had her bring him a pitcher of the brew she had made. He drank it while he told her he loved her, and was glad she was now in business. Whenny continued to serve customers into the evening. The barrel was empty, so she dragged it into the house to protect it. When she came into her room, the grandchildren were asleep on the floor, their clothing and the sleeping cloths around them. They had eaten half the meat and saved the rest for their grandmother, covering it with a banana leaf and putting it under her mat. She had almost stepped in it while going to sleep beside them. Whenny wrapped the money in her headscarf and put it under her head to sleep on, should anyone break in during the night.

In the morning, Lamont did not stir. He was alive, but he had shallow breaths. Whenny took his jar of waste to empty. The children swept the courtyard and gathered up the calabash bowls the customers had used for their drinks. They carried them to the wash basin, filled it with cold water and soap and scrubbed out the bowls. The sorghum mash barrel was empty and sitting in the front parlor, but a second one was behind the curtain in the sleeping room fermenting away. There would be a good business again tonight. Whenny was afraid that when her brother passed, the relatives would take this dwelling from her, as she had no papers saying it was her business place, or any lease showing she was renting it. She also worried that the customers would molest the children, once there was no man present to protect them. For today, it was enough that they had food to eat and supplies to make their liquor. She had no plan for what would happen when Lamont passed.

As the evening went on, the crowd continued to come and go. The second barrel was almost empty, one string of colored lights had gone out, but the flashing mirrored ball continued to draw in customers. She would raise the price of the remaining liquor, since it was apparent there was no shortage of customers. When the last group left, Whenny checked on her brother. He was gone, his hands pressed in front of his face and his nose black with dried blood. She was saddened, but more so because this business and her security were gone. When Lamont was living, he was no trouble to anyone and the bar could stay open when she needed the income. No one visited him, maybe she could just move the body to a different room, say the small storeroom, and continue to operate without his relatives taking everything.

She sat in the darkness with her children sleeping and made plans. At last she hit on an idea. What if she was to just care for someone else's brother who was in the same condition? No one would check, they would continue to fear the disease. She could work out a swap, say with someone who did not want to continue to care for a young relative who had HIV and was taking up space? She would have to be very careful, but she saw how it could be done. She would make the switch on a day when most people were at work, or occupied in their homes. She just needed to locate that certain family or relative who needed a break from their imprisonment. They would have to do the transport; she could use the barrel that was now empty. Whenny went to sleep and slept better than she had for months. In the morning, she locked up the bar, put the children in the bedroom, and locked them in while she went to locate her next tenant.

Reuben, now a pastor at the Tabernacle of Blessing tent church, looked up from the communion table where he was setting up the bread and wine. He saw the profile of a slim woman in the doorway, pushing a wheelbarrow. Something registered with him that he needed to talk to her, and he left what he was doing and walked over. Whenny was shy to talk to the pastor who greeted her in her own language, smiling at her as though she was important to him.

"I am looking for a patient to care for, a young man who has HIV. I need a tenant in my house."

"We have many who would be grateful for a place to stay. But many cannot pay for board or a room."

"I can care for him without wages, but he must come quickly," Whinney said.

"I will bring someone to you tonight. What is your address?"

"My house is the Last Laugh Bar at the end of River No More Street. I am Whenny."

"Whenny, I will come and see you after the service. Should I call you first?"

"No. I have no phone and the children will be sleeping. Just bring the person and I will take care of them. It needs to be a man not older than thirty."

"I am sure I have someone in the church who needs a place for themselves or a relative. Even if I do not have someone, I will come and see you tonight."

Whenny looked Reuben in the face and believed him. He was a young man, probably not more than twenty years of age and he had eyes of amber with long curled lashes. He reminded her of someone she knew from the past. She did not ask any more questions but started to head back to her house. Before she could leave Reuben asked her if she had room in her wheelbarrow for some vegetables and bread. She did. He loaded up her barrow with a week's worth of groceries and waved to her. Whenny continued to the warehouse where she purchased 50 kilos of sugar and headed back to the bar, glad it was a downhill journey with the laden wheelbarrow. She was in good shape for a grandmother of 70 some years, she thought.

The service was well attended that evening. Reuben gave a short sermon titled "The Great Commandment," followed by the communion. He asked the singers to take over, and then he took off his robes and hopped on his bicycle to find his way to Whenny's house. At the Last Laugh Bar, the lights were off. Whenny unlocked the children's room and fed them. They were on the floor playing a game of *mancala,* using the seeds of a gourd for their pieces. Whenny pulled a blanket over her brother and his door was locked. She took Pastor Reuben over to one of the stools around the bar and asked him if he had found a tenant.

"Yes. I had three people in need of respite care for their relatives. The one I picked is 25 and he is in the first stages of AIDS. He can still take care of his bodily functions, but he is weak and unable to work. He was a schoolteacher before he became sick. His name is Beautiful."

"My brother has given me this place to run my business. I will lose it if his relatives know he is gone. They do not visit him, nor does anyone, but if I can help someone else, it will allow me and my grandchildren to have a home."

"I can bring Beautiful over tomorrow. What will you do with your brother? Perhaps you were thinking of a private funeral. We have a cemetery that we can use when that time comes."

"That time has come. I will not be able to be there, but if you can help me, I will take good care of Beautiful."

"I am here to serve the living. We will plan a private burial for tomorrow and I will pray over him now so you can say your good-byes. Should you want to visit the cemetery; the marker will read "Beautiful in Life."

Whenny led the pastor into the small bedroom where the covered body lay. Reuben knelt down beside him and said a prayer and a blessing as to how he had been kind to his sister and his nieces and nephews. Then he made the sign of the cross and hugged Whenny. She was crying, and wiping her eyes so the children would not notice.

In the afternoon, Beautiful arrived on the back of Reuben's bicycle, and her brother's body was removed in the covered wheelbarrow. Beautiful was a little taller than her brother, but shrunken with *the thins* and not difficult for her to fit into the bedroom. She had cleaned everything out to make room for him, giving her brother's things to Rueben to distribute at the church. Beautiful smiled at her and she smoothed his forehead and brought him a warm bowl of stew and nshima, a cool towel, and a mug of tea with milk. She told him the bar would be noisy in the evening, so he should get some rest during the day, if possible.

The children did not notice the substitution as it had been some time since they had any interaction with their uncle. She told Beautiful where the latrine was, but asked him to use an enameled pitcher which she would empty each morning and night, so they followed the same routine she had kept with her brother Lamont.

On Sunday morning, Whenny attended the service along with her grandchildren. She was able to put an offering in the plate

"Pastor, I would like you to have this watch. It was my brother's, given to him by our father. I cannot read or write, and I have no need of it, but I would like you to have it."

"Thank you, Whenny. I will pray for your family when I look at it. It is beautiful."

"You have been an angel to me when I had nowhere to turn. I am glad I had something to give. I will have to go now to serve my customers. Our guest is doing well and sends his greetings."

"Tell him I will come and see him soon. Thank you again."

Whenny left before the service ended to go and set up for the afternoon's customers.

Once her customers were busy with their drinks and the music was playing, Whenny stopped in to see Beautiful. He was feeling better and sitting up in the bed, with his newspaper in his lap. He had lit a kerosene lantern and was happy with the room, the bed, and even the activities of the bar. She gave him greetings from Pastor Reuben.

"How long have you been in business, and where are you from?"

"I started this business when my husband died, about a year ago. My brother needed assistance, and so he helped me and my grandchildren."

"Are you from this area? You seem to have a different accent."

"You are right. I grew up further to the north. My mother could not raise twins. She was worried about us surviving, my brother and I, so she separated us and gave me to a relative. That brother I have not seen since. My aunt died and I was passed to another family. I moved around and even worked in homes of foreigners until I was given to my husband as a second wife—his first wife was barren. And now I am a business woman caring for my grandchildren."

"Thank you for taking me in. I am glad I am of use to your family. My name is Beautiful."

"I am Whenny, and you are welcome."

Whenny brought him yam chips and a hardboiled egg, as well as three chicken wings. She asked if he would like sorghum beer, but he said tea would be better. She wanted to ask him about his work, where he had taught, and other questions. But she would wait until he wanted company.

Monday was Pastor Reuben's day off. He stopped by the Last Laugh Bar to check in on Whenny and to comfort Beautiful. Whenny welcomed him and took him to the room. "Pastor, I am feeling much better. The woman has taken good care of my needs. How can I thank you?" Beautiful said.

"This is not my doing. Thank God. I am glad to see you comfortable. Is there anything I can bring to you?"

"If you ever have a bottle of lotion, or some oil for my skin, that would be a great comfort. It pains me and will not stop. Also, if you have any drawing paper, and a pencil, or charcoal, this place is interesting and I would like to sketch some of the customers, as they are pretty occupied, and I should be able to get some good likenesses. I haven't felt like drawing in months, but the creative spirit is coming back."

"I'll see what I can do. It will be a week before I am able to get out here again. Is this a good time for you?" The pastor asked.

"Yes. I am better earlier in the day, but not too early. Thank you, Pastor."

Whenny let the Pastor out and fastened the door. She had overheard the part about the oil for his skin and thought she might be able to fix something for Beautiful out of shea butter and cooking oil, with a little cinnamon to give it a fragrance.

She checked in on the children and told them to bring her their clothes so she could wash them. Each of them stripped down and handed her their shirts and skirts, then wrapped in a sleeping cloth to wait until the clothing was washed and dried. They had a little radio they could listen to as the day passed and the clothing dried on a bit of wire fencing near the fire.

The still was warm with its fermentation, the chickens were scratching away in the yard, and the Last Laugh Bar would be filled up with evening customers. There was time to get her hair plaited, if her friend Bernice would remember and show up. It was Whenny's big treat to have someone work on her hair to make her feel she was attractive, and catch up on the news. She was so grateful to have the security of a man staying in the house, even though she could not share this information with anyone. She switched her metal ring to another finger as a reminder to not mention the trade she had made.

Bernice walked down the edge of the road headed for The Last Laugh Bar. She saw the enormous red lips of the sign at the end of the street, and the ball sparkling in the sunlight. Whenny was her only customer for the day, and she had stored up good gossip to share.

Whenny kept an eye out for her friend and when she saw her coming, which was easy to tell, given the bright auburn hair color Bernice was sporting, she gave a sigh of relief. This had been a good week. True, Lamont had been late, but he was suffering, and his death was expected.

Beautiful made Whenny feel safer and needed, and the grandchildren would soon have enough food to eat and enough money to get them all a pair of sandals. Whenny was a frugal woman, but knew enough to save for a dry day, of which there had been many in her life. Bernice saw her waiting and waggled her hips to acknowledge her. They were soon talking, with Whenny propped on a kitchen chair, her hair sectioned off for a traditional plaiting. She had poured a glass of Fanta for her friend and was sipping the remainder of the bottle. She didn't want the children to see her—as they would all ask for a sip and she had only bought one bottle.

"What's it going to be today? A bridge, a tower, or maybe a wall of spikes?"

"Bernice, I leave it up to you. Make sure I can sleep on it though. I am not so foolish as to think I can perch my neck on a neck rest for the night, at my age."

"Woman, I have no idea what age that would be. Are you ready for the shaved widow's cut, or is there still a little life in this old body?"

"You are right. I am glad to be alive. Make this hairdo the "I am grateful" hairdo. Whatever that would be."

Bernice cocked her head to one side then began to braid. She had no one to help her and it was six hours later when she finished. The hair was crisscrossed into a pattern around the crown of her head, with a basket of neat rows ascending to the back. Just at the top of her head, the hair narrowed into a smaller pattern of tight weaves, then sprung free into a fan of black, before being gathered together again at the base of her neck.

Whenny did not own a mirror, but she could see the upsweep in the one Bernice had brought, and loved the way it accentuated her eyes and her forehead. She could see her long curled lashes and the curious amber eyes that so many people remarked on. She felt pretty, and loved, and hugged her friend, asking, "How much do I owe you?"

"Didn't you ask for the 'I am grateful hairdo?"

"Yes."

"Then there is no charge."

"What!?"

"Aren't you grateful?"

"Of course. I am very grateful."

"Then we are both happy. I wish you well with your business, and I will see you again soon. I am going." The women hugged and Bernice headed back up the street, her auburn flame of hair nodding from side to side as she walked.

When Whenny brought Beautiful his dinner of *nshima* and fried bream, he whistled at the transformation the hairstyle made.

"Who is this impala woman coming into my room? Am I dreaming?"

Whenny laughed at the young man flattering her, and was even more pleased when he asked if he could sketch her picture. That evening as the grandchildren walked in their clean clothes to buy penny candy, Beautiful captured the silhouette of the bar keeper with his graphite pencils. Beautiful told her he had studied art at the school in Burrisfuro with a great teacher named Bwalya Leibitsang. He had lost contact with his tutor, but the man had inspired him to become a teacher. Bwalya's wife taught math, and that is what he taught when he became a tutor. He had always wanted to thank the couple for the education and inspiration they gave him, but he didn't know how to reach them. He would make a note of this in his journal before going to sleep.

Beautiful was tired, but pleased with the results, and couldn't wait to show his portrait of Whenny to Pastor Reuben the next visit.

Reuben came down River No More Street on his bicycle, balancing a tray of art supplies and a pad of paper. He wore jeans and an argyle sweater vest over his striped shirt. When he saw Whenny, he did a double take. Her hairstyle took twenty years off her age, especially from this short distance.

He looked at the drawing Beautiful had done, and asked if he was willing to do one for him, if he wasn't too tired, and was willing to work from a photo. Reuben wanted to surprise his mother with the gift of a portrait of herself and his father.

"I can do it if you give me plenty of time, and are not in a rush. I have been feeling good these past days, but I can't guarantee anything. And thanks for the lotion. It really helped. My skin is not so painful," Beautiful said.

"I will get the pictures for you. And as for the lotion, I didn't get around to that. Whenny must have provided it. I can't take any credit. I did get you some drawing supplies. They are in the sack at the end of your bed when you are ready for them."

"Thank you. And thank you for locating Whenny. She has been a godsend. I am better than I have been in months."

Reuben saw the children sprawling on the blanket inside the sitting room as he left, and waved to them. They were looking clean and better fed. He silently blessed Whenny for the work she was doing with them and with Beautiful.

It was over a month before Reuben brought the pictures for Beautiful to use to make a portrait for his parents. Meanwhile, Beautiful had been having strange dreams each night. He described it as a vision of a small girl with a pure heart. He fell asleep thinking about her. She shared with him how her life had ended when she was five. At first, Beautiful would ignore that she wanted to talk to him, and he would think it was a manifestation from hearing the children at play outside his room—never seeing their faces.

One day, Beautiful took out his drawing pencils and began to sketch how the dream child appeared to him. As he continued with filling in her outline, as well as her features, and finally completing the details, the dream became very vivid. He decided he would record what he had been told the past month, and see if it made sense to anyone else. He had to tell it from her point of view, as she was speaking directly to him, or another who might want to listen to her story. Beautiful was a Believer, but this dream was so real, it also had to be acknowledged, and who better than himself to fill her need? He wrote down her words in his notebook.

Hello. My name is Lily Wonder. I wanted to find someone to write my story because I never lived it. You see, I died when I was 5 years old. My mother named me for her dreams that never were fulfilled. She is thinking of me tonight, and I have to return to her. If you or someone else will write this story, she can read it and know that I will never really die. I will be here waiting for her and all who care to join her someday. I know I have sisters and brothers, and my aunts and uncles as well. But this is about me, Lily. My story, as told to me by my mother Myrna, and verified by my father, began at Christmas time. My father recalled that it was a year of drought. More than half his cattle died, and he was never sure whether the rest would be *hainted*. Demons and witches thrived in the bush and covet what a man holds too closely. I am getting ahead of myself, for you see, you really have to start my story with my grandparents. They were quiet people who did not stay inside much, but lived in the open savannahs watching their cattle and telling stories. Their history was a long and winding path that led them to contentment, much as I hope my tale will do.

No one owned two sets of clothing. Everyone raised cattle, searched for honey in the bush, had a dog or two that helped them in their work, and married when they could afford a wife. For some, the bride price forced them to delay, and they saw other men getting ahead with sons and a legacy. That is what my father hoped for when he heard about my mother.

Myrna was a girl raised in the larger village on the outskirts of town. She was a beauty, they say. She had rounded features and a dazzling smile, full hair that was soft and luxuriant. She was loved by her parents and at an early age, she began to attend school. The colonials were ruling the country then. She went about in a raffia skirt, playing with her friends and enjoying her life. She had a desire to learn, and so she bribed her brother Stephen, who was attending school, to teach her from his books. He did. She soon could read and write and was writing his essays for him.

When she was thirteen, she was awarded a scholarship to go on to secondary school. My coming ended that part of her life. She did not complain about it, for she had me. From my earliest memory, I sat on her lap tracing letters in my palm, hearing about English flower gardens, and learning how people lived in other parts of the world. She taught me to sing my alphabet, and count out my beads. I knew my father had wanted a boy, but he too was willing to see me learn to read and to tell him stories of things he had never heard about.

My father was always tired when he came back from caring for his cattle. He did not ride a donkey or horse and walked miles each day to find them pasture and clean water. He would notice if any of them was dropping weight or needing medicine. He made his own medicine from the baobab tree bark. I always wanted to know how each cow was doing. Since he loved his cows, I paid special attention to learn their names and talk to him about them. I talked to him in front of the fire until my mother called me to the hut to sleep.

Father never took me with him to the outlying bush, but he listened to me when I named his animals, and how many more there would be by the time I was grown. I would tell him that when I married, I would bring him 15 cows as my bride price, which made him laugh, since no one had ever given more than 10 cows for a wife in the history of his family. He told me he had a twin sister, and she was given away when she was small because the family had so little. I never asked him what he had given for my mother, but I knew he had schemed to get her for his wife.

My uncle Dodge once bragged how he had helped capture her, the smartest and prettiest girl in the whole village. Once when Father went to the cattle auction, he brought me back a small cup made of metal that had a flower painted on its side. He told me it was a lily. Mother never corrected him. I drank my water from it each night. Now, for this telling of the story, which I haven't written before, I need to make sure that everything is put in its place. It won't due to have my other sisters or brothers coming too soon, or leaving abruptly, as I did. Each of them had a very different tale than I can tell, for you see, I was wanted up until the time I came. Then I was a disappointment.

My father had pursued my mother, taken her from her school and family, and planted me inside her. He had meant to plant a tree, and instead, he received a flower. A useless flower. That was me. I learned to bloom and I was loved. Maybe you can love a child too much and they get taken back by the gods, or you can love them too little, and they die. However it goes, I was dead within two days of having the sickness. I never saw a doctor. We didn't have medical people out at the cattle station, and by the time we reached the clinic, I was gone.

I was fortunate that I made it to five—just when my parents thought they had me secure. My mother was also pregnant when I up and left. I can remember nothing of it, except the feeling of lightness and the unexpected wailing, with me looking down and thinking how little I looked. When I was alive, I really thought I was a pretty big girl.

When I was departing and saw myself on the mat, I was a lot smaller and thinner than I thought. I wondered who would take care of the doll lying beside myself on the mat.

But I am going off the path. Mother went ahead and had another girl, and that's when I realized what a disappointment I had been to my father. He had really concealed it pretty well from me. With the second girl being born, father thought he was cursed. He looked at the new baby like it had been a trick of some sort. When mother had two more girls, the drinking started.

Father's herd was growing. The cows were fat and sleek. Mother was healthy and adored her little flower garden of girls. There was Pansy, Iris, and Daisy. Rose came much later, after the twin boys had been born, also another boy they named Royal Festal. Rose was the last child, and for some reason, father doted on her.

My father was getting on in age then; his wife was beloved in the cattle station. He then took another wife during this time, but she didn't seem to have the knack for keeping life in a child. She gave birth to four, but only one survived and Royal was not a healthy child. His legs crumpled inward and he walked in a curve, unable to move straight ahead. My mother helped the second wife with all the chores. When she was nursing the babies, she made sure her milk would not give out. My mother even helped nurse the child that did survive, even though she had babies of her own to feed. Mother also helped this woman to think more of herself because she was very young and often provoked the husband with her carelessness.

I have to say, my mother generated love in our home. Some people can add yeast to a bowl of flour and create a mountain of bread. My mother had the ability to add love to a dry place. Her little flower garden flourished. I should tell you she named the boys Kindness and Self Control after the gifts of the spirit. She also gave them western names, Reuben and Samuel. Each of them grew up with a desire to understand their world. They respected their father, protected their sisters, and adored their mother. Later, they married women from the school they attended, except for Royal, who left his family to attend culinary school where he learned to bake and ended up marrying his teacher Hen.

My mother was going to see London and visit her old tutor, Wellington Taylor. My father would not allow this, so she must wait for the future to come. I could tell her that I have seen how their lives turn out. It is surprising how life can be, but I will say no more about that, as it is not my tale to tell. It is worth the trip, however. I would tell my mother, Myrna ,that, if she could hear me. Sometimes I think she does, but often, she is closing the door to the spiritual world to get on with her busy life as a mother.

Let me get back to my life as a child at the cattle station. You cannot believe how sweet it is to be a child in Africa, growing up with animals, open space, and long days of play and adventure. I did not know it was so sweet when I was there, but now, as I observe life in other places, I know what I had was the best. Even my leaving was not difficult. It would have been so much harder had I had babies to leave, or even a husband or a best friend that would lament my going. As it was, I departed just as a new child was ready to be born. My father was sad, but he was also hopeful he would have his son. He was pained by my leaving. My mother suffered, but she also had hopes in the new child coming.

Altogether, it couldn't have been better managed. I think it was the flies that made me sick. Flies were maybe God's big mistake. They pester the animals to the point of madness, and humans cannot escape from their hovering. At last, you don't even notice them on your food or your eyes. But then sickness comes. Somehow, they are part of this.

I was small when my mother sewed me a doll. I wore it in my *chitenge* and cared for it as any mother would her baby. She was a doll with no eyes or mouth, but she had arms and a soft body and a tuft of cow's tail hair on her head that I could comb and plait. Best of all, Mother sewed her a tiny blanket and a dress that looked like the pictures in my book. I named the doll Fancy, for that is what she seemed to me. When it was springtime, I gathered seed pods from the palm and made holes in the dirt to play *mancala*.

Sometimes in the evening, my father would bring out his board and play *mancala* with me, carefully counting out the seeds so he would come out the winner. I liked the feel of the smooth round seeds in my hand, and the pile of them in the cup at the end of the game. We also had a game made of a checkerboard with a herd of tiny cattle that you had to protect and win back when the other player captured them. And so our evenings passed in front of the fire in the dirt courtyard of our home.

Now, I am watching my mother teach other women to read, just as she taught me when I was four. She is patient with them, helping them trace the letters in the sand several times before they try it with the pen. Many of them have not done fine work before, so it is difficult for them to hold a pen at first. When they make their first letters on paper, they are so proud. I always wanted to write a book one day, to share what I have seen in my short life. I guess that is what I am doing now, as I get you to record my thoughts. I will call on you again to record how it was that my mother and Aunt Violet met the grandchild who was mixed. Guess what? She was given my same name, Lily Wonder. So my story goes on. I don't want to get ahead of myself, as time here is different than earth time."

During the daylight hours, Beautiful recorded the story of this departed child, wondering if his talk with Whenny had influenced the dreams he had of Lily, or whether his imaginings were part of his illness. The descriptions were so real, the names came to him as though he had read them in the newspaper. When he did not hear from his Lily Wonder for several days, he took out the sketchbook and began to fill in the details of her face and form. One day when Reuben was visiting, he pulled out the sketchbook and showed it to the pastor.

"That is my sister Rose. When did you see her?"

"This is out of my imagination. I have a dream girl who visits me almost every night and compels me to write her story. When I am gone, I will leave it for you to read. She is as real as anyone I have ever met. You will think me mad, and maybe I am. I have caught everything else since I became positive with HIV. But her story comforts me as I think about my passing and what has been my life, and my experience as a human being."

"I would like to read that. Does she come to you every night?"

"Not every night. When I draw her picture or try to imagine her life as a child departing so young, she responds, letting me know what her reality was. She is a beautiful spirit who can go to different places and experience all time in a single moment. I don't want her to leave me, but she says she will when we all stop grieving her passing. She thinks that will happen soon."

"I have never had that experience of seeing the future or the past so vividly, but I do know we have angels who look after us. Maybe she is one of these. You seem to be more creative and more alive than anytime that I have known you, Beautiful."

"Yes. I can tell that because I want to draw and to paint and to portray what my inner self knows. I have also lost the sense of regret and despair that plagued me when I was first diagnosed. Then I wanted to end my life, the sooner the better. This dream child makes me want to read the next chapter. It may be the last, but I am going to enjoy it. Some of this may also have to do with Whenny. She tells me every day I am a gift to her."

"She says the same thing to me about you. She deserves to have a kind spirit in this place. She is the hope of these children she is raising. I pray for her and for you, and what will come from this exchange. Keep all your writings, as your vision may help others. I am going now."

"Goodbye. I now look forward to the night, and my dreams of Lily."

"Lily? That was my eldest sister's name. She passed away twenty years ago."

"Really! What a coincidence. I will give her your greetings, if she passes my way in my dreams."

Whenny nodded goodbye to Reuben and continued to empty sugar into the vat of spirits she was brewing for the week's brew.

Lily Wonder appeared again to Beautiful that night, after the lantern was out, and the fire was almost out. He could see nothing, but the presence was as real as Whenny sleeping in the next room, with her slight snore.

I'm back. I was telling about my life at the cattle station and the sweet times I enjoyed. When I woke in the morning, it was to the sound the rooster crowing and of my mother dishing out the corn porridge we call *nshima* onto the enamel plates. Mother would rise before dawn to start the fire and get the water boiling. At her wedding, her mother had given her an enormous iron pot with three legs. This pot was always on the main fire, with water heating in it. From this pot, she would dip water for making the morning tea. My father liked to have bread and red bush tea with a lump of sugar and some cream in it. For the rest of us, my mother, myself, and the orphan child we called Mpala, there was *nshima*. We ate it from one dish, set out on our kitchen mat in the rainy season, or outside when the weather was good, which was most of the year. The dogs would watch us eating from the dish, licking their chops, but knowing to stay out of range until everyone was finished. When my mother cleaned the cooking pot, she would gather the small chunks of cooked porridge for me to give to her chickens. They would come flapping down from their coops where she kept them at night. If she had leftover bones, these would go to the dogs. The men would head out with their cattle to the pastures where they grazed during the day. Then we took our baths, using the rest of the heated water.

We had a very secure ablution block with water above us in a bucket to rinse, and the tub with its loofah below to the water we rinsed with. When we finished bathing, we would carry the bath water to the plants in the yard. We had beans growing, followed by tomatoes, and then groundnuts would push up. We had an orange tree and a cashew tree with its broad round leaves coming from smooth branches weighted down with bricks so it would produce shade and we could reach the fruit when it was ripe. Mangos also grew in a grove of trees behind the washing area. Each plant had a set amount of water that we would pour around it from the calabash. The cashew tree received five calabashes of bath water, while the orange tree base was always damp from cooking water, wash water, and bath water. It was about the only orange tree I can recall in the cattle station.

Along the gutter and beside the inside wall were lilies taller than I was at five. They were red and orange and yellow in color and each had a drink after we bathed.

Out front at the end of a well beaten path beyond the small courtyard and wall were the calf pens, and the corral for the cattle. The valley sloped away below the pens. Along our house was a smooth gutter that caught the rainwater and carried it to a storage tank. The tank was made of clay and was black from the fires they used to make it water tight. It was taller than my father and looked like a huge ball at the side of our house near the gardens. The gutters were warm and sloped along the ground at the base of our round house. We liked to sit in them with our backs against the wall, and feel the heat of the sun. When we were able to print, we could use the outside of our house as a blackboard to make the map of the world, and our letters.

With the three baby girls, there were plenty of clothes to wash. She would soak them first then scrub them with a washboard and green bar soap. The baby clothes were washed first, then the linens, and finally, my father's work shirt and trousers. We had a scrub board my father had brought my mother that made the soap rub into the cloth and the dirt come out. When they were clean, we rinsed them, twisted them like a piece of dough, then hung them on the bushes and wall of the courtyard. My job was to keep the chickens from jumping on them and soiling them. This was an easy job for me, as I learned to use a slingshot to shoo the chickens away with pebbles thumping on their feathers.

After washing the clothes and putting them out so they would dry in the sun, there was wood to gather, floors to sweep, the courtyard to sweep free of leaves and debris, and the garden to weed. If someone had made soil on the ground, we would pour sand on it, then scoop it with a leaf into the garbage pit. We planted the normal crops; some grew at the same time. Beans would sprout up two days after the first rain fell, followed by tomatoes, then the groundnuts, and finally, the mangos ripening on the mango trees. All of the vegetables grew under a canopy of banana and cassava leaves, if the rains came. We kept the goats out using thorn bush fencing that could be put around the plants, the same kind used for the corrals at night.

My father, Festal, would split the larger wood and make tool handles from the thick limbs. We had a walking stick, a hoe, and a pick axe for land clearing. He borrowed a saw when we needed one from the neighbor who was a carpenter as well as raising cattle. My mother showed me the impala he had carved for her from the white mahogany wood when they were expecting me. It was delicate but strong, and smooth from wear.

I can still see the rows of cooking fires dotting the darkness of the village before the sun rose. When the sun came up, the roosters ceased their crowing, no doubt thinking they had brought it about. The birds would sing at first light. The sun came up in a rush of heat and light. At this time, the birds ceased their singing and the waft of scented lilies was in our yard. Each of them would unfurl in the sunlight. After I was bathed, my mother would have me sit between her knees and plait my hair into corn rows or other designs. I could feel the baby bumping against me as I pressed near her stomach. We had a mirror over the table, but I could touch the braiding and feel how regular it was. When I pulled on my dress and my sandals, I was ready for the day.

In the morning, many of the girls went out to gather firewood or to carry water. They usually went in small groups, carrying the jerry cans on their heads and trekking to the watering hole. I was very fortunate that we had a large cistern to hold our water. Once a month, if we had no rain, my father would hire the neighbor to bring barrels of water on his donkey cart and empty it into our tank. We did not lack for clean water, except during the time of drought, when the waterholes dried up and even the cattle could not find water to drink. We could see the buzzards circling as they waited for a gaunt animal to finally drop.

During the day, the orphan child, Mpala, would gather firewood and drag or carry it to the house. He would also weed the garden with the hoe, gather stones to line the gutters on the ground around the house, and do any tasks my mother needed done. He did not speak the same language as our village when he came, and my father said he had come from somewhere west where wars were going on. He slept in the storage room on a mat and helped keep the compound free of litter and rodents, which he loved to kill with the slingshot he had made of a piece of wood and some old tire tread. I think he was around 8 or 10 years of age. We called him Mpala which is antelope, because he could run and jump like one.

Let me tell you about our house. My father had built it himself, starting with clearing the ground, then assembling a set of mud blocks carved out of the earth and set to dry in the sun. The bricks were not kiln dried in their first rondavel, so they had to be careful about keeping it plastered so the rains would not wash away the walls. It had a thatched roof made of the long grasses that grew near the river some distance away. In time, my father was able to purchase the harder bricks from the local merchant who made them, and they enlarged the size of the house, using the older rondavel to store the kitchen pots, firewood, and their tools. We had a hoe, a storage jar, and a length of rope, two cooking pots, a brazier, and a small set of dishes, a tea pot, our mortar and pestle for grinding the *nshima*, and a set of red harness for the donkeys my mother bought. He was working on making a double set with his leather punch and the leather he had cured when my mother surprised him with a store bought set. The home-cured leather smelled like dead rats. He used bird droppings to soften the leather. There was also a pile of reeds in the storehouse that Mpala could weave into mats. I would play in this room and had a miniature brazier and a tiny cook pot made of clay which I used to cook food for my doll. Sometimes my friend Precious would come over and we would play house together. I never let her be the mother. She had to be the baby or the customer. If we played store, I was the clerk, the mother, the teacher. I wonder if she thought then I was too bossy, and later, when she had my doll, she was the boss of all. My mother gave it to her when I passed, and not to my sisters.

Precious was a good friend. We made designs in the sand with stones and sticks, shared secrets, and sometimes caught a locust and would tie ribbons to its legs so it made a beautiful kite as it tried to fly away. We would keep the locusts in a small basket in the storeroom and try to feed them something so they would not die. Sometimes the rooster would jump up and grab one when we forgot to shoo him away, and our game would be over. The locusts were not always around, but if you dug in the ground, you could sometimes find one. They were longer than my hand and their wings were like window panes of silk. We also had termite mounds among the mango trees that were higher than my father's head. We would hide behind them, climb the sides to poke sticks in the holes, and often found shiny stones the insects had dug up while making their mounds. These stones were the semi-precious garnets that predicted diamonds were beneath the earth, I was to learn later. These mounds were shade on the hottest days, and we pretended they were castles or tall buildings that we had seen in my books.

I liked the singing games we played. We also would pull the rope out of the storage building and play jump rope, although it wasn't easy because we were not allowed to cut the rope and it was too long for single skipping. It was made of thin cords of cowhide and plaited into a single strand. I would tie it to the cashew tree and then turn it for Precious to skip rope. My favorite game we played, other than *mancala,* was hopscotch. I used my smallest coin for my marker, and Precious used a broken comb. We could play this for hours and had to be reminded to do our chores. Sometimes Mpala would join in and he always won, he was so graceful.

When I learned to read, I would read to Precious. She did not have a mother who knew book, so I could tell her anything, turning the pages slowly and making up stories. One day my mother caught me doing this, and said she was going to get me a pen so I could write down my stories. I passed before she had a chance to buy a pen. There was one in the village, but she couldn't risk it going missing. Ours had long since run out of ink.

We did not have many people in our village who were different than ourselves. We had heard of the colonials, but by the time I was five, the country was changing its name, its boundaries, and we were making new rules to live by. My mother told me one day I would go to school and I would vote. I didn't know what vote meant, but I would tell Precious that she had my vote, because it made the adults laugh and poke each other when I said it. I didn't know if it was possible for a girl to vote or to get a vote, but it made my mother smile.

I have told you how my house looked. It was round and made of mud bricks with a straw roof and a floor that was smooth as a pot. Surprisingly, the floor was made of cow dung. Once it was laid and pounded, Mpala polished it each day after sweeping and you could see a reflection when the door was open. The house also had an opening to let light in, but we kept it closed because of the flies. Flies do not like the dark, so inside, there were no flies, unless the door was left open. We did not have the brazier inside because my mother said this was a danger. Sometimes it was cold as we had no furniture except for a small table and our carved stools. These were heavy and dark, made by a carver in the village. Each person in our house had a stool. Mine was very small with a little cross on the leg made of cowry shells. I could see it in the night if the moon was out and I had left it in the courtyard.

We slept on mats on the floor, and I slept beside my sisters, each of us nestled against the younger one's back. Mother would tuck me in and I was asleep before she climbed into her bed. She was usually up before I was. My father would bathe in the evening and sometimes I heard him asking my mother to scrub his back with the loofah, or sponge. We grew these in our garden under the platform and when they were big, we gave them to the neighbors. I liked how their vines crept over the mounds and made spirally circles on the ground.

Our garden also had groundnuts. You may call them peanuts. These were so good roasted on the flat iron tin over the fire, or boiled in a pot in the cold weather. We had to watch that the termites did not eat the roots of the plants in our garden, and this is one good thing about the chickens, they loved to eat the bugs. We would cluck to them when we saw any ants or termites near the house and the flock would rush over. When the rains came, the ants moved their nests and the chickens filled their craws with them.

My mother was heavy with the baby when I last remember her, but before that, she had lots of energy and would make some little pots of the clay from near the river. These would dry in the sun and I wanted to be able to do this one day. I liked the feel of the silken mud on my hands. She never let me go near the river, because of the danger of a crocodile. I never saw one, but she described them as enormous lizards that would gobble me up like the geckos did with the flies on our walls. I shivered at the idea of such a huge lizard, and imagined it would get me in the night if I didn't keep my sleeping cloth wrapped tightly over my head. Maybe that is why I never suffered from malaria. I was too busy warding off the crocodiles!

My friend Precious had a mother and an aunt who could weave incredible baskets out of grass. Precious said her mother was going to make one big enough for us to get inside and keep us safe, but she never did. She would make the flat winnowing baskets with patterns of brown circling the center grid. Her aunt made round baskets that came up like a pot and on some there were lids attached with a thong of woven grass. Some pots were so tightly woven, they could carry water. We had two tiny ones they made for us to play with and to put termites in. Some of the older women would use these tight little baskets to store their roasted mopani worms, then snack on the dried caterpillars in the late afternoon when they made their pots of tea, before they prepared food for the evening meal together. These worms were good, but not available except in the rainy season in the mopani forests further south. We always had a good supply of them. The traders would bring us gifts when they came to visit during the dry months in July and August to trade for our cow skins and dried beef.

One day Mpala carved me a whistle. I was blowing on it when my father came home and he was not pleased. He told me to give it back to the boy; I was never to receive a gift from a boy without it being presented to him or to my mother. I was embarrassed and a little angry at this. I never knew why this was a rule, nor did he explain. Mpala never gave me anything else after this and we stopped playing in the storage building. Mpala joined the herdsman that spring and no longer worked with my mother.

My mother had a sister named Violet. She was a tall woman with eyes like the moon. She didn't come to see us often, but when she did, she brought gifts. She brought cloth and a sewing machine for my mother and books for me. She brought us pens and a notebook, which was where I started my stories. My mother taught herself to sew and was soon making repairs to the clothing of everyone at the cattle station. She was also able to piece together curtains for the openings in our house and hung them on sticks so we could let the light in without the insects.

Mother made a cloth for the table, a shirt for my father, and many other things, just by seeing a picture and then copying the design. After I was gone, she taught other women this skill— men as well. This was the beginning of her earning some money for herself and how she was able to occasionally order a book, buy a pen, and even provide shoes for her children to come. The last gift Violet brought was a kerosene lamp, which my father grumbled about for the next 30 years. Violet said little to me, but she gave me lots of hugs and listened to me with all her heart. When she had her children, I was already departed, but I know she always wanted a girl like me. She said she would name her Lily Wonder.

Now, you may be asking where I am now. If I told you, you wouldn't believe it. So I am sticking to the things you can understand of my earthly home. Let me tell you how life went on with my Aunt Violet.

Violet lived in the village close to what is now called the capital in a town called Blancville.

When Violet sent me a letter, I began to think about her more often. Everyone dreams of being remembered, and to receive a letter was a great honor. I put it on the wall in our sleeping room. I thought I had missed how much she cared for me, and how important her sister was to her, for she didn't like to travel. Violet would also fuss with my mother's hair, something no one in the cattle station had done. She would sit my mother down and wash her hair, lavishing on shampoo and conditioners made especially for delicate curly hair. Then she would massage her head, finally braiding it in loose coils and fashioning them into a crown that was cool and regal. Even my father had to smile at the transformation, for Myrna was a beauty. The hair piled up above her bronze-gold forehead accented her silhouette and the long lashed lids above her large tilted eyes. From Violet, as a child, I learned that family counts, and can be counted on.

You will hear from me again, for I am bound to my family until they no longer grieve or mourn my passing. Until then, I can see what is going on in their lives, but I can only watch. –

Beautiful was awake before it was light, eager to record the story of his Lily. He could remember so many details and his pen flew across the paper jotting down the scenes and the interactions. He wanted to meet these people and comfort them with what he knew of their lives. Did everyone have such a vibrant force that surrounded them? This child gave him energy and hope. Each appearance brought back memories of long forgotten joys and some disappointments that he had suffered. By seeing what her life had meant to her, he was strengthened to make his last days count. He asked permission of Whenny to draw pictures of her grandchildren, of the bar, of herself. He recorded his struggles with HIV isolation. Each day as he logged in what was happening in his narrow world, he longed to understand more, and to let people know that he was somebody, that he mattered—that each of them mattered. Somehow, he conveyed this to Whenny and she took on new life. She was mistaken as the mother of the children, rather than their grandmother because her love and her caring gave her a new light. She took time to listen to him and to them, and they began to want to learn and to excel.

Beautiful began to give mini lessons in art to the children, and to welcome their visits to his room. He was meticulous about his hygiene, and his skin and hair improved as he watched what he was eating and drinking. Soon the children were learning to read and to write. The girls practiced their letters and each of them shared the single book their mother had purchased with her income from the still. As the children learned and began to observe, Whenny too, wanted this ability to read and write. She dictated her story to Beautiful, then he would have her read it back to him, and record it all; the daily events, the calamities, the miracles of maintaining life when the odds seem all against you.

Their lives were becoming intertwined. Reuben saw the change that love was making in the life of Beautiful and asked permission to speak in one of his sermons about this transformation of the young man with AIDS. The day he gave his sermon on Beautiful, Festal and Myrna attended the service. As he held up the pictures of the children, there was the picture of the dream girl. Both of Reuben's parents gasped at the likeness. It was their Lily Wonder. She was working a miracle in the life of this dying man. They wanted to talk to Reuben after the service but he was called away for an emergency.

Whenny was so pleased with the education her grandchildren were receiving. The girls could now read print and tell her what a notice or letter said. She closed up the bar a little early on Saturday and went to attend the church service because Reuben was going to be talking about Beautiful. All the children were bathed and dressed in gingham shirts and jumpers, all were wearing sandals and had their hair washed and combed out. She was feeling pride as a grandmother, and wanted them to be seen and admired. As the service ended, she was proud that she had been able to help Beautiful, and the gift that he had given the family. They didn't stay around after the service, but headed back to the Last Laugh Bar, singing one of the catchier new praise songs they had learned.

When they arrived at the house, Whenny had a sudden premonition, and went straight to Beautiful's room. The door was ajar, and the place was a shambles. He was lying in a pool of blood. Whenny pulled the comforter over his body. Both of the barrels were missing, along with the wheelbarrow, the Dutch oven, and the brazier, as well as her new sewing machine and all the clothing and blankets. Missing too, were the months of journals, recorded sketches, and writings of his relationship with the visionary girl, Lily Wonder and the Last Laugh Bar.

It looked as though Beautiful had died trying to protect her home. She locked the children into the parlor, and headed back to the church to notify Reuben and get his advice. It had been too good to be true, her life had never been so sweet and she had never known such love from a man as she had received from Beautiful, as he lay dying, then recovering in her little home at the end of Water No More Street.

Reuben listened to Whenny tell of the death of her houseguest, and the stolen items. She could hardly contain herself as she rushed through the story. No plan came to mind as to how to care for the children. She could not report the thefts or the death to the police, the room was contaminated by Beautiful's blood, no one would clean it for her, and she did not want to risk her own safety as she was the only one the children had to care for them. She and Reuben knelt in prayer and looked for a solution. As they were praying, Festal and Myrna came into the room. They had wanted to help Reuben with his farming plans, and he had asked them to drop by after church.

When Festal looked at the woman kneeling on the floor, he was taken aback. She looked so much like his mother. Her posture, her hair, even the way she pulled her head back and arched her neck. As she stood up, he caught sight of the watch on Reuben's wrist, and within minutes, a mystery over sixty years in the making was solved. That had been Festal's father's watch. Lamont, who had passed away, was his youngest brother and Whenny was Festal's twin. The two of them wept in joy. They had each felt guilt their entire lives because they thought the other had been given away and lost forever.

Whenny was given away when she was six years old to a family in the Gulf to be a servant in their household. Festal had been sent to the fields to be a cow herder. Briefly, Whenny shared her current dilemma, and the answer was simple. Lamont's brother would have inherited the house, and that brother was Festal. They would go back to the place, release the children into the care of Myrna and Gift, and if necessary, they would burn the building to purify the land. Festal was thrilled to

find his twin alive and with family besides. He hugged her and hugged
Reuben, and hugged Myrna, then started all over again. This was an
unveiling of biblical proportions. He was a blessed man. Whenny felt the
same, and the two of them joined arms as they walked down the street
to release the children, Reuben and Myrna following behind.

Reuben pulled back the comforter and saw his friend Beautiful lying
there. He called his name, and heard a slight moan. "Bring some water,
he is not dead, he is just banged up and bleeding. Maybe he can tell us
what has happened."

Festal helped pull the man into the light and they rinsed his wounds
with the water and wrapped his bleeding head in a towel. Myrna
diverted the attention of the children to the tuck shop down the block,
and gave them some coins to buy gum and a bottle of Fanta to share.
The men cleaned up the man as best they could and gave him water to
drink. Within minutes, he told how he had been robbed, and that the
men were the same who had been drinking in the bar the night before.
He asked about the couple who had come in, recognizing them from the
sketches he had made.

"Beautiful, we have heard about your dreams and we want to know
more. This is not the time, as you need to heal. The woman who has
been caring for you is my sister. You are not to worry. We can repair the
house, and we will get some medicines for you."

"Whenny, come and stay with us until we get this house back in
order. We will send the cart for Beautiful and he can live in my rondavel.
It is good that we came in time. God is good." Reuben and Stephen
followed up on the information about the thieves and the goods that
were located at the far end of the cattle country. They heard from Rose
that someone had brought her the sketch books, thinking it was her in
the pictures. She had read some of the stories and was amazed at how
clear a description the Dream Girl had given of the lives and places. She
knew Royal would want to read them as well, as he had a talent for

writing and had a plan of writing the biography of his mother Gift.

CHAPTER 45

MYRNA AND THE ENDOWMENT

Several members of the local affiliate had met at the large mango grove to go over meeting the international team that was coming to Copperfine. The local coordinator had asked Myrna and Festal to be present for the meeting, as the national coordinator would be present. Festal was not able to attend, but Myrna was there to meet him. The national coordinator did not show up that evening, and when he did, almost a week later, he went over the procedures again for welcoming the guests, getting them to their housing, and preparing the host families for their arrival. Their names were difficult for the people to recall. He warned the homeowners that you could not keep track of them by their clothing because they dressed alike and they also changed clothes frequently. Sometimes you could recognize them most easily by their voices or their laughter. They tended to smile and laugh a lot.

It was late afternoon when Myrna returned to her cottage and hung up her cardigan, built the fire, and prepared for the night. Gift had gone to visit her aunt that she had discovered in the displaced persons' camp. So, Myrna was alone in their home. She realized how much she counted on the company of Gift, and sharing the day's experiences with her. She made herself a cup of tea and ate a few leftover yam chips, then cleaned her teeth, and pulled the curtain back from the window. Looking out, she reflected on her what her education had meant to her. She had been impressed by her tutor, Wellington Taylor, and his idea of being the *Prince of Love,* had given her a model on which to build her hopes. She and her family had become a beacon of hope and knowledge in the community.

Her sons had made it possible for her husband to unite with his twin and restore a relationship that poverty and powerlessness had broken. She had a daughter, college educated, who would be able to administer an academy for women so no other girl in the area would have to be denied an education. Each of her children was involved with each other and respectful of their differences and their common bonds as brothers and sisters. They had united tribal groups, ages, and gender. With the addition of Lily Wonder into the family, even racial lines had been united. She had to say that she would never have imagined how beautiful the lines laid down for her would be, and tomorrow, her sister and her husband would see the family honored. She did not regret that her own Lily had passed away. The child had been a blessing beyond measure.

As she said this to herself, a breath of fresh plumeria scent blew into the rondavel and she felt a tremendous relief and a joy enter her spirit. She went to the rondavel where Festal was sleeping, and saw he was sitting at the wall of the compound. He, too, had scented the perfume of the tree growing above their Lily's grave. He was also in a state of oneness with how their lives were being spun into a tapestry of love and peace. They were looking forward to meeting the new Lily Wonder and getting to know her story, and what she would bring to their lives, even as they had moved from the wonder of reunion with Whenny, and knew that there was a plan to all of this. Myrna kissed her husband good night, and they went to their sleeping places to wait for what the morning would bring.

The mattress was sweet with the new grasses they had stuffed into it during the dry season. Myrna pulled her cloth over her face and turned to the wall. Festal was sleeping in the small rondavel alone tonight and she was wondering if he was missing having her close to him.

Morning came suddenly on the plateau. The rooster had scarcely finished his clarion call and the donkeys were still braying a love song when the heat of mid-December sucked up all life from the air. Myrna pulled herself out of bed and felt the welcome coolness of her polished floor. She gathered her clothes from where she had left them and hung them on the peg near the bed. Today, the local people would meet the international team. The coordinators had asked her to wear her traditional dress. She pulled it from the trunk in the storage room and smoothed it out on the bed. When the fire was going well, she drew a few charred coals out of it and carried them to the iron, put them inside, then ran the bottom of the iron over a towel to make sure none of the soot remained on the bottom.

On the small table, with a cloth laid down, she pressed her dress for the welcoming. Her hair was pulled into a nylon scarf then wrapped in a fanciful bow shaped headdress of the same material as her skirt and wrap. She caught a glimpse of herself in the mirror and applied a small amount of kohl to her eyes and some coloring on her lips. There was bound to be a number of photos taken, she had learned this when she met her first international team. Slipping on her sandals, she finished her cup of tea and two slices of bread, then headed for the village square. Festal was going to feed the animals, then dress in his *abaya*, and join them later. Her friend Priscilla met her on the path. She too, had her traditional skirt and top with her hair braided, then pulled into a wrap that resembled a mortar board in its shape. The two laughed to see each other so fancified.

"As if anyone will know who we are," they laughed. "Two classic women that have outlived most of our peers in cattle country." Royal had driven out to Blancville to pick up his Aunt Violet and Lily Wonder and bring them to Copperfine, just in time to see Myrna receive the endowment for her school. Festal was there, dressed in his best *abaya*.

Festal was charmed by the little girl, who promptly sketched him— complete in his tribal dress, and surrounded by fattest and most beautiful of cows. He let her lead him around the school site, commenting to him on what was most important to see. When it was time for the ceremony, the chiefs invited Priscilla, Myrna and Festal to be seated with the dignitaries. As they were seated there, waiting for the ceremony to begin, Gift arrived and Myrna signaled her to join them on the podium.

The gathering consisted of about one hundred people. The village chiefs came, along with several school children, the magistrate, the affiliate members, and the team of 14 volunteers. All of them had cameras and began immediately taking pictures of Myrna and Priscilla. The women were glad they looked so colorful. There were speeches, a prayer, some songs, and then one of the women from the team stepped forward. "I am from England," she said. "I have been asked to bring a special book and a special letter from my country. The person I am seeking is Myrna Chitundu." Myrna felt the heat come into her cheeks as she recognized her maiden name and the diary from her school days.

Myrna stood to acknowledge she was the woman, then the English woman continued. "My name is Sarah Taylor. My father Wellington Taylor left an endowment for a school for girls in the care and name of his prize student, Myrna Chitundu. I am here to present this to you. I am his daughter. We have permission from the Ministry of Education to commence the building of that school, which is why this team is here in Copperfine."

The audience broke into applause and unexpected tears ran down Myrna Chitundu Phiri's face. Her daughter, Rose, who was seated beside her, handed her a tissue. Cameras flashed and the pictures were on the news by evening. Myrna took the hand of her friend Priscilla and was so glad her sister Violet and Lily Wonder had been there to share the joy. Gift loved the ceremony and the pomp. For now, Myrna's heart was full and she turned to the village chief. He nodded his head and rose to announce that the land would be donated for the project, and the team would begin the foundations the following morning, once the engineers laid out the corners. Then he signaled the children from the middle school and they began their dance of the impala.

A dozen small boys and more mature girls jumped and gyrated to the music of the drums and the rattles the dancers wore around their ankles. Each dancer wore a neat costume of antelope skin whose sepia and white patterns highlighted the golden brown bodies of the young dancers. They were rhythmic and aware of the impact they were having on their audience as they leapt into the air, or hunted the elusive antelope. The girls were modest and alluring in their trained choreography. The music, the people singing, and the overflowing happiness of the international team, was contagious. Myrna could smell perfume of the plumeria wafting over the celebration. She did not dare to look at the diary that had held so many conflicting thoughts about herself, her Uncle Dodge, and the marriage suitor. Over time, everything had worked out. She had been able to use her education to love her husband, and produce children who cared about others and themselves. She had stopped worrying what her family thought of her marriage, and realized each of them had hurdles to overcome in their own lives.

Other girls would benefit from her attendance at the all boys' school. Even her pain at the death of her Lily was gone." All is Well' was the good word that floated into her mind as she swayed to the music that glorious December day, just fifty years after she had arrived in Copperfine, a new bride of 14, with her husband Festal, and they started their life together.

Rose excused herself to leave while the dancing was still in progress. She knew little of her mother's time in the secondary school. But she knew if a tutor from England was impressed enough by a student to create an endowment—that was something. It made Rose want to know more about her mother's history. She was intrigued by the writings Beautiful had done. This endowment would bring students and funding to their area. She would report all of what she had learned to her husband Henley, who took such an interest in this small community. There would be photos to share with her work mates at the ministry, many of whom would have seen the pictures in the news.

Another celebration would follow when her mother returned to visit Grandmother Beatrice and the remaining family in Blancville. Violet gathered her purse and her grandchild and followed Myrna towards the waiting car. They were going to have dinner together then head back to the house. Festal would be driven back to the house and dropped off by Royal, after insisting that he wanted to have some time alone and that they should and enjoy their dinner without him. Festal kissed Myrna and told her not to hurry. She had a lot of catching up to do.

Violet wanted to get Myrna's opinions on what to do with the extensive art collection of Bwalya's. His widow Karin had expected to be able to advise her, but she was now in serious condition and unable to travel or be of much use in business matters. So Violet had turned to Myrna and Festal. They had spent some time thinking about the paintings and how they might best be marketed. The decision was to open a gallery, a gift shop, and a coffee place in Blancville, and have the girls run it, with the help of Royal. Violet was also concerned about the business that Joseph had left her. The women and Festal advised her to get Rose's husband who was an attorney to review the situation. At dinner, they chatted about the trip to Holland and the changes that were taking place in their family.

After the ceremony was over, Rose went back to her husband to report on the event, while Royal drove his father back to the rondavel. Festal changed his clothes, then went down to feed the calves while Royal drove back to town to pick up the family.

CHAPTER 46

INDEPENDENCE

Festal looked down the long drive leading to his calving pens. Each year, as his family grew and the number of cattle increased, he had extended the distance from his house to the corrals where the youngest of his calves were kept. Each of his children had taken turns naming the animals. From the first time he had led his new bride to the small brush corral where orphaned calves bedded down, Festal had been touched by the tenderness of young girls towards the small animals.

He first felt affection for Myrna when he saw how she stroked the sides of the calves' faces and wanted to brush them free of the mud that stuck to their sides. He felt like he was being stroked. When Myrna had been gentle with the bar girl he brought home to help with the household chores, he had seen a new possibility in the girl. His bitterness at being outmaneuvered by Dodge had subsided. Festal had never talked to Myrna about what her dreams or expectations had been. Today, he saw some of them coming true. Respect.

His women had come up with the idea of the women's co-op, which had transformed the climate of the village. Neighbors began to treat each other with kindness. He had grown old here in comfort. His daughters brought him joy. His sons became pastors and formed a community church that reached out to the orphans and the widows. He saw the village chief praise his family and a school founded in Copperfine because his wife had been a scholar and earned the respect of her tutor. His name, Phiri, was part of the title for the academy. Festal had won over his sister–in–law and her husband by his faithful care of his family, and the values he passed on to them. He was humbled by the survival of his children when so many had been taken. His daughter Rose was a college graduate and all of his girls had developed into fine women who were skilled in different ways.

Whenny was a blessing to her grandchildren. The fact that he was the one who could help her, was a miracle of God's grace. He could not think of anything he would change or want as he watched the calves line up for their milk in the tidy calf pen. In the heat of the late afternoon sun, he felt his life was sweet. He lay down to rest a bit before going up the hill to the house he had built. The grass was fragrant in his face as his calves nuzzled him, and he saw the slow cloud of darkness open and light appear. His body felt nothing but peacefulness and release. He had been a man.

The sons, along with their mothers, continued to minister to the women in the community until the academy for girls was built. Myrna and Gift then moved to Blancville to join Violet in caring for her grandchild and opening the Impala Gallery and Gift House. A coffee shop run by Royal was built adjacent to it, with fresh Danish daily. A new chapter had opened in their lives with expected visitors from Holland, new clients, and a closer family bond, even as Festal's life closed with a sigh of contentment—that he been loved, and was no longer afraid.

ABOUT THE AUTHOR

Suzanne Popp was born into a large military family that traveled across the United States in her early childhood. She was raised in the country and has a love of rural life. When her brothers went to Vietnam, she and her husband Ken went to the Peace Corps following graduation from college. In West Africa, she taught English and African literature at a Post Secondary Teachers Training College in the Brong-Ahafo Region of Ghana which borders the Ivory Coast. Students ranged in age from 18 to 45 years of age. Some were working to become certified after years of pupil teaching, while others wanted to gain entry into the university and were working on the 'A' level exams. During the vacation periods, she traveled over 16,000 miles overland in Central, East and Northern Africa by native transport, and witnessed the rapid change of governments from colonial occupation to independence. As a woman, she gained admittance into the households of young wives and mothers of all beliefs; she shared in their joy and their hardships, and listened as they poured out their dreams of a better future to her.

Suzanne has returned to Africa many times, and been actively involved in the education of girls and vulnerable children, as well as building homes for those in need through work with VillageSteps, the charity founded by her family for the education of orphans and vulnerable children, especially girls, and Global Village, the international branch of Habitat for Humanity. Suzanne is a mother, a grandmother, and an advocate for literacy and humanity in emerging countries as well as locally. At home on her horse farm in Enumclaw, Washington, she writes, is active in the arts, and serves as Director of VillageSteps, the charity founded by her family. This is her first novel, and she hopes you will find it encouraging and let her know how it affects you.

16146427R00151

Made in the USA
Charleston, SC
07 December 2012